Jealousy

THE COMPLETE SAGA

BY

LINDA BRICKHOUSE

This is a work of fiction. All of the characters, organizations, and events portrayed in this novel are either products of the author's imagination or are used fictitiously.

www.melodramapublishing.com

Library of Congress Control Number: 2007943734
ISBN-13: 978-1934157138
ISBN-10: 1934157139
First Edition: May 2009
10 9 8 7 6 5 4 3 2 1

Book Interior Design and Layout by candace@candann.com
Editors: Melissa Forbes, Candace K. Cottrell, Brian Sandy

Chapter 1

THE BETRAYAL, FALL 2003

Petra, enjoying a peaceful moment with her family, draped her lean chocolate legs across the love seat. Staring from Chaka, the man she loved, to her children, she smiled. She noted that their daughter Chanice was the spitting image of Chaka, down to the tiny markings along her jawline. As CJ caught her attention with his comical antics, she thought, *Wow! This is what life should be about.* She watched Chaka entertain the children as though he were a peer rather than their father.

An annoying chiming in Chaka's pocket interrupted the serenity, but Petra refused to acknowledge the intrusion. She slid to the floor beside them, hoping to make the best of this time together.

CJ was tired of playing games. He wanted his gifts. He leaned closer to his father's side.

Chaka pretended not to understand CJ's body language and continued playing with Chanice.

"Daddy, come on," CJ said, "it's my birthday. I didn't get a party, and you said my gift would be extra special this time."

Chaka shook his head and smiled at Petra.

Petra had chastised her man earlier that morning when he'd made the promises to CJ. "Stop promising these children things," she told him. "Because they don't let up until they are satisfied." She wanted to rub it in a bit but knew that Chaka would only mimic her know-it-all attitude.

Quickly, Chaka grabbed his son in a bear hug and lifted him into his lap playfully. "You want your gift, huh? All right. Suppose I tell you I forgot to pick it up, will you be mad with your forgetful daddy?"

CJ's eyes bulged from their sockets. Immediately, he tried to hide his disappointment.

Chanice jumped up from the floor and took off toward the den, just off the living room. "Don't believe it, CJ!" she yelled. "He didn't forget nothing. Your gifts are right here in these big bags."

Chaka gripped his son a little tighter, holding him to his chest, while Chanice yelled out for him to come before she opened his gifts herself, and Petra laughed as CJ tried to squirm his way out. Chaka finally let go, and CJ flopped to the floor.

"Don't open my stuff, Chanice. This is my day. You can't open my stuff. Mommy, whup her and she'll stop."

Petra shifted once again, deciding she'd better referee, or there would be a fight between those two.

Chaka grabbed Petra by her small waist and leaned into her arms. He licked his peach-colored lips. "Kiss me, pretty lady," he whispered.

Petra felt her pulse quicken. "You still know how to make me smile." Slowly, she stole the quiet moment to kiss.

As each second ticked away, the kiss deepened into something more inviting. His tongue danced in and out of her mouth, and she chased it with hers. Slowly, they wrapped themselves into a tight embrace right there on the floor, oblivious to the children in the den, or even the world outside their cozy home. Petra lived for these times, the ones that Chaka couldn't take back.

The chiming shattered their moment, and Chaka struggled to silence the annoyance without breaking their connection.

As soon as he leaned back into her arms, the chime sounded again. Petra leaned away from him, her brows tightly knitted.

Chaka glanced at the screen and shoved it back into his pocket.

"Either answer it or turn it off," Petra barked as she sashayed from the room.

Chaka met Petra at the door leading to the den. "Why you leaving, girl? I was just about to show you something." He chuckled.

Petra didn't slow her movement. She just nodded.

Chanice and CJ were busy trying to get the stuff out of the biggest Toys "R" Us bags they'd ever seen, and two jewelry bags. Everything was wrapped, except one box that Chanice claimed for herself. "This has to be mine!" she screamed at the top of her lungs. "Daddy always gives CJ one gift for my birthday, and this time he's giving me one for CJ's. Look, Mommy. It's pretty."

The phone chimed again.

Chaka couldn't believe his eyes as Chanice shook the chain in Petra's face.

Petra could feel the heat rising from her toes. The gift was way too expensive for their daughter, and it certainly wasn't something she herself would wear. Before Chaka could open his mouth, Petra snatched the chain for a closer examination. It was a diamond-cut link chain with a medallion that read DADDY'S GIRL. "Oh, so that's what she calls you now? Don't bother to say a word. Just go answer that damn phone before I break that shit too," she whispered through clenched teeth.

"Yo," he barked into the phone, his eyes on Petra.

Petra couldn't hear a word from the person on the other line, but she was certain it was Eve. Chaka's face and ears had turned red, and he wasn't having his usual jovial conversation. In fact, he had turned his back on his family to listen to the caller.

Chanice bounced from one foot to the other, trying to take it from her mother's hand. "Mommy, it's mine." She watched her mother glaring at her father.

Petra watched Chaka's face for any clue as to what he was about to do.

As Chaka took steady steps back into the living room area, she stepped into the doorway and stood nose to nose with the man that swore to love and protect her.

"Your disrespect for this house and your family is ridiculous. She calls, and you hop up and go running. The acknowledgment of your bitch is a betrayal, but the fact that she has so much power over you is intolerable."

"Petra, everyone in this room is a fucking adult. We made our choices. If you want out—fuck it—just leave!" Chaka took two steps away from her.

"Is that it, Chaka Dubois? Is that the only answer you have for me, the mother of your children, the only woman that loves you—just leave, if I can't hang?" Petra stepped closer to him, disgust in her eyes.

"What do you want me to do, *P*?" Chaka reached for the doorknob.

Petra wedged her back between the solid oak door and Chaka. "I want you to stay home. For once put us before everything and everyone else."

Chaka shook his head.

"What do you mean, no? Chaka, today is your son's birthday, and you leaving him to go take care of your mistress. Go explain to them that she comes first."

Chaka stood there ashamed that he'd allowed so much drama to enter their home. "Petra, I love my children. I take care of this house and everyone in it, including you. The only way I can do that is by doing what I do. I work those streets and the life that comes with it. Why, all of a sudden, Eve bothers you so much? You never cared before."

Petra's chest was heaving. She tried to get her emotions under control. "I've always cared about your relationship with her, but I put it aside because of my love for you. I know that was the second dumbest thing I've done in my life."

Chaka stood closer to Petra now, his anger out of control. "OK, so what was the dumbest?" he asked, assuming he already knew the answer.

Petra pointed toward the kids. "They are," she responded, hoping to hurt his feelings.

Chaka didn't bother to respond. He knew it wouldn't help. Besides, Petra had gone too far. This fight was over, and he was better off getting out of the house before he did or said something he'd regret. He slammed the door, and every picture on the first floor rattled.

Chaka's thoughts were all over the place as he went to deal with the latest situation. He just couldn't chance another battle with Eve. They were just getting to a place where they seemed to understand their purpose to one another, but this new dependency was creating a new dimension to their relationship. First she called whining about the car, and then she called back to tell him the tow company hadn't come yet. Then she called a third time ranting about him leaving her for dead.

Instead of telling her to call Quinton, he figured he'd handle things himself and eliminate the bullshit. As the sign welcomed him into Brooklyn, he called Quinton to update him.

Chaka didn't find Eve when he got to where she claimed she'd broken down. He circled the block. The idea that she'd called him but didn't wait for him weighed heavily on his mind as his call to her went unanswered. Twice. He was beginning to lose his temper.

Just as he was heading back to his car, he heard someone call out to him. Standing next to his luxury silver vehicle, he smiled at the two brothers approaching him. They were family, and he greeted them as such. As Chaka embraced the taller of the men, he felt the handle of the gun against his side, which made the hair on the back of his neck stand.

He disregarded that and turned to offer the same welcome to the shorter brother. Just then, he felt the barrel of a weapon pressed into the center of his stomach. He winced. "Oh shit!" He looked into his friends' eyes. "What the fuck is this?"

Before Chaka could get an explanation, he heard the shot, and felt the agonizing pain soon after, a searing fire that radiated to the soles of his feet.

Tears slid from his eyes, and a haunting sound escaped his mouth. People he'd trusted came to kill him.

Quinton pulled up on the avenue just as the shot rang out and witnessed Chaka's body fall to the ground.

Getting into the thick of things, he jumped from the car and began firing at the men. The barrage of flying bullets from the men didn't slow Quinton's pursuit, but the men leapt over the low wall behind the church and hurried off into the cemetery.

Quinton yelled at Chaka's corpse, "What the fuck happened?"

Chapter 2

THE RAGE

Anissa was the first one at the door the moment she heard the glass rattle against the wall. Eve stood and flew in the direction of the disturbance.

"What the fuck happened to you?" Anissa yelled.

Quinton pushed past her and headed up the stairs two at a time.

Eve wouldn't allow herself to think it was anything more than some street shit as she headed back into the sitting room.

Anissa stood still a little longer, sure that something terrible had happened.

Before she could make a decision, Eve was back at her side. "Yo, where is Chaka?"

It was Anissa's turn to look dumbfounded as she watched the expression on Eve's face change from indifference to concern.

Quinton was in the room above them, slamming doors and dresser drawers and stomping back and forth. Mentally, he rehashed everything that had happened in the last few moments and he couldn't come up with a suitable answer, except, it was time to go to war. Sweat poured from his head into his eyes as he snatched his clothes off and put on black army fatigues. Q tore down the stairs and found Anissa and Eve standing in the same spot as when he'd first walked into the house.

By the time he hit the last step, Eve was in his face demanding answers.

"Where is Chaka?"

Quinton didn't acknowledge her. He moved her out of his way and headed into the basement. He hit the switch, and light flooded the entire area.

Anissa knew for sure that, whatever the situation was, it was only going to be made worse if Quinton was heading out the door with heavy artillery. She heard the ventilated door open, and silently she prayed for his safety.

Quinton had pulled the X-harness shoulder holster from the hooks and immediately reached for his twin signature Smith & Wesson .357 SIG's. He loaded each gun with a clip and on impulse loaded a round in the chamber. The vest was sitting on the floor when he noticed his cell phone was vibrating. "Nah!" he yelled as he sent the annoyance shattering across the room.

Anissa jumped the moment she heard the vault door slam shut. *It was only a matter of time before he came back upstairs and walked out of the door*, she thought. Quinton was standing directly in front of her when she opened her eyes, afraid to say a word.

Eve stood in Quinton's path and cranked her neck. "I asked a fucking question—Where is Chaka?"

Quinton stared at her, allowing her to really see the hate in his eyes. "They got at Chaka. Right now I don't have time to tell you all the details. When 'jake' brings his punk ass here, just act like you don't know shit."

Anissa fought back the questions in her mind and quickly reached up and hugged Quinton, hoping this wouldn't be the last time they see one another.

Eve hung her head, a little angered by Quinton's tone toward her, and by the time she found the courage to speak, he was heading out of the door.

Buck was awakened by the sound of his phone, and by the time he answered, Sasha was on the line crying uncontrollably. Between the hiccups and the sniffles, he could hear her saying someone had been shot, but he couldn't make out the name.

"Yo, girl, take a deep breath and tell me who was shot."

"Chaka," she managed to blurt out before she started crying again.

Buck lost his patience. "Where?" He slammed down the phone.

It was a jolt to his system once he made sense of everything. In his car he struggled to keep himself from losing control. He reached for his cell phone and realized he'd left it in the house. There was no way he was heading back, especially since he'd just entered the Interboro Parkway.

Traffic was flowing at a normal pace, but Buck was in a hurry. By the time he reached the exit, he'd all but sideswiped two cars and he didn't give a damn. Bushwick Avenue, from Eastern Parkway all the way to Granite, was lit up with police cruisers and flashing lights. Traffic was being re-routed to keep the streets leading to the murder scene clear.

Buck headed the only other place that could offer him answers and hoped Quinton could tell him more than Sasha did.

Eve opened the door the moment his foot hit the concrete steps. "Where in the hell is he?" she yelled, tears clouding her eyes.

Anissa raced to the door, hoping to at least get a few answers, but was disappointed when he yelled back at Eve.

"Where the fuck is everybody?"

Anissa tried to settle the screaming match before things got out of control. "Buck, Quinton left here about an hour ago. All we know is, Chaka has been hurt, but he didn't tell us anything else. He hasn't called or been here since, and I'm very worried."

Eve quickly turned on Buck. "While Chaka was out there getting hurt, where the fuck was you? I mean, everyone has come through here except you, and now you come, acting like you all concerned."

Buck turned on Eve. "You one stupid bitch, and before it's all said and done, I hope Chaka finally puts your ass on the street, where you belong." He stormed back to his car.

Anissa was startled by the hate in Buck's words and embarrassed by Eve's accusations, but there was nothing left to do except close the door and wait it out.

Buck couldn't control the rage and anxiety building, especially after Eve attacked him for not being with Chaka. "Shit!" he cursed in the car alone. *Where is Quinton?* he thought, not allowing himself to believe Chaka was dead. Nah, he decided there was no way Chaka was dead. Shit, they were supposed to die old men, spending the money they'd accrued over the years.

Before long, Buck was back to trying to figure out who had done this to Chaka, and the only name that made sense was Earl. For years he had been walking in their shadows, creating drama either in the streets, or with Eve. As soon as the idea entered his mind, it festered and bugged him. For years Eve had been sneaking behind Chaka's back with Earl, and this was one of those times he prayed she wasn't up to her usual tricks . . . because he wasn't sure he wouldn't murder them both.

Buck entered the block with the intentions of either getting his own answers or finding someone that might lead him to Quinton.

The streets were crowded with people watching the scenario play out, and Quinton sat on the steps of an abandoned building, blending in with everyone else.

Buck, a look of danger in his eyes, emerged from the crowd only inches from Quinton. "Who?" was the only word he trusted himself to say in front of all the strangers trying to see.

Quinton hunched his shoulders and hung his head in reply, hoping Buck wouldn't lose his temper before they had a chance to talk. They couldn't afford to call attention to themselves, especially when he was holding more artillery than the cops canvassing the block. Slowly he rose from the battered steps and weaved his way through the crowd to meet Buck on the sidewalk. It was an unspoken language that "Excuse me" or "Pardon me" couldn't express, as people moved about them, getting out of their path.

Chaka's still body lay uncovered on the black tar, and Buck didn't have the courage to take a glance over his shoulder to see the truth of his friend's death. He lowered his head into his chest, hiding the tears that escaped. With each step he felt shame and then rage that it was Chaka and not him lying there. Buck's thoughts were clouded with questions. *Isn't it my responsibility to take care of the crew? Ain't that how it's always been since the second grade? From our first bake sale to our first dope run, I was the muscle, and somehow I hadn't taken my job seriously, and Chaka is dead because of me.* He stood still in the middle of the street, ready to kill.

Quinton recognized the slope in Buck's posture and knew it was only a matter a time before Buck surrendered to his confusion and anger. He picked up the pace as he headed to his car, hoping his friend would at least hold on a few more steps. "Don't start, nigga. We almost there. Besides, we got too much shit to do before this night is over," Quinton whispered and rammed his shoulder into Buck's back, forcing him forward.

Quinton's door hadn't closed when Buck yelled, "Yo, what the fuck happened? Who did this shit? And don't hunch your shoulders again, nigga. I know you can talk. Start fucking talking."

Quinton didn't acknowledge he'd heard the first question. Instead he pulled into traffic and initiated an entirely different conversation. "The twins will be here in two hours. By then we should have everything else in place."

Buck slammed his hand on the dashboard, drawing Quinton out of his calm. "Everything ... like what we don't even know happened. I spoke to that nigga Chaka, and he was supposed to be with the kids today celebrating. Just tell me, how did he end up back in Brooklyn?"

The streets rolled on before Quinton hit the parkway heading toward the airport. Again, he steered the conversation away from Buck's questions, hoping Buck would calm himself. "Beating on my shit ain't gonna help this situation, you fucking brute, and hollering ain't gonna get you any answers until we all together. I'm only gonna tell this shit once, and then we going to work. The first thing we need to do is go see Petra and them babies before she get word from someone else."

Buck threw up both hands in surrender. Although Quinton was making sense, it still didn't sit well with him that he had to wait to find out any details. "I'm not waiting two hours because you don't want to repeat yourself. Say what you know now and repeat that shit for the rest of them later. I swear, Quinton, this shit got me 'aggie.' I'm ready to just kill every lame we've ever had beef with."

Quinton nodded his head, and together they sat alone with their thoughts.

The twins Danny and Dave were under pressure the moment the phone calls began filtering in from New York, but the only one that held any weight was Quinton's message—"It's a red-eye situation. Chaka's been hurt." It didn't take them long to head out to the airport, leaving their families wondering exactly what had happened.

Confused by the severity of the situation, Dave paced back and forth, while Danny stood at the baggage carousel.

"Yo, what did Q say exactly?"

Danny dropped his head in frustration. "The same message you got is the one I got. I don't know how badly Chaka was hurt, and I haven't been able to reach Buck since we landed." He snatched both bags off the assembly and headed to the exit.

Dave followed quickly behind his brother and walked right into Buck's solid chest. "You one big muthafucka," he hissed. "Too big to be standing in front of doors and shit."

Buck shook his head.

The twins continued on their path to Quinton's car without any more words. Between Buck's ashy skin and Quinton's look of death, they knew the situation was probably worse than they expected, but neither was ready for the words that left Quinton's mouth. There was no trace of sorrow, as he kept talking, afraid that if he stopped he might break down.

Dave stared at Danny, who rocked back and forth, rubbing his hands together.

Before long, they pulled up to the only place that seemed right since they'd known one another as friends—IS 271 yards. They each leaped from the car.

Dave's haunting words brought them back to reality. "Eve told Chaka her car was broke down, but when he got there, she wasn't there."

Quinton only nodded.

"OK, so what you saying?" Danny interrupted, trying to connect the dots. "She may have set him up?"

Quinton hunched his shoulders. "I don't know."

Buck hadn't said anything since they'd gotten out of the car. He sat on the tiny slide and watched things unfold.

"That could only mean, if Eve did this, Earl snake ass is the triggerman." Danny pieced things together for them all.

It was a unanimous thought shared by everyone except Quinton. He'd actually seen the killers and had watched them get away.

Buck grew tired of the mindless chatter. He was ready to send both Eve and Earl to hell.

Quinton said, "We can't jeopardize everything, trying to get revenge. If we do this, we have to be smart about it."

Buck's anger spoke with nothing less than contempt in his heart for Quinton's last statement. "We can't jeopardize everything? Are you listening to yourself? Chaka wasn't just a figurehead in two empires legal and illegal. Muthafucka, he was our friend. Shit, our brother. Don't you remember the oath we took right here back in the sixth grade? We were the Baker Boys," Buck screamed. "If we do this, nigga, both those bitches is dead already, and that's a fact you may as well get use to right now."

Quinton stood. "It was never a question if we would step to our business.

The question is, How? … so that none of us are suspects, when it's all over. Besides, you can't bully us." Quinton pointed at the twins. "Sometimes you've got to stop and think, and as for my loyalty to a childish oath," he yelled, "muthafucka, don't you ever question it again."

Buck rammed his shoulder into Quinton's stomach and tackled him to the black plastic foam mats. "Bully that, bitch! And I'll question you and anyone else that can't remember this shit didn't start with money. It is always about friendship first."

Quinton rose up on his elbows ready to fight but thought better of it. Now wasn't the time. There was a missing piece to the puzzle, and they needed it before they even thought about revenge. "I hope that helped you feel a little better," he said as Dave helped him to his feet, "because there are still two facts that need addressing. The shooters weren't anyone I recognized right off, and two, we don't have any proof that Eve set Chaka up."

Danny was ticked off. "She had to have done it. Who else would have known where Chaka was headed? Who else had so much hate in their heart for us, besides Earl? And, more importantly, what bitch is greedier than Eve?"

Dave believed it was just a matter of asking Eve. "Let's go see Eve. We know Chaka's dead, but does she know?"

Quinton shook his head no.

Dave said, "Let's go to the house and tell her, and see what she says. What's the worst that could happen? She'll confirm what we already believe to be true. Fuck it! We don't have shit to lose."

Eve was sitting in the living room area when the group walked through the door. One by one she watched as they each greeted Anissa. She noticed no one had even offered her a head nod. *It's OK,* she thought, *because the moment they see Chaka it would all be different.* They'd be back to kissing her ass. Fuck it, if they weren't going to be civil, then neither was she.

She turned her attention to Quinton. "Where is Chaka?" she asked with an attitude.

Danny answered while Quinton left the room. "He's on his way to Kings County Hospital."

Eve stood up. "So if he's going to the hospital, why the hell didn't you call me so I could meet him there? Fucking stupid!" She tried to push past Danny.

"Nah, Eve," he interrupted her. "We need to know what happened, why Chaka was out there."

The question stopped her, and she spun around to face Danny. "What the fuck you mean, why was Chaka out there? Where the fuck was he?"

Buck leaned forward on the couch, and the slight movement caught everyone's attention.

Dave didn't bother to hide his disgust.

Eve, looking for some help, or a sign of what they wanted from her, shifted her head in Anissa's direction. "What the fuck? You come in here asking me questions, but no one is willing to tell me what happened to Chaka or where he was. I know where to get my answers." She looked for her car keys. "Oh shit," she whimpered. "He was on the avenue looking for me. My car broke down. Oh my God! Did something happen to him while he was looking for me?"

Everyone in the room sighed as they watched Eve break down.

"I was pissed off the tow company was taking forever, and Chaka didn't answer his phone right away. I kept calling, but by the time he answered, the tow company was pulling up. I was so mad, I decided not to call him back." Eve heaved as she explained what happened.

Buck wasn't convinced that Eve was so upset. She still hadn't asked how Chaka was doing.

Quinton didn't doubt her tears, but they certainly didn't confirm her innocence, especially after they'd heard Chaka's last message on the answering machine. 'Eve, where are you? I've been out here riding around for a half-hour.

If you don't hit me back, I'm leaving.' The line disconnected, and everyone was left with their own opinion about what happened after that call.

Eve began hyperventilating. "Where is he? Quinton, say if he's OK!" she yelled.

Before anyone could speak, the police were banging on the door.

Eve rushed out of the morgue feeling lost and confused. "This wasn't supposed to happen," she said out loud to Anissa. "I called Chaka to pick me, and now, look, he's dead because of me. They think it's my fault he's dead. Don't you see how they treating me like I killed him?"

Anissa didn't bother to respond. She wasn't so sure it wasn't Eve's fault either. All it would have taken was a phone call, and maybe Chaka would still be alive.

Eve sat quiet for the rest of the ride but swore that before the day was done she'd tell them all, it didn't matter what they thought. She didn't mean for him to get killed.

Chapter 3

THE FUNERAL SERVICE

No matter how many times Quinton rehearsed the words, he couldn't believe they were true. This was Chaka's going home service, and that just didn't seem right.

He dodged the reflection of his face as he stood in front of the mirror. He stared at his suit and fixed his tie. The tears in his eyes were for his shame and guilt. Part of the night he'd paced the floors trying to think of the right words to eulogize his friend. The other part of the night he listened to the twins telling stories about their youth. Even Buck had gotten caught up in remembering places they'd gone or things they'd done. Quinton listened as if he wasn't a part of the memories. He was hoping they'd all get drunk, and tomorrow it would all be a bad dream.

As the sun rose and he looked around, he knew this wasn't a bad dream. It was all the truth, and the direction of their lives were forever changed.

Confused, hungover, and exhausted, Quinton chastised himself. He talked to himself quietly. *If I hadn't been flirting with some girl, maybe I could have saved Chaka. Shit, the bitch wasn't even pretty. I heard that shot as I turned into the block. Didn't I see those two muthafuckas standing over my homie's body like they had a right to kill him? Didn't I watch in shock as they dodged my bullets and disappeared over the low wall?* Fuck it!" he yelled out as he snatched the tie from his neck. "How the fuck come you didn't hit at least one of them muthafuckas?"

Defeated, he sat on the bed. His mind shifted gears as he thought about Earl and Eve. *They did this*, he convinced himself, even if he wasn't willing to admit to his crew. "They killed my boy," he said loud enough for Anissa to hear as she walked into the bathroom.

Quinton called Anissa from the hallway, "Have you spoken to Eve?"

Anissa didn't bother to enter the hallway. She yelled from the kitchen, "Yes, she'll be there. Quinton, she said she couldn't stay here, knowing that you blamed her for Chaka's death. I mean, can you blame her? All her last memories of him are of a fight over something as simple as the car breaking down."

"Whatever. That girl caused Chaka's death, and if you don't understand how, there's no point in talking to you either."

Anissa stayed silent until Quinton called for her to get in the limo, and they headed to the church.

Eve had been sitting alone in the church as she stared at Chaka's portrait. She wondered if she was the reason for his death. "Could all of this misery be my fault?" she whispered. "You have to know I didn't mean for any of this to happen, and no matter how many times I say it, no one seems to care, especially, your crew. I don't know which one of them hates me the most. All I know for a fact is, I called you to the block, but I never meant for you to die. Besides, now that you're gone, I don't have anyone. It's almost like I'm a plague and no one wants to be near me. What am I supposed to do? My entire life was built around you and representing you."

Eve stood on weak legs and walked to the casket.

You don't get it. I may have stayed with you because of the things you could give me, but I never would have wished this on you. I would have never given up the only thing in my life that made me important. I was your woman, and now that you're no longer here, I may as well crawl in a hole. Even Anissa is looking at me sideways. I'm so sorry. I never would have been so reckless if I had imagined this could have happened.

Anissa tiptoed in the sanctuary, unaware that Eve was already there. She quickly seated herself in the rear, not wanting to interrupt Eve's last few minutes alone with Chaka. Anissa realized that Eve was suffering as great a loss as anyone else.

Just as the thought materialized, Anissa watched Eve slide to the floor. "No, baby, you can't stay down there. No matter how hard it is, you still have to represent him to the bitter end. You can't let those people walk up in here and see you broke down like this. Get up. We have to find a restroom to fix your makeup, because you can't go out like this."

Eve nodded and pushed herself off the floor.

Eve and Anissa re-entered the church and were surprised that, in the short time they'd been gone, so many people had filled the church.

Quinton shot Anissa a curious look as they took their seats.

Anissa ignored him, believing that the situation would work itself out, but she had to be supportive of Eve, especially since no one else was. It didn't matter that they didn't always agree. They were still friends, and until Buck, the twins, or Quinton could prove otherwise, Eve deserved their support.

Eve sat quietly to receive condolences from all kinds of people, some offering a brief story to their relationship with Chaka, others just viewing the body and offering a quick head nod in her direction. She immediately recognized every member of the Dirty Dozen. "And then there were thirteen," she whispered to Anissa.

It was a true statement, but it was an odd thing to say, Anissa thought.

One by one they walked to the casket. Some made the sign of the cross and moved away, others just lingered close enough to see before stepping away.

From the rear of the church Buck looked for anything irregular. Quinton stared at any unfamiliar faces, hoping to see the killers, and Danny and Dave both were hoping Earl would come through the doors.

Eve had witnessed several women crying as if they were mourning their husband. A few even had the audacity to kiss his corpse. One woman had the nerve to declare her love for Chaka. But no one outdid the elegant, dark-skinned woman that sashayed down the aisle to Chaka's casket. Everything about her seemed different to Eve. The way she walked, even the way she was grieving, wasn't overly done or pretentious.

Eve and Anissa quietly observed the stranger.

It bothered Eve that everyone else had at least acknowledged who she was. Meanwhile, this woman hadn't bothered to even look in her direction. The slant-eyed woman held onto the sides of the casket and wept. She appeared oblivious to the stares as she walked back up the aisle into Buck's arms.

"Who is she?" Eve whispered.

Anissa watched as Buck seemed to be consoling the woman, instead of the other way around. Just as she turned to answer Eve, Quinton walked over and held the woman as Buck wiped away his tears. And Danny and Dave flanked her side as though they were her personal bodyguards. This woman presence was beginning to bother Anissa.

Eve noted everything as a betrayal. She seethed in her seat as she watched them build a wall of support for the stranger, but they hadn't even offered her a tissue during this whole time. "Fuck them," she mumbled under her breath. She leaned upright in her seat, preparing to confront the group, but the ushers began closing the doors, signaling that the service would begin. She silently prayed that things would hurry along between the hollering women and the stranger. She wasn't sure how much longer she could hold herself in check.

Quinton finally, stood to speak, a piece of paper in his hand. Slowly, he began reading until the tears blurred his vision. Unconsciously, he cleared his throat, trying to rein in his emotion, but it didn't work. Frustrated he stared at the portrait of his friend and spoke from his heart. "No man could suffer a greater loss than the one I have to live with today," he said in a shaken voice shook, and the dam broke and the tears flooded his face. I could stand here and tell you all about our fallen brother, but every one of you knows exactly what he means to you. Go away with your thoughts of him, not someone else's memories written down on a piece of paper."

By the time he took his seat, he noticed everything had changed. Anissa was sitting next to him waiting to comfort him, Buck had disappeared, and the twins were both heading for the door. Even Petra had begun to tiptoe back up the aisle.

Buck's temper flared as he listened to Quinton break down during the eulogy. Sitting in the pew, he lost all control. Instead of crying out, he stormed from the church. He wanted to hunt down Earl and kill him. Stomping back and forth, he thought about all the deaths of his friends and family members. He cried over the loss of his grandmother after her long bout with cancer. He thought about the loss of Angela, the girl who taught him the meaning of love.

His thoughts roamed over countless faces and ended with Chaka. Angry, he wondered why loving someone always meant losing him or her. The only thing that would give him peace would be to kill Earl. He envisioned himself choking Earl until his body went limp.

Passersby openly stared at the imposing six-foot man storming back and forth, talking aloud, and swatting at an imaginary figure. Nothing was more heartbreaking than watching the gentle giant transform into a haunted beast that seemed to be going mad.

Dave and Danny showed little emotion during the funeral. Despite their feelings of helplessness, they were committed to the next step. Repeatedly the two scanned the church, gazing over familiar faces and trying to place a few of the not-so-familiar ones. Dave was searching for anything that might give a clue. Danny was searching for Earl. The twins had rationalized the whole scenario days ago, and the conclusion could not have been clearer. They had made a huge mistake allowing Earl to live.

Over the years, even in their differences, Chaka refused to go after Earl, even protecting him from the death he deserved. However, Earl's repayment for the protection was to kill his protector.

As frustrated as they were, Danny and Dave couldn't walk away this time. Earl had made too many threats for them to let him live. He would die, but not before they armed themselves correctly. The Baker Boys were losing a friend, and the Dirty Dozen was losing a figurehead.

Chapter 4

FREEDOM FROM MY ENEMY

Earl Clement watched the smoke rise high above his head as he sat celebrating the death of his enemy. His cold, beady eyes barely slit, he swayed to the beats of melodic steel drums. It was if they were pounding out his story. A story filled with loneliness, pain, and later mistrust, he reasoned in his narcotic haze.

"Chaka was supposed to be my friend, but time proved he would never be anything more than an enemy. It feels like yesterday, except our lives have changed so much."

Occasionally Earl would blurt out some obscure statement, as if anyone in the room was supposed to understand him. The woman in his lap half-listened, not caring in the least bit, as long as he continued to show her a good time.

"I got plenty of bitter memories with that muthafucka," he whispered, "and the only sweet thing I ever had he stole from me too. Eve." He hoisted the bottle to his lips. "I remember wanting to fit in so desperately. I trusted every word Chaka said, only to find out later that I was being used."

The mention of Chaka's name finally caught the girl's attention.

"I was new to everything in this country and afraid of just about everything in it too, but my father was determined for me to get an education here, despite the fact that I looked different and walked different. Shit, back then I even dressed different." He laughed. "I wasn't a trendsetter like I am now."

Even the young lady laughed, thinking Earl was kind of charismatic for someone that seemed so sad.

"Chaka called his crew the Baker Boys 5. They did everything together, selling cookies to classmates, partying, and selling weed. I thought accepting their friendship was a blessing, but later I learned my hardest lesson about curses." Suddenly Earl stopped talking, like he was no longer bothered by the drama of it all.

In his relaxed haze, Earl giggled to himself as he thought about better times. The crew changed him from the weird-dressing outsider with a heavy accent to a street hustler in less than a year. With Chaka's influence, Earl took over his father's illegal business, and they began getting money together. It was only natural that Earl trusted the crew with his life, and they took him in and trusted him with some things. Chaka never really shared his motives with Earl, although by the time Earl figured that out, he'd been ousted from the group.

Now that Chaka was dead, Earl hoped to embrace the original remaining members of the Baker Boys 5, and the members of the extension of their success, the Dirty Dozen. He wasn't opposed to a hostile takeover. This was his chance, and he wouldn't allow fucked-up emotions to get in his way. For too long he had accepted living in the shadows, trying to get along while other crewmembers flourished. They flaunted their success, while he struggled to get just a little more than enough. He was tired of being the outcast from a kingdom he helped to build.

There was no possible way Buck or Quinton would accept that he had nothing to do with Chaka's death. Telling them the truth about Chaka didn't matter in the past, and it surely wouldn't make a bit of difference now. He intended to use their anger to suit his needs. He would do to Chaka's crew exactly what Chaka had done to him.

Slowly his resentment took over his relaxed mood from earlier. He wanted to forget he'd ever given Chaka a second thought. Looking around the room, he decided that even without the Baker Boys 5, he had managed to do well. Counting his blessings, he lit another spliff and waited for the high. Earl willingly allowed his mind to wander back through his teenage years.

Earl remembered when the idea of the Dirty Dozen was formed. The moniker was a rip-off from the movie scripted by Lukas Heller and Nunnally Johnson.

They were watching the movie together in Chaka's basement. Chaka got excited as the end credits began to roll. "It's basically a suicide mission in them streets hustling," Chaka said. "But the truth is, our training starts at birth. We live behind the enemy lines, and the promise is the chance at having money, material things, and a temporary sense of freedom."

"Yeah, we could make our own Dirty Dozen," Earl declared, catching the wave of Chaka's excitement. "We could expand the business into other states, with a leader for each state all reporting back to us."

Chaka had agreed, and the Dirty Dozen was born.

"Who would have believed a plan so simple could have worked so well? And here I am sitting on the outside, celebrating that nigga demise."

Again Earl got quiet as the memories took over.

Fall 1995, Chaka's Plan

It was a cool day. The wind was whipping trash around as the four men stood just outside the fence of Ocean Hill projects, waiting for a few senior citizens to pass. Chaka and Earl stood side by side, while Quinton and Buck faced them. Earl, wishing he could drop the bag and run, handed Buck the nylon knapsack and waited for the chaos to begin.

A paneled van sped up onto the sidewalk where the boys were standing. Doors flew open, and the cops jumped out.

Earl took off past two police officers that exited the rear of the van. Chaka tried to run into the street and was clotheslined by the huge forearm of another officer. Meanwhile, Quinton stood still and threw up his hands in surrender.

Buck took off running with the bag. Before the cops could get close, he leaped over the black iron gates and slid past the wooden benches and concrete tables.

Earl watched the mess unfold from the parking lot between two cars. It looked like Buck would get away, but only moments later, he saw the cops pushing Buck toward the van.

Earl was so engrossed in watching Buck, he had allowed an officer to creep up on his hiding spot. Fear almost made him shit on himself when he heard the cuffs clink against the lock. The idea that he was in the middle of this caused him to re-think the reason he was there in the first place. He couldn't go to jail and vowed to do everything in his power to stay out of the system.

Chaka, Quinton, and Earl sat on the freezing curb in handcuffs, waiting for another paddy wagon to arrive. Chaka kept giving Earl dirty looks during the entire ordeal. By Quinton's own expressions, Earl figured they believed he had set them up, but no one ever asked him anything.

Buck was placed in a cell separate from the rest of the crew, Ms. Sadie came down to the precinct and took Chaka home, and Quinton's father showed up with a belt for him.

Meanwhile, Earl went untouched. No parent was called, and he walked without a desk appearance. Earl knew this was the beginning of the end for him and the Baker Boys 5. Later, that week, he tried to explain things to the twins, especially since they were the only members of the crew that hadn't gotten arrested. Earl remembered the coolness Danny showed him, and Dave walked away while he was talking.

Success had never been an accident for the Dirty Dozen. It was a chore, and the original Baker Boys had done things for the Dirty Dozen that was unheard of for men twice their age. And it was always Chaka who would sacrifice anyone and exploit anyone's integrity to get the end result.

In less than ten years since their quest to be millionaires, the Baker Boys branched out over eleven other states throughout the U.S.—New Jersey, Connecticut, Pennsylvania, DC, Virginia, the Carolinas, Florida, Georgia, Texas, and Louisiana. Fourteen men reaped the rewards, and the only one to ever suffer a loss was Buck.

Once again Earl was mentally cataloguing the Dozen's success and how they managed to make it work.

Every man representing the Dirty Dozen in one of those states was a native New Yorker. The plan was simply to succeed no matter what. No man was on his own, even if he was his own man. He had ten other counterparts to help him in any endeavor. Their initial product was drugs. Nothing they wanted could happen without capital, and these soldiers understood fast that money could be made from the forbidden, untamable desire to get high. They exploited it and studied the old American gangsters to make the transition.

Chaka loved to debate about the gangsters from the '20s that were now respected families in the new America. He thought it was ironic that Prohibition had made these men multi-millionaires, and the money had turned them into respectable men. He used that knowledge and the thoughts of each man in his circle to better run the vision. They also became well-bred businessmen with real estate in every one of the places they hustled. Strip clubs, mini-malls, and minor recording studios were among the list of businesses they held down.

By the time Earl finished thinking about all he'd missed out on and how he'd been used, he wanted everyone out of his space so he could begin his own plan. It was to get every dollar that he felt he was owed. It was clear the dirt had been kind and profitable to Chaka, and even in his death, most people didn't understand the level of hate he inflicted to get exactly what he wanted.

Chapter 5

THE LAST RIDE

The Dirty Dozen's last ride with Chaka at the helm revealed a slew of fully restored classic vehicles, from Cadillac El Dorados to Lincolns, Buicks, Monte Carlos, and one 1955 Ford Crown Victoria, which led the pack. It was the first car Danny ever owned, thanks to Chaka's weird sense of nostalgia.

Chaka had given each one of the men in the Dirty Dozen a used, beat-up hoopty, to symbolize the state of mind they were leaving behind. "We were all beat up by society and left to rot, but beneath the rust and flat tires is a beautiful body," Chaka used to say.

The process of remodeling the car was about pride and commitment. The commitment showed in all the vehicles that trekked from the church to the cemetery. Their pride lay buried behind the sorrow of losing a friend, a mentor, and a great business partner. Side by side, the Dirty Dozen flanked the open grave, each member alone with his grief.

The last amen echoed as mourners threw roses atop the casket. No one moved. It seemed there was something more to say. This couldn't be the only way to remember someone as loyal and smart as the man who had turned boys into millionaires.

Quinton quickly looked around the cemetery and realized Petra had left. His gaze wandered across the street. There she was, an ebony woman with sad eyes and a broken heart standing near the rear of the truck, observing the last rituals of the service. She too mourned Chaka's passing, accepting that she would love him far beyond his grave, probably for the rest of her life.

Petra wondered how she had become Chaka's secret while Eve became his public woman. Somehow she had allowed him to push her into the shadows even though he had loved her first. The bitter taste of jealousy and deceit made her angry, but her fear of losing him had kept her quiet. She needed Chaka, and she vowed to accept his love at all costs. Now she realized she had sacrificed her own self-love and worth for the illusion of a loving relationship.

Petra was losing the battle. Controlling her anger was more difficult with each second that ticked away. In the church she'd spied Eve looking at her, but she refused to acknowledge her. She noticed Eve's face had twisted up. Today wasn't about Eve, she tried to convince herself. This was Chaka's funeral, and she wouldn't do anything to disrespect the memory of her children's father. She imagined that one day soon she and Ms. Eve would get the opportunity to see each other again.

Petra knew there wasn't a soul alive or dead who could deny the love she shared with Chaka. He had invested everything in their relationship. She didn't want to be angry with Chaka. After today she only wanted to remember the good things she loved about him.

Petra had grown used to the way he smiled when he was happy. She loved the way he held her close while they slept. She couldn't have wished for a better father for their children. More importantly, he was her shoulder to cry on, and her friend. When the world felt like it was resting on her shoulders, he held her up. He encouraged her to continue with school when her family claimed it was a waste of time. She wanted to host the parties he and his friends gave, to be a part of the life he kept a secret, but she learned to encourage him from the other side.

Caught in her memories, she imagined Chaka's face the very first time they met.

Almost tripping over her feet, she stared into the face of the clear-skinned boy. She couldn't decide if it was his big expressive eyes that held her captive, or his black, wavy hair. All she knew was he was fine.

Sasha yanked her across the street and began the introductions for the double date she had asked her to attend. "Chaka, this is my study buddy, Petra," she said with the biggest grin on her face.

Instead of speaking right away, he stared at Petra.

Instantly, she felt self-conscious and began straightening her clothes.

Finally, he responded, "Hey, nice to meet you," and extended his hand.

Petra nodded, but didn't extend her hand, out of fear she would do something dumb. Sasha pinched her friend, hoping to get her into the date.

"Ouch! Oh, nice to meet you too."

The date was clumsy for Petra. It was her first since she began school, and Chaka, being American, made her a bit uncomfortable. This was one time in her life she wished she didn't have an accent and wished she knew all the right words to say at the right time.

Sasha would always tell her, "P, no one notices your accent, because you rarely say anything."

Petra would only smile and try to imitate Sasha, but with the slight singsong lilt to her voice, she always failed.

On their first date, Chaka encouraged her to speak, asking her question after question about her studies, the island she was from, and the life she wanted when school was over. It took him years to admit to her that he wasn't listening to her comments. He was attracted to the way she gestured with her body, and in love with the soft, confident sound of her voice.

The date was almost a disaster. Conscious of every move she made,

Petra nervously dropped her fork, and twice she almost knocked over a glass of water.

Sasha and Buck sat across from the couple, observing everything, separately wondering if their first date was so weird.

To make Petra feel comfortable, Chaka pretended not to notice.

Petra's memory faded as reality set in. Chaka had made his choice, and she hadn't been chosen. No amount of wishing, hoping, or praying could change that fact. All she would ever be was the mother of his children. Drowning in her thoughts, she wondered who would offer her condolences and share memories with her, the outsider.

She'd lost the fight years ago and surrendered to his will. Living without him wasn't an option, so she accepted his reasons for being with Eve. Nothing she could do would make him leave Eve. Her tears had made him angry, and her silence moved him out the door completely. Desperate to hold on to him, she allowed his wants to supersede her needs. She prepared meals, washed clothes, and did whatever he asked of her. She was the perfect example of a good West Indian girl, raised to take care of her home and cater to her man. Nevertheless, she wanted more. Deep down she should have demanded more, but having a part of him was better than not having him at all.

Petra had come to this country in search of the American dream. Chaka had vowed that he would not stop her from achieving it, but had never figured out how to be the man she needed. She remembered Chaka once trying to explain his love for her.

"My love for you should be obvious," he said. *"No other woman can declare that I have given her the best part of me—my children. Do you really think it was a mistake that you became pregnant?*

"Having Chanice changed the direction of my life forever. Hearing her cry for the first time made me different. I wanted to cut off my arm, if it meant it would make her happy, not so she would be quiet, but so she would never feel another ounce of pain. Maybe in the beginning I did things to jeopardize our love—running away instead of working things out—but even then that was to ensure you met your goals. I loved you then, and I love you more now. There was never a competition between you and another woman. You are the woman that I live for, and I will continue to ensure that our children never want or need anything."

Petra had heard every word he spoke that day, and she knew he spoke the truth, but she couldn't accept it without the commitment. In her heart she always hoped he would make her his wife.

A glare from someone's headlights shook Petra from her memories as she stood watching the procession from across the street.

Quinton hurried to the waiting limo and ushered Eve and Anissa inside before quietly closing the door. Without explanation, he dashed across traffic to where Petra stood and held out his arms, offering her his condolences. Forcing himself to shut out his own pain, he tried to be strong for Petra, knowing she needed someone to help her through the tragedy of losing her lover, her children's father, and her best friend.

Chaka's death was overwhelming, and the shattered woman that clung to Quinton stamped her feet and cried uncontrollably. "Why?" was all she trusted herself to say.

Quinton understood Petra's need to know why. He held her tighter, praying his arms would be enough until he could find the answer to her question.

As Petra stood there crying and shaking, she remembered the voice of her daughter yelling, "I want my daddy."

The image of her son CJ, staring at her, afraid to ask why he couldn't come to the funeral popped into her head. Unsure of how to go forward, she cried until there were no more tears.

Her outburst rocked Q. His strength slid away as he held her tighter still. The tears welled up and spilled from his eyes as he breathed deeply, trying to gain some control over his grief. Unprepared for the breakdown, he wished Anissa could help him.

All day he had watched the difference in the two women Chaka had chosen. Where Eve was rude, crass, and disrespectful, Petra was reserved, classy, and almost regal. The outburst of grief nearly dropped him, and by the time she pushed away, he was ready to let go too.

"Chanice and CJ were not ready for this," Petra said. "Remembering him in a casket just didn't seem appropriate. The boy has not spoken one word since I told him about Chaka." She paused. "And Chanice just keeps saying she wants to see her daddy. I couldn't saddle them with this burden."

Both Anissa and Eve sat in the limo and stared out the window, stunned at the affection Quinton offered the stranger. Anissa was horrified.

Eve immediately recognized the woman from the church. The questions were now screaming loudly in her mind as she wished for the right answers. *Why is Quinton offering this distraught woman such comfort? Is she a friend of his or Chaka's? Most importantly, why is she getting special treatment?* The bitter taste in her mouth showed all over her face.

Eve had finally lost her calm facade she had fought all day to maintain. "Who is the fucking ugly bitch?" she yelled.

Before Anissa could think of an answer, Eve ordered the driver to take them across to the parking lot.

"The path is blocked by last-minute observers," the driver explained.

Eve spoke through clenched teeth. "Don't play with me! Honk your horn and go around those pretentious bastards." The anger she felt had ballooned. She was seeing red and welcomed a confrontation. She slammed her back into the cushioned seat and crossed her arms, like a spoiled child having a fit.

The driver took his job seriously. He silently prayed the young man across the street knew what he was doing. With respect for the situation, he said, "Honking a horn is forbidden in a burial ground. I'm sorry."

Eve glared at the driver through squinted eyes as she slid to the door.

Anissa reached for the handle just as Quinton opened the door. He practically pushed Eve back across the seat as he sat opposite her.

"Who is she?" Anissa and Eve both asked in unison.

The scowl on Quinton's face should have been a warning, but neither acknowledged the look and kept questioning him. Tired of the litany of questions, he easily silenced Anissa by meeting her glare head-on. Although he had not spoken one word, she understood his meaning—*Shut the fuck up!*

Eve, however, was relentless, speaking to him as if she had forgotten her manners. "Quinton, I asked you a question, and I expect a fucking answer."

"*Evil* Lynn, ask me no questions, and I won't have to tell you a lie," Quinton said, using his distorted nickname for Eve's full name, Evelyn.

"Self-serving son of a bitch," she spat just above a whisper.

Anissa's mouth flopped open as she watched the two people that meant the most to her insult one another.

"Evil, listen to me. I am not going to tolerate you much longer, so I am suggesting you get off my nerves."

The words eased from Quinton's lips, but the venom they held was clearer than the words spoken. She could push if she dared, but Quinton was in no mood for her theatrics. The emotions from the funeral along with the drama of having to continue on the path the Baker Boys had set for revenge weighed heavily on him. He wouldn't give Eve the chance to add any more pressure than he was already feeling. Staring at her, he wondered if she could have set up Chaka to be killed.

Chapter 6

Buck stayed behind at the cemetery to make peace with his fallen friend. Staring at the open hole, he waited for the right words to form. Nothing he attempted seemed appropriate. Every thought he had seemed unreal. Ashamed, he allowed the comforts of rage to engulf him.

The old sparkle in his eyes was now replaced by emptiness, and his contagious smile hid behind his cold heart and menacing glare. Pacing, he cursed the wind that swirled around him. "You protected Earl's bitch ass for too long, and now look," he said. "Your arrogance made you believe that nigga didn't have the heart to get at you. You ignored every one of his threats, but look at you now. He's living and you … " Buck didn't have the courage to complete the thought, let alone speak it.

"On everything I love, I promise that nigga's days are numbered. He better start praying so he can get into heaven, 'cause he's gonna die."

His tears poured down his face, and guilt rode him as he begged Chaka for forgiveness. Buck believed he had failed his godchildren by allowing their father to die.

In the cold he made more promises, hoping that they could somehow change the direction he knew he was about to take. Friendship was the only constant in his life. Quinton, Dave, Danny, and Chaka were his responsibility, and he had failed them, like they had failed him so many years ago.

Buck couldn't find the courage to walk away just yet. Instead he sat on the cold ground and allowed his thoughts to be carried back to a time when he questioned the Baker Boys' love for him.

Buck Serving Time as a Youth, 1996

The first night locked up was the worst. The constant sound of metal slamming was mind-altering. It stole his breath away, his stomach clenched, and his heart pounded. Fearing the unknown worked him over. The wide space was more than intimidating. Men were huddled together talking and making jokes as if they weren't serving time behind bars.

One kid was hankering down in a corner looking scared to death. The putrid smell radiating from him saturated the room. To taunt him seemed cruel, but occasionally someone would go by and throw something in his direction, and he would jump every time.

Buck was determined to stay out of unnecessary trouble, but he was hell-bent on remaining true to the man he was.

After months in jail, he was transformed into a hostile urchin. His face stayed screwed up in a scowl, and his eyes moved constantly as he watched for trouble heading his way. Nothing in his life had prepared him for the outcries of men in the night. Someone was always in some shit. The things going on behind the wall were hidden from family and friends on the outside, and the guards often responded when it was too late.

One day while preparing for a visit, an older man approached him and asked in his slow, gravelly voice, "Son, why you here?"

The question was simple, but the answer was complicated. How could he explain that he was there by choice? That he took the responsibility for the actions of his entire crew because it seemed like the right thing to do? No one would understand that, although his Grandma Bea's sad eyes and broken heart would probably haunt him forever. He had to stand up and be responsible.

Even now as he worked the words around in his head, it didn't seem so smart to have pled guilty. Sixteen months seemed better than everything else he was hearing could happen if he had waited for trial.

After waiting for an answer, and not receiving one, the old man left Buck to contemplate his response.

Jahson Holden, also known as Buck, needed to quiet the resentment that had found shelter in his heart. He contemplated all the things he had given up and decided that the punishment was far greater than the crime he had committed. His chance at a football scholarship washed down the drain the moment he heard the heavy iron doors slam. The girl who made him smile was probably out enjoying time with another man smart enough not to be caught. In addition—and worst of all—his friends were off enjoying their freedom, giving little or no thought to the sacrifice he was making in the name of friendship.

Two months before his scheduled release, Buck sat opposite the two people he had trusted most with his life. Clothed in an orange jumpsuit, his head hung low as he fought back tears and prayed the words he'd just heard were not true. The words were boulders placed on his heart. Through clenched teeth, he asked, "How did she die?"

"She was killed in a car crash last night on the conduit," Quinton explained. "Some nigga she was riding with was racing, and he lost control of his car."

Quinton could not help feeling that delivering the horrible news was like standing in quicksand. Next to Quinton in the bright orange chair was Chaka, lost in his own misery at being helpless to the man who had saved him more times than he could count.

Although Buck was the only one serving time for possession of marijuana with intent to sell, Chaka, Q, and Earl were just as guilty. In retrospect, Buck had the most to lose by going to prison, but he did what was natural when it came to his partners. He protected them. He had been protecting Chaka since second grade, so this was just another step in the course of their friendship.

Chaka chose his words carefully. "I can only imagine how you feel."

Buck exploded. "Nigga, you can't imagine my pain. The thoughts of Angela are the only reason I'm surviving this bid." The depth of his words could have sunk the Titanic. "The day the judge sentenced me, I asked you for one thing. Please protect her until I come home. Both you muthafuckas failed. You sitting here imagining my pain, and this nigga sitting here looking at me like he going to break down and cry. Fuck that shit you talking!"

Buck leaped from his seat, bitter, resentful, and angrier than he could ever remember being. In jail, there was no room for weakness. Despite his attempts at holding his tears at bay, he was breaking down.

Later, back inside his cell, he collapsed and allowed the tears to flow like a raging river. He banged his head on the concrete wall and bit his tongue to keep from screaming. Blood gushed from the sides of his mouth as he held his mouth open but refused to let any sound escape.

He opened his eyes and saw the letter just inches from his face. It was in Angela's neat cursive. Leaning forward, he grabbed the envelope, hoping to make the words of her death less true. He was searching for a clue that she would not be alive by the time he received her words of encouragement. In some bizarre way, the letter had taken him to her. He pictured her as she wrote the words he would remember for the rest of his life. They declared love for all eternity.

Boldly she described missing his gentle loving touch and needing the opportunity to try all the things they'd only imagined doing. She begged him to forgive all the things she had done in his absence, explaining that nothing could erase the purest and most innocent love she had experienced with him.

She had ended the letter by promising to see him in her dreams. That last line of the letter brought the hulking physique of a powerful man to his knees. Love was such a small word, he rationalized later, but it had the ability to destroy everything in its path. The only woman to love him was unprotected. Now she was gone. Shame, rage, and now a lost love had taken over his miserable existence. Buck cried and begged God to send her back to him.

News of his approaching release should have been a happy moment, but instead he began re-evaluating the direction of his life. He resented his crew. They had failed him while he had given up a chance at a good life. He'd wanted to prove all the people who predicted he was headed for prison wrong. Instead, he had helped the prediction come true. He had broken his Grand Bea's heart.

On the day of Buck's release, Chaka sat in the beat-up Monte Carlo, waiting for his brokenhearted friend. Finally there he was standing at the electronic gates. From a distance, nothing about Buck seemed to have changed, except that he had bulked up, and his glare was more menacing.

Standing next to him, Chaka realized Buck *had* changed. Their greeting was cold. There was no excitement in his eyes or even a hint of happiness that he was a free man. If there was ever a time in Chaka's life he wished he could change a bad decision, this was one. Not knowing what to say to change Buck's mood, he said nothing.

Chaka's quietness revolved around the fact that he didn't protect Angela. In his selfishness, he had not even bothered to speak with her, outside of the pleasantries of seeing his friend's girlfriend in passing. Privately he was a little jealous of Buck's strength. Buck never stopped trying. There was no situation too big for him. When they were younger, the pudgy kid with crazy fighting skills would not allow anyone to pick on him without a fight. It wasn't the same for Chaka, who had been the target of more than one bully, but meeting and befriending Buck changed that forever.

Chaka was never able to shake the fact that Buck had to save him from getting jacked almost every day of his elementary school years. Instead of being grateful, he resented it when they were older. He hated that Buck could go anywhere and most men either moved out of his way or greeted him politely, simply because of his intimidating height and girth. Even standing next to him had its rewards. A woman could give Buck hell, but a nigga didn't stand a chance. That's why Sasha had dubbed him the gentle giant. Meanwhile, Chaka always had to earn respect.

Chaka was happy he never had to explain why he harbored such feelings. Men didn't discuss the things that made them weak, or the animosity they harbored from their youth, but seeing Buck now made him ashamed of the things he had done to hurt his friend.

After Buck was seated in the car, he asked Chaka to drive him straight to the cemetery where Angela was buried.

Buck searched the grounds until he found the stone dedicated to Angela Plumbton. Without fanfare, he knelt and kissed the bronze-colored plaque. There wasn't a tear left to shed or an apology left to ask for. He sat quietly until he could allow the words to form. He poured out his heart and promised to love Angela for all his days. No woman could claim her place in his heart. The minutes that passed were like seconds as he thanked her for loving him and being his best friend.

The air that escaped from his lungs burned as he vowed to make the guilty pay for the pain they had inflicted on his beloved. Just as quietly as he walked to the grave, he found himself wandering back to the car.

Chaka's meaningless chatter forced Buck to accept that, no matter how angry he was, he needed to control his emotions. He couldn't allow anything to interfere with his plans.

As Chaka and Buck arrived at Grand Bea's place, Chaka climbed from the car and handed Buck a set of keys. "These are for the car, and the others on the ring are for you when you're ready," he announced, like it was some big surprise.

Buck hunched his shoulders in response and turned to leave his friend standing on the sidewalk. Buck's homecoming was uneventful. There wasn't a group of people waiting for him or even a home-cooked meal.

After a few days he took a chance and left the house. Not two blocks from home, he ran into Chaka's mother. Ms. Sadie put an end to Buck's self-inflicted exile. She summoned him to her home to have a talk.

The moment he stood in her kitchen, she turned and smiled. There he was, the teddy bear, trying not to look as sad as he felt. Understanding his loss, she wanted him to feel and know she would always be there for him. Opening her arms, she wrapped him in a mother's hug and rocked him until she was ready to let him go.

Ms. Sadie's reception made Buck feel loved. For the first time since being home, he was sorry for staying away from the house he had spent so much time at as a child. In his anger he hadn't given thought to the other people who did love him and wanted to know he was OK.

The petite woman placed a platter full of his favorite foods before him and watched him eat. She couldn't have been happier to see that he still loved to eat as much as she loved to feed him.

Giggling, she reminded him of all the times she had to cook extra because he pretended to be taking food to his grandmother. Buck would eat the food long before he got home.

"Buck, it's not easy to accept losing someone we love, either in death or if they just move on to someone else. But it's better to know that special connection than to wonder about it all your life."

Ms. Sadie wanted to encourage Buck to move beyond his grief, so she wanted to be sure he understood her point. "I am proud you haven't allowed the setback to cripple you, and for that, I could not have chosen a better friend for Chaka. My son is a better man for having you in his life. I remember not being able to get any of you to leave as children. Do not allow your disappointment in them to stop you all from growing. I know they let you down, but you are as incomplete without them as they are without you." She hugged her surrogate son and begged him to try to forgive his brothers.

Buck listened to everything she said, and even tried to forgive them, but the pain wouldn't subside.

Days later Buck leaned back in the barber's chair relaxing, wondering if he had the courage to forgive Chaka and Quinton. Laughter and complaints buzzed throughout the shop, but it was the peaceful feeling that helped him make up his mind. Being home and able to do something as simple as go to the local barber and talk bullshit seemed like a privilege after all he had been through. He watched as mothers dropped off their sons and talked to their favorite barber, and little kids running back and forth, waiting for their turn to get in the chair. It all brought back memories of him, Quinton, and Chaka as young men.

Later that day Ms. Sadie was all smiles when she saw Buck enter the room. Although she had asked him to forgive Chaka and Quinton, she didn't think he would show for Chaka's birthday party. Standing there in her elegant cocktail dress, she couldn't wait to show the rest of the boys her surprise for them. The healing could truly begin, as long as they were in the same place at the same time.

Despite everything, Chaka wanted to appear unmoved by the gesture of seeing his burly brother in the walkway, but his ears turned red, and his eyes glistened as he bowed his head to hide his joy.

Chaka rose as his friend strolled toward him in his black leather pants, matching leather shirt, and fedora pulled slightly over his right eye. The two men embraced as though they hadn't seen each other in years. More than anything, they knew this was not about time. This gathering was about forgiveness.

Quinton observed the camaraderie. *This is a long-overdue welcoming,* he thought. He could now relax and enjoy the night.

A cameraman captured the scenes as the men sat side by side, laughing and clowning around. Ms. Sadie posed for a picture with the young men, kissing each one as if it would be their last time together. She proposed a toast to Chaka, wishing him a happy birthday and a peaceful life with his closest friends. Each man understood the meaning and bowed his head, paying their respect for the wisdom bestowed.

The night went by quickly as each man danced with every woman brave enough to shimmy nearby. Chaka was smiling because he knew just how much his brothers meant to him, and Quinton was elated that his right arm was now intact.

Buck left that night feeling as if he had eased a small burden. He marveled at the number of women who found him attractive. In his state of bereavement, he didn't even bother to appear available. He had stumbled about, restoring his Monte Carlo and staying away from anything that would remind him of his loss. Now he understood the other part of staying away that he had missed—the tender touch of a good woman.

Just as he was about the pull off that night, Sasha came out of nowhere. "Hey, bad boy," she teased.

He had seen her since he'd come home and meant to call her, but it always slipped his mind. Amazed at seeing her, he leaped from the car and pulled her into a huge hug. He twirled her around. "Damn, Sash! You looking good."

She laughed when he let her go. She blushed, tossing her hair back and thinking the same exact thing she always did about Buck, but she didn't dare say it. All her teenage life she had a crush on him, and he never knew it. In fact, she kept the secret from everyone.

"Thank you. When did you get home? And why haven't you been to see me?" she said all in one breath.

He lowered his head, but kept his smile in place. "I've been home a little while, but I wanted to get my head right before I started visiting my peoples, you know?"

"That doesn't excuse you," she answered, her hands on her hips.

Buck ended up sitting next to Sasha in her apartment, listening to music and reminiscing about their days of playing in the middle of the street. He couldn't help thinking, *Things are beginning to get back to normal.*

Several weeks later Quinton leaped an inch off the ground as he got his first look at Buck's restored Monte Carlo. The coffee-colored exterior gleamed, and the ivory-colored interior with coffee piping complemented the driver's smile.

"Damn, big boy!" Quinton said. "You have made this baby pretty as hell."

Buck nodded. He had done well in restoring the car. The excitement etched across Quinton's face eased his reservations about his color choices.

"What you name her?"

"This is Miss Mable. She got an old soul with a hot-ass body, and pretty as any of tomorrow's next best things."

"Nigga, you did all right restoring this pretty bitch. I'm ready to go get me a Caddy and see what you can do with that."

Buck leaped from the driver's seat, allowing Quinton a chance to really see the detail he had put into his ride.

Quinton sat down and got familiar. He turned on the ignition and listened as she purred. He slammed the door, reclined, and adjusted the mirrors. If Buck didn't get in, he would be left right there, because Quinton was ready to ride.

"You better get in, or I'm gonna leave you standing right here," Quinton yelled.

Buck laughed as he sat in the passenger's seat.

"Let's go to Atlantic City. Give me the chance to open her up and see what she can do."

Buck smiled in agreement, and they glided into traffic. The car sat suspended in mid-air, and the tires stroked the pavement with the touch of well-skilled lover. Buck nodded his head to the words that flowed through the Alpine speakers.

Quinton smiled as he accelerated on the parkway, weaving into one lane and dashing into the next with the agility of a panther. He yelled above the music, "This must be what it feels like to ride on a cloud."

Buck laughed. "Just remember, this is my ride. You got to get your own."

The flow changed as they found themselves on the New Jersey Turnpike. Quinton stopped at a rest stop to fill up the tank. In his excitement, it hadn't occurred to him to invite Chaka along for the ride, but shit, he would tell him about it when they got back home.

Buck shook his head at his friend as he watched Quinton push Miss Mable to full throttle on the open highway. Her smooth response impressed Quinton even more as he sailed past exit sign after exit sign.

The tollbooth clerk uttered her approval as she claimed the fee.

Buck leaned over his friend and began flirting. "Hey, shorty, can I see you again?" he asked with a sincere smile.

Her giggle and wink answered that question. Buck pressed a laminated card into her hand and asked that she give him a call.

Once they left the turnpike, twenty minutes went by before Quinton got the nerve to ask his friend about a time not so long ago. He hadn't apologized yet for not holding up his end of the bargain when Buck got locked up, and he wanted him to know he knew it. He also understood Buck's distance, and didn't want anything to come between them. Quinton valued his friendship without any reservations, even though others thought he was a brute.

"I can't tell you how sorry I am for not protecting Angela better, man. I truly hope you can forgive me. I know how much you loved her, and it's really good to see you flirting and getting on with your life. I also have to believe that anything I say now is not good enough, but you must know, Buck, I would have done anything to take away the pain you felt that day."

The words rang true to Buck, but he was still angry that the time for him and Angela had come and gone. Gritting his teeth, he finally spoke his first words of forgiveness. "I have to believe that you wouldn't have wished something so miserable on me. But, most importantly, I have to accept that Angie is gone."

Quinton was awestruck by Buck's response, but there was nothing more to say. The next few minutes of the ride, they happily reminisced about the past.

Before they realized it, the neon signs of Atlantic City were welcoming them.

Four hours later Buck was driving back to New York with a serene feeling in his heart. During his bitterness and exile he had forgotten the realness that he felt being around his friends. Snoring beside him was one of the men he felt he could bare his soul to and never regret it.

During the party he had taken a first step toward forgiving his friends, but now he was ready to move completely forward.

Chapter 7

HOW THE BAKER BOYS DO IT, 2003

Later that day, after the funeral, Buck, Danny, Dave, and Quinton met at the park to play basketball, just like they always did, to work out their problems. After playing three games of street ball, Buck was left with a swollen lip and scuffed knees; Quinton had scraped off the skin of both palms; Danny had torn the seat of his black slacks, trying to keep up with Buck; and Dave, going for a lay-up, had run headfirst into the pole. If the reason they were there wasn't so sad, it might have been comical to watch them play.

Earl knew exactly where they would end up. Every time they were upset, they went through this ritual. This was as common as Quinton's compulsion to repeat everything twice, and the twins' penchant for having a trunk full of liquor to douse any pain. Buck, however, was the wild card, even back in the days. He wasn't one whose actions could easily be predicted.

The brown bag rattled as Danny checked the amount of liquor left in the bottle. Memories flooded them as they each remembered why they were there in the first place. Chaka always said that wasting liquor was like wasting good pussy—just a sin and a shame. Instead of the tradition of pouring out liquor for their dead brother, they raised their plastic cups and recited Chaka's words as if they were their own.

Earl's false bravado and his poor judgment made him waltz over to the men standing on the playground. He wasn't welcome, even though it was a public park. The reverie ended and angry men stood there, each wanting an opportunity to kill the man they suspected was responsible for harming Chaka.

Quinton pushed past Buck, sensing the danger, and spit collected in the corner of Buck's mouth, as his eyes went from sad to pure evil. Earl was living on borrowed time, but they had to put some distance between the murders. The streets were watching, and no one wanted to take any unnecessary chances with the justice system.

Earl raised his palms, as if surrendering to some unwaged war. "I'm only here to offer my deepest sympathy," he said.

Quinton's eyes glazed over, his heart raced, and his palms burned to slap the shit out of Earl. Knowing he needed to remain calm, he waited. Dave and Danny both closed the circle around the culprit they knew was responsible for their pain.

Buck was the one who finally found the words to respond. "We heard you," he said, a menacing glare on his face. "We appreciate your heartfelt sympathy. Now please leave."

The snarl that came after Buck's words should have sent Earl running to his truck, but he stood firm. This was Earl's moment, and he planned to take it. Quinton didn't have any patience, and Buck was just a fucking brute. The two together couldn't out-finesse him at this game, or so he thought.

Earl sneered at Buck. Everything he knew about the crew was hand-wrapped and delivered to him by someone held in high regard, someone inside the circle. "Damn, nigga! You would think your big, dumb ass would have learned. Since your man is gone, anybody can be touched."

Earl knew they suspected he was the cause of Chaka's death. He also knew they would wait before they went gunning for him. No matter, he was planning to come after them first. But Earl let his mouth get his ass in a world of hurt.

Buck punished him for being dumb enough to say what he thought. Earl didn't even get a chance to pretend to reach for anything, let alone defend the rain of punches. The first blow shattered his nose, and the second cracked at least two ribs. The countless stomps to his body following his collapse left Earl unconscious. Buck put more effort into each blow as he relived the cries he'd heard at the church earlier that day.

"You one dumb muthafucka," Buck said to him. "I guess playing in traffic ain't dangerous enough for your simple ass." Buck was kicking Earl's ass and talking shit like it was an old-fashioned get-the-belt whipping.

The other men standing nearby prayed Buck would kill Earl, and the shit would end in peace. Street justice would have been served.

Danny laughed hysterically. The moment made him want to kick Earl's ass too. Feeling a little vindicated, Dave got in a good shot to the head before they walked away.

When Earl finally came to, he looked around to discover he was alone. His ego had been stomped, snatched, and damaged almost beyond repair. As he struggled to rise off the ground, he finally realized Buck's weakness. Damn the investigation, and fuck who knew what. There was no way he would have allowed his nemesis to live another day.

Holding his ribs, he stumbled to his car and smiled, knowing Quinton and Buck would be joining the beast that set this rivalry in motion. The sight of his blood as he coughed was the serum he needed to make his words ring true. Someday soon Buck would turn against Quinton, giving him the chance to murder them both.

Chapter 8

Eve noticed Chaka's jewelry immediately, but she didn't bother to give him a second look, until she saw him standing next to Anissa laughing. Not waiting for an introduction, she pushed into the center of the group and extended her hand to Chaka. "Hi, my name is Eve." She rushed on. "How do you know my girl?"

Chaka accepted her hand but didn't bother to answer any of her questions. Instead, he smiled and introduced himself. Immediately, he recognized her beauty, but it was her brazen attitude that attracted him to her. "I'm Chaka. This is my crew." He pointed at the rest of his boys, staring in her eyes.

The deejay cranked up the music, and all conversation ended as Eve and Chaka bounced across the dance floor. Chaka didn't mind dancing a little, but he wasn't for working up a sweat, no matter how great the music was.

Without Eve realizing it, he went to lean back against the wall. He was mesmerized by her tight body jamming to the music. He kept thinking, *She might be some fun if I could convince her to take a ride with me.* As soon as he considered the thought, it occurred to him that he'd seen this pretty young lady before with Earl. Damn! He'd stepped into a gold mine and he wasn't even trying to. He wondered if she knew who he was, because things could definitely work to his benefit if she hadn't figured it out yet.

Buck had finally come off the dance floor with a shorty, and Chaka was eager to talk, but he didn't really want anyone knowing exactly what he was up to. Instead, he continued to walk Eve for the rest of the night.

Anissa woke up late the next afternoon, wondering why she was not in her bed. Panic set in, until she got her bearings. Glaring at the broad, black back of the man lying next to her, she prayed she had not gone home with a stranger. Anissa raised the blanket and was relieved to see her bra and panties intact.

Quinton rolled over and barreled into her as she leaped from the bed. He smiled at his guest as she stood there practically naked, wide-eyed, and terrified.

"Good afternoon, Ms. Anissa," he said, his voice groggy.

"Hey! How did I get here? How come you didn't take me home?" Anissa had just met this man the night before at the club. She knew he was friends with her old buddy, Chaka, but still, she couldn't believe she agreed to spend the night.

"First of all, your ass is heavy, and you sleep like the dead. Secondly, I didn't take advantage of you while you slept. I laid your ass down before you caught a cold."

Anissa rolled her eyes at the demanding jerk that lay there, looking good as hell. "Do you ever ask anyone to do anything? Or do you just pull them along and bark orders?" She looked around his room.

For a man, it was a tastefully decorated room, with a gold-plated wrought-iron bed frame, matching side tables with lamps, and the biggest television she'd ever seen in a bedroom.

"Nah. Normally I club a woman over the head and carry her where I want them to go. Sort of like what I did to you last night."

That afternoon they slept in turns. Anissa watched the rise and fall of his thick, defined chest and long neck. She stared at his expressions as he dreamed. She pretended to care about what he dreamed about when he slept.

The truth was, she needed anything to take her mind off his fingers playing with her in her most private place.

While Anissa drifted off to sleep, Quinton kneaded her breasts, measuring the size in his large hands. He palmed her ass and finally flipped her over to climb on top of her, forcing her to open her eyes.

"Dammit, you Neanderthal! You could have waited until I woke up." Anissa pretended to be angry, but couldn't wait to feel him inside her.

"Take those things off," he demanded.

Anissa eased out of the bed. Nervous, she slowly removed her sexy panty and bra set. She stood there, less than perfect, in front of his lustful eyes. Somewhere in her subconscious she found false bravado and issued a challenge. "I am showing you mine. Now show me yours."

Quinton slid from under the covers and dropped his drawers as if he was the most confident man alive.

The sly grin that etched across his face made her laugh aloud. "Why are you standing here looking like you stole the cookie out the cookie jar?"

"This is why." He pressed her to the wall with his body. Softly he touched her until she surrendered.

By dropping her guard, she experienced the ultimate pleasure. Any place his hand touched, his mouth followed. He seemed to be practicing or preparing for something. Just as Anissa expected the experience to be less than fulfilling, Quinton made her purr. He traced the length of her arm with his finger and brought the palm of her hand to his mouth. Using his tongue, he traced a small circle in her palm.

The simple act seemed a bit bizarre at first, until he blew in the same spot, causing her to tingle below the waist. Next he sucked her middle finger slowly, allowing his tongue to lead the trail. There was nothing masterful about his skill, but he did have superior instinct. He wanted to make her remember his touch long after he released her.

While Quinton toyed with Anissa's body, he whispered for her to open her eyes. At that moment, he touched her breast. She thought she would melt into the floor. He allowed his finger to trace along the dark inner circle of her nipple, and his tongue followed. No words could describe the pleasure she felt as he stroked her nipple with his mouth, applying just enough pressure, and alternating between sucks and teasing licks.

Suddenly, she felt the dam break, and juices flowed down her legs. Her back arched all by itself as she pulled him to her, and soft pants escaped from her mouth. Her chest heaved as she gasped for air.

Quinton took both nipples into his mouth at the same time, forcing Anissa to whisper curses, and she stroked his head and continued to moan.

He leaned away from her, just a bit, to look up into the face of the woman he would possess after today. Anissa closed her eyes and tried to relax from the tension Quinton had just created.

Just when her breathing seemed to find a normal rhythm, he slid his hand between her thighs. The moistness that covered his long finger was all the encouragement he needed. As soon he pulled his fingers from her fold, he slid his tongue in its place, and her mouth flew open as she stared down at the body that kneeled beneath her.

Quinton hoisted her from her wide-legged position and placed her in the center of the bed. Not one moment was wasted as he climbed between her legs and took pride in every moan that escaped her lips. He felt the pressure she applied to his head and knew that he had found another source to pleasing her.

She was short of begging him to just fuck her, when she felt the pit of her stomach do a somersault. The heat rose from some unknown place as she covered him in her juices. Anissa had experienced sex before, but this was her first orgasm, and no way could she live without feeling like this again.

She leaned up on her elbows and stared at the comical look on Quinton's face. "What?" was all she could trust herself to say.

"I'm a Neanderthal, but you must be a mermaid, because you just tried to drown me."

Anissa hunched her shoulders and smiled.

"Look at you. A half-hour ago you stood in front of my bed, all shy, like it was the first time you had taken off your clothes in front of a man, and now you lie here naked and unfeeling to my emotions."

Anissa laughed, offering no answers, and happy with her recent discovery. Quinton straddled her as she stared at the slight curve of his hardened penis.

2003

The ringing of the phone broke Anissa's pleasant memory. She debated whether she should answer, but knew the annoyance would only persist. She raced across the room and picked up the phone.

Quinton's baritone voice broke through. "Hey, babe."

"Hey."

"Are you all right?"

"Yes," she answered.

"Were you asleep?"

Angry that he had not come home the night before, she sighed. "No, I wasn't asleep. I was just wondering when you were coming home." The tears slid from her lids.

"Maybe I'll see you tonight."

Anissa didn't argue. She had learned that it was wasted energy. He wouldn't respond to the vilest of her attacks, and only punished her sexually when she was utterly disrespectful with her taunts. Nor did she wait for an explanation. She just hung up. That was the one thing that made him angrier than any words she could form at that moment. It didn't seem appropriate to tell him that Chaka was no longer there for him to impress.

So many nights she wanted to ask what Chaka had done to warrant so much admiration. Even Buck had the ability to get Quinton to leave a warm bed on a frosty night. But Buck reserved his intrusions for the issues that they had to handle as a group. Chaka, on the other hand, used his friends. He wanted them at his constant disposal, but they all had to wait for his compliance.

Just as she began to cry openly, she heard the sounds of Eve moving about in the kitchen. "Don't mess up the kitchen, greedy," Anissa yelled from the living room. "I just cleaned it."

Eve walked over to her friend and stared at her face. "Why are you crying?" she whispered.

"He didn't come home last night. I'm just so tired of waiting for him to see my worth. I'm more than a dumping ground for his semen. I deserve to be happy, don't I?"

Eve stared wide-eyed. She had to be careful. Anissa was always the levelheaded one in the friendship and the main reason the two couples lived under one roof and shared the expenses down the middle. Far too many nights passed when either she or Anissa would be at the other's place.

To stop all the unnecessary yelling and questions, Anissa convinced Chaka and Quinton to live together. The women would only end up in each other's houses anyway, and privacy was a matter of her and Quinton residing on the second floor, and Eve and Chaka claiming the third floor. The ground floor served as a dining and living room area with a full kitchen and bathroom.

"Go wash your face, Nissa. Quinton hasn't changed since the first day you met him, and he ain't going to change if he sees you hysterical that he didn't come home last night."

Anissa understood Quinton had to deal with his issues but didn't want to be sacrificed while he found a way to cope.

Twenty minutes later Eve was lying in her four-poster bed when she heard the front door slam. Seconds later she rose from her lying position, ready to run into Chaka's arms. Grief erupted as she realized those were not his footsteps. Chaka would never again come through the door. Now he was gone and she was alone. The thought provoked all kinds of insane questions.

As Quinton searched for Anissa, he peered around the door and found the bedroom empty. He reasoned Anissa must be upstairs with Eve. He would not climb the steps, and he refused to call her. She had to have heard him come home.

Anissa could not bring herself to move. She wanted him to return home, and now she wished he would just leave. The confusion that tore at her heart made her lean back into the chair.

A few hours later Quinton went searching for Anissa and found her asleep in the oversized chair. His heart ached that she had been waiting for him and he had come too late. He kneeled at her feet before hoisting her into his arms. The small display of affection reminded him of their first night together.

Lying next to her, he sniffed her hair, kissed her forehead, and silently promised to be a better man to her.

Anissa couldn't miss an opportunity that might not ever return. She leaned into him, kissing first the tip of his nose, and finally his lips. She forced him to lie on his back as she straddled him. The moisture returned to her face as she peered into the sadness of his eyes. His hands touched her face, and she pecked at the center of his hand as the tears dropped from her eyes.

"Don't cry. I'm sorry," he offered. He wanted to assure her everything would be fine, although he wasn't so sure that was true.

Every day brought another wave of emotions and questions, but tonight he surrendered to the woman who held his heart. She couldn't talk. All she could do was cave in to the need to feel his arms wrapped around her, to touch all the places she had missed lately.

Anissa peeled away her nightgown and pulled the belt on his robe. She sat perched atop his erect penis as he held her hips. At a turtle's pace, she lifted and lowered herself onto him, refusing to look away. She had hoped to steal a piece of his heart just for herself. With precision and control, she lifted one hip and lowered the other.

There were times he would make her beg him to just stop teasing her and give her all of him. Tonight, though, the tables had turned ever so slightly. Quinton lost the battle of wills and closed his lids to allow the feelings to capture him.

"Open your eyes," Anissa whispered.

He felt her muscles tighten and relax as she rode him into a fury. He could only surrender to her request.

"Tell me you love me, Quinton," she begged just as she felt the familiar feelings that came when she was about to climax.

Quinton complied once, saying the words as if he would never get the chance again. As the last word left his mouth, he roared, and Anissa's chest thundered against him.

They clung to each other all night, afraid if one let go, the other would not be there in the morning. They cried together, realizing that life could very well change for them after that moment.

Chapter 9

Chaka had taken Eve from the only place she'd ever lived—her momma's house. He gave her money and other material things while he ran the streets and did his dirt. Gone were the days of spending time with her or caring about her day. If he paid her any attention, it was to criticize or chastise her about something she hadn't done right. Although she didn't like the way Chaka treated her, Eve lived with it, believing it was all worth the drama, if she could live like a queen. Leaving wasn't an option because being with him had gotten her many of the things she didn't want to live without—her home, with furnishings supplied by every expensive company she could find, clothes that cluttered two walk-in closets, shoes, and all the accessories any woman could ever want.

Immediately after sharing his bed, Chaka began playing another game Eve wasn't prepared for. If she showed any resistance to his behavior, he wouldn't come home, staying away for days at a time, until he knew she was damn near stir-crazy.

Eve learned the game and found a way to cope. She began provoking him when she wanted to run the streets. He'd set up rules and she'd break them, because he would always come looking for her.

After one particularly bad argument, Eve came up with a plan. He could call her any name in the book, but she'd hold her corner until someone better came along. She could handle a few insults, while she continued to rape his pockets and save her love for another.

Eve's plan involved her living life like a single woman. If Chaka wanted to go around acting like he wasn't her man, then she saw no reason to act like she was his woman. She figured Earl would be a good candidate to start off her single woman life again.

Although Chaka was the only lover she had who could whisper from across a room and make her cream, she hated him, but she just didn't have the courage to leave. She wanted to smear shit all over his face when she found someone more deserving of her love and affection, but no man seemed suitable, so an affair with Earl seemed like the best revenge.

It didn't take long for the affair with Earl to get out of hand. Since Earl didn't have to take care of her financially, he was very attentive. He wasn't the man she dreamed about at night, but he was affectionate and always catered to her every whim. If she wanted to spend three days on the beach, he provided the relaxation. When she wanted to see a play, he made it possible. They just had to see it outside the city limits. If she just wanted to lie around, he was right there to hold her hand.

The night of Earl's Christmas party, Eve, pregnant and unsure of the father, was forced to recognize that all her game-playing had landed her in the middle of a deadly triangle. Earl seemed like the right person to blame, because Chaka certainly wasn't going to let her have an abortion.

But Earl didn't give a shit about Eve's feelings either. Despite his attentiveness, his real motive for getting involved with Eve was to have bragging rights over Chaka, the man she'd left him for.

Eve fucked Earl at the Christmas party that night, hoping to relax him before she revealed her pregnancy, but apparently nothing she could do or say would have made a difference to him.

"Bitch, please! You come in here talking about being pregnant. Fuck that shit! Tell your man he about to be a daddy."

When Eve wouldn't leave and demanded that Earl speak with her, he threw his drink directly in her face. As an afterthought, he said, "Come see me when you handle your little problem."

Dumbfounded, a few people openly gawked, while others just did not care.

With a broken spirit, Eve left the party. She got home and thanked God that Anissa was asleep and Chaka wasn't home.

In the shower Eve scrubbed her body as though she would never be clean again. Exhausted, she went to bed, only to dream about the mess she had created. In her dream, Chaka was choking her senseless, and Earl lay inches from her body, breathless. Common sense prevailed. She knew if she even attempted to tell Chaka about Earl's disrespect, then he would have a hundred and one questions, and she might get an ass-kicking. She promised herself that this secret would ride with her to her grave, along with all the others.

Eve certainly hadn't thought the situation out completely. It hadn't occurred to her that Earl might betray her and tell Chaka himself.

The next morning Eve opened her eyes and feared that her worst nightmare was about to come true. Chaka's face was beet-red, and his eyes matched his face. Somehow he had found out about her actions from the night before.

"Tell me your dumb ass didn't go to that party last night."

Eve couldn't trust anything that came from her mouth, so she just breathed deeply, preparing for the drama.

"I know you're the most self-centered bitch in the world, but to go to Earl's party and think for one minute it was going to be a secret was the second dumbest thing you ever done."

The puzzled look on her face confirmed that she needed to know her first dumb move, but Chaka ignored her pained expression.

"You want that nigga, right? So, guess what—I am gonna send you to him. Get up!" he shouted, pulling her by her hair. He tossed her a pair of jeans and a sweatshirt.

Eve hurried into the items, thinking he would kill her right then if he knew for sure how far things had gone between her and Earl last night.

Chaka held her at the base of her neck, pushing her about until they worked themselves to the front door. In the heat of the moment, he didn't bother giving her a winter coat or shoes. He pushed her through the door and calmly told her, "Go see Earl!"

Eve stood there horrified by Chaka's cruelty. They'd been down this road before, but not once did it occur to her she could find herself without a place to call home. The winter wind whipped through her thin clothes, and she really began to understand the severity of her situation.

"I'm standing here barefoot and pregnant, in the cold, with no place to go," she whispered, as if hearing the words would make them less true. She turned to knock on the door, but saw Chaka through the glass pane standing there, his 9 pointed at her face.

She lowered her head, not in shame, but in arrogant anger. Nope, she wasn't about to be scared by Chaka's theatrics. She twisted the knob and found herself locked out. The smirk that filled his eyes was evil as all day.

Eve's angry smile struck a chord in Chaka. He had learned that she was medieval if pushed too far.

She banged on the door and begged him for a pair of shoes and at least a jacket, so she could get off his property.

Chaka tossed the ratty sneakers a spring jacket on the carport.

Grateful she wouldn't die of pneumonia, Eve gathered the things and left. She walked around the neighborhood for a while, finally retracing her steps and entering the house through the basement.

Chaka was on the third floor and didn't have a clue that Eve would have the balls to come back after he'd tossed her on the sidewalk.

On her way upstairs, she stopped in the kitchen and grabbed a butcher knife. His actions had forced her to a place she did not dream existed in her. Slowly she crept to her bedroom and watched Chaka as he lay with his back to the doorway. She stepped lightly to the edge of the bed.

Just as she found the courage to pounce, Chaka leaped from the bed in a battle stance and slapped her.

As the tears stained Eve's face, her head went slamming into the wall. She found her bearings and raised the knife above her head. The force behind the blow she intended would have killed him if she'd hit her mark. The deranged look in her eyes and her sinister grin were enough to prove she intended to kill her benefactor that day, if he didn't kill her first.

Anissa and Quinton came into the house as the screaming erupted from Eve's mouth. Neither Quinton nor Anissa raced toward the mayhem. They'd both become accustomed to the wars waged on the third floor. They carried their grocery bags to the kitchen, but Chaka's raised voice alerted them that it was more serious than usual.

"Bitch, you want to cut me?"

Eve swung the knife in an arc and nicked his shoulder.

The punch Chaka delivered sent Eve sailing across the room and smack into the walk-in closet before she slumped to the floor. He then grabbed her shirt, lifted her to her feet, and took her to the door, where he planted his foot in her ass, sending her past the threshold and into the hall.

Quinton reached the landing first, and Anissa was huffing and puffing as she followed as quickly as her feet would carry her.

Chaka stopped them both. "There is no need for a family conference. This bitch has finally worn out her welcome here."

The defiant look on both Eve's and Chaka's faces left them bewildered. In a short time, something had gone terribly wrong. The sight of Chaka's blood caught Anissa's attention. She raced about to gather materials to clean his wound and bandage him.

"You'll get yours, muthafucka!" Eve yelled hysterically. "I promise, one day you're going to get yours!"

Chaka laughed. "That lame bastard Earl, he's too weak to come up against me. If it will make you feel better, tell him to come see me."

Eve's sobbing stopped at the mere mention of Earl's name. He was no longer an option after he had insulted her beyond repair. "Earl ain't the only muthafucka that can't stand your bitch ass! I'm sure of that." She wobbled down the steps.

"Well, stupid, when you find the muthafucka dumb enough to go up against me, tell 'im to come see me."

Anissa completed the task of repairing her man's best friend as quickly as possible, and then raced down the steps. Eve had disappeared. She prayed that wherever Eve went, she would be OK.

Eve's face stung as the wind blew around her. She felt like an idiot, with no place to go. Everything she'd owned was sitting in that house with Chaka.

Not long after she'd started dating Chaka, her mother had warned her. "That boy doesn't care anything about you. Open your eyes, *mi hija*, because Breito was your winner," she'd said, referring to Earl, "and you leave him for money. That's not right, but you will see."

Eve knew she couldn't go back to her mother's. She didn't want to deal with her sister looking at her in disgust and her mother gave her the I-told-you-so attitude. She decided the only person that might give her a hand was Earl, and she didn't hesitate to call him.

Of course he'd rescue her, if it meant another opportunity to rub Chaka's face in the drama. He'd surely find an apartment and even pay for the abortion. In fact, he'd do everything to make her life easy, especially since she'd given him a victory over Chaka.

Eve immediately recognized that Earl had stipulations for helping her, which made her angry. She really thought they had something more than just a fly-by-night relationship. Eve decided, no matter what, since she'd been a pawn in everyone's game, she'd go to the person who could afford her the thing she wanted. And that wasn't Earl. He was still struggling, trying to get to where Chaka had just left.

As the days crept forward she decided she had to get back home to Chaka and his money. It didn't matter if she had to grovel for a while.

It didn't take long before the streets started murmuring about the breakup, but before it could get out of control, Eve was back riding in his car. "You can be angry with me, but the truth is, none of the women you chose will be able to live down my presence in your life."

Chaka laughed, but he'd been thinking the same thing lately.

"Even you taught me that your money isn't always represented by the car you drive, but the bitch sitting in the passenger seat. What other bitch you know make you look as good as I do?"

Chaka sat quietly and listened. He knew she was a brazen bitch to begin with, but surprisingly she'd been showing him she was listening to him too. He flipped the script before she could continue. "So I guess I get you out of this, but what do you want?"

"I get what I want—a chance to make everything right between us," she answered with a straight face."

Chaka nodded. He recognized the game but didn't bother to bust her.

After that, things slowly went back to their usual love-hate dependency. That was the last breakup that truly threatened their relationship, all the others being petty squabbles of control that didn't do much to change their tumultuous affair.

Chapter 10

EARL'S PLAN: GETTING EVEN, 2001

After Eve betrayed Earl for the last time, he vowed that she would pay for neglecting him. Not to mention, every lowlife knew that he was shunned by his archrival, Chaka. Desperate times called for desperate moves, so Earl managed to quietly leave New York to set about his plan for revenge. He headed south to align himself with some get-money soldiers who were making a name for themselves.

Ian, Earl's cousin, was having a little trouble staying focused, and Earl needed a new start. Helping his cousin seemed like a win-win situation. He would help set up shop and show him the best way to turn profit on even the worst product, and in return he'd make a little money and establish his own crew.

As the business grew, an unspoken debt was rising. With newfound dollars in Ian's family, egos and confidences soared. Ian began to buy into his own hype, setting his own plans into motion. The timid curiosity he felt about Earl had snowballed. The time had come to ask questions.

He asked Earl one day, "Why you really down here in the Dirty when you could be home in the Rotten Apple making money?"

Earl's answers were always barely truthful. "I was having a hard time finding real soldiers willing to put in work."

Ian understood that answer. He had taken his share of losses, until he got the right crew together.

Earl witnessed Ian's crew develop from meager street urchins to real money-chasers. He fantasized that if he just had a few good men, he could really show Ian how New York cats put themselves on display.

Ian imagined that if he offered to help Earl set up better at home, he could eventually snatch the business from beneath his feet and make Earl into an earner for him instead of a boss. Grime and grit were staring each other in the face, but they had no clue they were both just dirt.

Days turned into weeks, and weeks into months. Ian finally broached the subject of helping Earl get on his feet. The topic came on the heels of Ian seeing his first million dollars, free and clear.

"Cousin, listen. We have everything on sound footing. It's time you went back home and paved the way for us to expand."

His words were clever enough. Earl became an actor in a matter of minutes. Faking surprise at the generous offer, he shook his head slightly. "I didn't come down here for you to help me in New York. I came to get my head right before I went back and re-established for myself."

Ian, in his own arrogance, couldn't see the trees for looking. Earl was playing him, but greed was in Ian's way.

Ian smiled pleasantly. "There are plenty hungry cats down here looking to get a hand up in the world. You need soldiers that don't give a damn about the reputations of cats running the streets in your hood, strangers somewhat to the area, and I got that here. You could pick any six men and clear town and country on their eagerness to make money."

Earl covered his face with both hands to hide his smirk. He'd caught his mouse. When he uncovered his face, he looked pained and spoke through labored breathing. "If we do this, we have to come to some sort of agreement."

Ian grinned as if he had just hit the lottery. "OK, whatever you deem fair is payment enough."

Earl was willing to reward his cousin a king's ransom for his efforts, knowing he intended to break the terms as soon as he was strong enough. Ian accepted without fuss, thinking it would be easy enough to snatch the entire pie from Earl when he was earning the right numbers. Ian was counting on his soldiers staying loyal to him. Meanwhile, Earl was counting on Ian's greed to cause a straight-up mutiny. The terms were negotiated, and the deal was sealed as they puffed on fat, neatly rolled ganja. No shaking hands and toasts, just puff, puff, pass.

As quietly as Earl had left town, he returned to New York with a new swagger and his killing squad. Earl was delusional when it came to his real potential. He had learned, while sitting about in the South, that patience was important. Even more important was the element of surprise.

Patiently he watched the self-proclaimed Dirty Dozen operate. Quietly he learned the habits of the main crewmembers. Earl had deemed Buck the weak link and decided that, even if he killed Buck, they could still operate without the muscle. Every man was willing to hold his own when it came to his money.

Quinton was smart enough to handle the business, but he lacked the finesse to keep men loyal without the use of humiliation and fear. Earl believed if Quinton was at the helm of the empire, he would ruin it by his own tyranny.

That meant Chaka had to be dealt with properly, since he was the real threat. But there couldn't be any proof that Earl was the true murderer. Earl was experienced enough to know that as long as no one could prove his involvement in Chaka's death, he would have a fighting chance at taking over the Dozen's entire operation. Money could quiet any suspicion, and killing a nigga was the answer to blackmail.

Earl had been circling the wagons for months. He thought about everything from the actual murder to the reaction of the crewmembers' women. His first order of business was to learn the habits of the targets. Eve, he imagined, would be his sweetest victory. The chance to see her broken after Chaka was dead and buried would be the best revenge he could have for her betrayal.

When Earl learned that Chaka housed another family only a short distance from Eve's watchful eye, he was stunned. His undying dedication to Eve was tarnished, but Chaka's blatant betrayal of her made him somewhat sympathetic. He would use that information for a better day.

Although Chaka's children's mother was pretty, she was definitely not as beautiful as the sultry, sexy Eve. One quality intrigued Earl. She seemed to operate as though Eve didn't exist, going grocery shopping dressed as a parent of two children bound for success, and meeting her man at the door with a hug and kiss before sending him out into the world. She wasn't caught up in the gutter-fabulous lifestyle Chaka could so readily offer. Even her home was just ordinary and understated in comparison to the gigantic brownstone Chaka shared with Eve.

True to a hustler's creed, Chaka had kept her away from the game. She lived just far enough away to be invisible, but close enough to touch. If all else failed, Earl would make Chaka pay with the loss of this comfortable place he had hidden behind Eve's back. Further investigation revealed that seeing his children every day was Chaka's only habitual act. The nigga even shredded his bad boy persona when he came home.

Earl became bored with Chaka and his daily regimen, but he needed an opportunity to shake up the Dozen's foundation. Trailing Buck seemed like a good idea, but Earl could never catch him slipping. He had no bad habits worth mentioning.

Quinton was proving to be the easiest of the trio. He was a day walker, and at night he went home, to the club, or to visit one or two of the women he had stashed around the city. Earl surmised, if he moved too quickly, Chaka and Buck would band together and flood money into the hands of nosy neighbors to find Quinton's killer, but it was the only move that made sense, and he was the easiest target.

This was proving to be a project that Earl might not be ready to handle alone. His crew was keeping a low profile, but they were also itching to meet some of the natives. Getting a woman was difficult if you didn't have any bread, so Earl knew he had to fix things quickly.

It became clear almost immediately which member of his six-man crew was a ladies' man. Pop seemed to know his worth too. Maybe it was his cat-like eyes, black skin, and pretty, spinning waves. The country rooster made the city chickens cluck loudly every time they passed by his yard. Unbeknownst to Earl, Pop was sexing one of Buck's lady friends regularly.

Sasha began seeing Pop after she realized Buck would never commit to her. She had told Buck about the incident at Earl's Christmas party, hoping it would help him make a choice and be with her as more than one of his many flings. However, it didn't pan out the way she expected, and her hopes dwindled into nothing.

After months of hanging on, she began hanging out in the streets and becoming less available to Buck when he got around to calling. She'd met a country boy, and although she knew he was not the one, he was doing her justice in bedroom.

In her search for true love, Sasha was betraying trusts. The fact that she may have spoken out to the wrong man never occurred to her as she began telling all of Buck's dirty little secrets to Pop.

Pop was listening and doing his own mathematics. He was certain that a time would come when this information would land a golden rainbow at his feet. Pop's plan worked well—share a little information, pay her a little attention, cater to her freaky nature, and wait for her to tell everything else.

Everyone seemed to be plotting on someone else's weaknesses, but not everyone could win this deadly game.

Chapter 11

Eve cried in the darkness, wishing she and Chaka had just one more night together. She talked to the picture of him that rested on her dresser.

"Why can't you just come home one more time?" she begged the portrait. "I need to hear you laugh at me for one misguided attempt at something or another. I need to feel your cold feet against me while I complain. Please?"

There was no one who could fill the void Chaka left behind. The miserable thought occurred too late. She really did love him. She had been running in a circle for the intimacy she already possessed, which became clearer through her tears, the pounding of her heart, and the tantrum that rose in her soul.

The moment she heard the glass breaking, Anissa flew up the stairs two at a time, Quinton right behind her. She burst through the door to see Eve's body crumpled on the floor.

Quinton said softly, "Come on, baby girl, you can't lay here in this glass."

She covered her face, ignoring him.

"Get up!" he demanded.

Still she ignored him.

"Get your simple ass off the floor before we have to go to the emergency room tonight!" he yelled.

"Fuck off, you black bastard! It should have been you lying dead on the ground instead of Chaka."

"You're absolutely right, but in the meantime get your special ass off the floor until I clean up this mess."

She leaped at Quinton with the agility of a panther. Nanoseconds before she clawed his face, he snatched her hands. "Now that's the evil witch I know and love," he said.

The truth in her words intensified the guilt he carried. The hurt in his eyes was evident to Anissa, but Eve didn't give a damn about his feelings.

Selfishly, Eve wished Anissa was suffering the loss instead of her. Short of telling Anissa that, she glared at them.

Anissa's anger was burning a hole in her chest. "I don't understand how two people who love one man so much could be so mean to one another. You both need to accept that we are the ones left to deal with Chaka's passing," Anissa said. "Eve, wishing it were Quinton isn't going to change shit." She turned to Quinton, her eyes blazing. "You hollering, it should have been you? Well, where would I be? You didn't give that thought before you started changing places?"

Turning around she left Quinton and Eve, hoping they understood the damage they were doing to one another.

Quinton pretended to have the answer. "Evil will probably be the victor in that battle."

"Stop calling me Evil, you bastard!"

"I'll be calling you Evil until the day you bury me next to my best friend. Now get your evil, silly ass out of here until I clean up this mess."

His last words shut Eve's mouth. She had not given any thought to Quinton also suffering a loss. She was there as he cried openly at the funeral, yet it still didn't occur to her that anyone might miss Chaka as much as she did. Slowly her outburst subsided, but she wouldn't let his emotions change her mind.

Several days later

The smell of Chaka's favorite cologne enveloped Eve the moment she opened his closet door. Determined, she touched each thing as though it was him. She grabbed his favorite suede jacket, fingering the fabric, feeling the softness, and trying to stay just beyond the memories that claimed her every time she dared to look in his space.

Eve had to believe there was life after Chaka. Accepting it, however, was another dilemma. His money, his shadow, and his respect made her more than just another pretty face in the crowd. Torn between her fears and being loyal to him, she debated with her heart. When should she date? Was it even appropriate to clean out his closet so soon? What would folks think if they knew she wanted to move on with her life?

When Chaka was around, other people's opinions never mattered. He could change the temperature in a room the moment he opened his mouth. Solemnly she made a pile of coats, pants, shirts, and shoes for Goodwill to pick up the following day. In tears, she worked through the pain of losing him. She wanted to keep almost everything she touched. Giving them away was like giving away the years they had shared together. She tried to pack the boxes without seeing anything. She decided to keep a bottle of his favorite fragrance and all the photo albums.

There were two albums. Looking inside one, she found a hospital bracelet of a girl child named Chanice Dubois. Suddenly her faith in their commitment was shattered. The date showed four years ago. Inside the album there were also recent pictures of the child. She had a smile identical to Chaka's, and the pattern of her freckles was identical to his.

The pounding in Eve's chest forced her to look away. There was no way in life she could put the book down and walk away. She had to confirm her suspicions. There had to be an explanation. This child was too young to have been born before they met, and too old for Eve not to have known she existed.

There was a piece of hair in the compartment marked BABY'S HAIR, and a navel cord in another compartment meant for that.

Eve thought she would go insane when she saw the picture of a smiling Chaka and a woman who seemed happy. The woman looked familiar, but she couldn't recall why at that moment. She needed to piece this scenario together. Her breathing quickened as she tried to find a legitimate reason for the display of photos. Tears formed but refused to flow, as she held the album close to her chest. Anger began to coil in the pit of her stomach. The anger she had felt the morning of his funeral returned as she realized he had betrayed her. He had a child with another woman and kept it a secret. He had violated their relationship, and now she wondered what other secrets he had taken to his grave.

Before Eve allowed the rage to fully claim her, she lifted the second book. The very first page in Chaka's handwriting declared: My first son. Chaka Xavier Dubois weighed in at nine pounds and eleven ounces. At birth he was twenty-two inches long and the color of paste. She held the book, hyperventilating over the realization that he had two children. "Holy shit," she whispered. "This muthafucka has two children." *I'm sitting here unsure of how to act, and he was playing me for a fool.*

Quinton came into the house as Eve began screaming. He raced up the stairs without thinking. She was kicking boxes and throwing clothes about as she cursed. Her hair was wild on top of her head, and her eyes were red as beets. At that moment he knew she must have found something to prove Chaka had a family separate from her. Her words were more than a declaration of the truth.

"I can't believe all this time you've had children hatching all over the place! I can only imagine how many times you waltzed in here from being with your children and lied."

Eve stopped ranting suddenly. She turned to see Quinton standing in the doorway. She sneered at the image that bothered her more than Chaka being dead—Quinton alive.

"You knew, didn't you?" She rushed on before he could explain. "You knew about his bastard children and never said a word."

Quinton didn't feel like he owed her any answers.

"I've hated you for more years than I care to admit, but now I have good reason to hate. You helped him betray me."

He stood still with his head hanging low, allowing Eve her right to vent. She didn't want or need a shoulder to cry on. She needed to place blame. Quinton didn't expect to feel guilty when Eve finally found out the truth, but the emotion claimed him as she blamed him for never mentioning the children.

It occurred to her that maybe Anissa knew also. "Does Anissa know too, Quinton?" she demanded.

"No," he answered without much thought. "If Anissa knew, you would have known before I could have gotten the words out of my mouth."

Eve crossed the floor to stand in Quinton's face. She had gotten so close to him, he could feel the negative energy dancing all over her.

"I suppose I should thank you for keeping all of his dirty little secrets?"

"Eve, this was never my secret to tell, and as for telling you after, well, that was information I didn't think you could handle."

Suddenly she was able to put together the missing pieces concerning the strange woman from the funeral, and the pregnant woman in the photos. "That was the woman at the funeral, the one you and Buck kept holding on to and comforting. You sorry muthafuckas! Y'all showed the bitch more loyalty than me, and I was his woman. Now I understand she was his babies' mama."

He tried to reason with her.

"Stop talking! You kept his secret because you never believed I deserved his love." She shook her head. Even in death, Chaka had managed to make her feel like a fool. "Well, it seems he earned everything he got in our relationship. He lied to me, and I did the same fucking thing to him."

Chapter 12

QUINTON'S SIDE

Hours later Anissa, mad as hell, sat in the passenger seat opposite Quinton. She said, "Quinton, you have to try to understand how she must feel. From his grave he was able to destroy all the love they shared by keeping this secret, a secret she had to discover all by herself while trying to find a way to live without him. She can't even confront him."

Quinton was pissed that Anissa even pretended to understand Eve's mind. She gave her opinion knowing that Quinton would be hurt, but she was on Eve's side this time.

"Every chance Chaka got, he berated Eve for being the woman he created, calling her money-hungry, but he started out giving her stacks to shop with in the beginning, then calling her self-centered when he made her his showpiece. You can say what you want, but the way she is acting right now is about the way I would if it happened to me."

Anissa sensed there was so much more going on besides just the love/hate relationship Eve and Quinton shared. The tension between the couple was strangling them.

Q could not believe Anissa saw logic in Eve's drama. Eve had been less than loyal over the years. Although his judgment and loyalty were measured by his long-time friendship, he still believed Eve's wrongs were utterly disrespectful. Chaka managed to keep his family hidden from almost everyone. There was not even a whisper in the air about them. Meanwhile, Eve's every step revealed a new scandal involving her and Earl. She wasn't discreet, and had never cared that much to be.

"You don't really know all the trouble she caused," he uttered.

Anissa's curiosity wore a hole in her mind as she debated the facts. Quinton began to show his dislike for Eve shortly after they'd moved into the same home. "Why do you dislike her so much?" She watched him shake his head and then open his mouth and close it again.

"Leave it alone, Nissa. Let it go."

Anissa turned her entire body to him. "I've asked and even pleaded with you to tell me the truth. Every other time you said leave it alone, and I did out of respect. Not this time."

The cryptic statement was code for an ultimatum. There were few times when she outright demanded anything from Quinton, but on those rare occasions, he couldn't deny her. He lowered his head into his hands. The deep breaths he took before speaking was a sign that the truth was a heavy burden he had carried on his shoulders for a long time.

"Chaka and I were having some problems," he began. "That is a long story going back to another time. By the time you and I started messing around, nobody was safe from the drama in the streets. Hustlers were catching cases for trafficking like fly balls, and sentences were coming with letters instead of numbers. The boys and I were looking for a safe exit. I personally didn't know any man that threw his hat in the game and just walked away with everything intact. Maybe you lose your values or quality of life, but either way, you suffer a loss. Call it being naïve, but we thought we could be different. It was just a matter of planning. We were pups in the game by the time I met you. Our real respect came from the things we did as kids to keep money in our pockets."

Anissa had heard the stories involving the Baker Boys 5, but she knew Quinton needed to build slowly. It was his way of doing things, so she stayed quiet and let him continue.

"We sold cakes by the slice, brownies, cookies, and anything else that we could cook in Ms. Sadie's kitchen. Natural as rain, we joined the drug game. It was as simple as selling a little bit of weed. Our reputation as the Baker Boys 5 took on an entirely new meaning. Then it was a little bit of whatever. Finally, we had a lot of everything.

"No one really knew Eve was still dating the lame-ass nigga Earl. Seriously, I don't think it would have mattered if Chaka had known. He seemed to want her trifling ass all the more after he found out. You and I were spending so much time together; it was just a natural reaction that Chaka and Eve would see one another. No one ever expected there to be anything more than a little fucking, especially since we all knew Petra was due to have Chanice any day.

"Anyway, they started seeing each other regularly, but your girl neglected to tell Chaka she had a man at the time. Buck found out some months later and tried to warn him, but Chaka wouldn't listen. When Chaka confronted her, she lied and the real bullshit began. All behind some snitching and some pussy, this shit got outta hand."

Quinton stopped speaking, as if to allow Anissa the chance to completely understand what he was saying. His hands expressed every word and punctuation mark when he continued with, "One night Eve was sitting in Earl's car when Chaka rolled through the block. He didn't say anything. He just tooted his horn to let her know he had seen her. She made up some story to Earl about Chaka harassing her or some shit, so later in the middle of the club, Earl pulled a gun on Buck, threatening to kill us if we kept fucking with his girl. Tempers flared and promises were made. That night there was no turning back. Buck and I left the club and headed home to gear up.

"Once we got back to the club, before either of us could make good on any promises, Chaka showed up. He was just as amped as we were, but I guess after waiting for Earl to come out, he lost his steam. He flipped shit, telling us Earl wasn't a real threat. Like jackasses, we listened to his bullshit. He convinced us to let the nigga live. When Eve came out of the club first,

Chaka snatched her up by her collar and whispered something in her ear. That ended that. When Earl came out, she was sitting in Chaka's car. Chaka stepped to Earl about his threats. Without raising his voice, he squashed the bullshit. That still didn't make me or Buck feel any better, though. We wanted at that nigga.

"Do not misunderstand, though. Earl was the man among his men, but Chaka was the bigger nigga back then. If it was about money, we were getting it."

Anissa took a deep breath. She wasn't ready for the details Quinton had laid at her feet. She knew about the beef between Chaka and Earl, but she thought it was simple rivalry. She never even knew Eve was seeing Earl on the low and couldn't believe that her best friend had kept all of this from her.

"We were all making money in the street," Quinton continued, "but Earl's name was spoiled years ago. He set us up to save his ass when we first got in the game. Earl could have showed out, but he was a lot smarter back then. The key was making money. No one wanted to lose his freedom over a bitch. Eve might have been Earl's girl before, but getting in Chaka's car that night changed that, and the rest is the drama that follows."

Anissa was stunned speechless.

"It didn't end there, though. That was really just the beginning. Chaka beat Eve's ass that night and dared her to go get Earl's simple ass. For a while Chaka and Eve had broken up, and since she couldn't get next to Earl any longer, she just kept after Chaka until he started up with her again. It didn't matter to Eve what trouble she created. Every few months it would be something new, and most of it centered on her interactions with Earl.

"By Christmas that year, Earl had re-established his crew and was really grinding hard in the streets. He had a tight little group of boys running with him, so he thought he could be disrespectful. Eve went to a party hosted by Earl. She was there for about an hour when Earl threw a drink in her face and told her to go call her man. He claimed it was about time they settled some issues. You ever hear the saying 'add liquor, act foolish'? That's the perfect description of Earl's scrawny ass."

Anissa saw where this story was going. She remembered part of the story, and the drama that took place afterward, but still she kept quiet, letting her man finish.

"Eve didn't have the heart to tell Chaka what happened, but one of Buck's lady friends witnessed the situation and called Buck to explain before it swept out of control. Buck didn't call anybody. He just showed up at the party and raised hell. Most of the cats at the party were men we grew up with, or crossed paths with at one time or another. They didn't have anything to do with the drama, and weren't about to get in the middle of another man's problems.

"Earl's crew whipped Buck's natural black ass that night, but not before Buck told him he would see each man personally. Buck pleaded with Earl to grow some balls and kill him, or he would see him again.

"After that night Chaka isolated Earl and forced him out of the area completely by supplying hustlers with the best work at the sweetest prices. The plan was simple—undercut anything Earl might have dreamed of doing. Niggas came at us looking for help when Earl did them dirty. Chaka, being the man he was, helped more than he turned away. It took a minute, but by the summer, Earl realized he wasn't getting any love in the streets, so he took his act somewhere else.

"But, of course, Earl couldn't just leave things. He had to smear a little shit in Chaka's face about good ol' Eve. She forgot to tell anyone she fucked Earl before the Christmas party, and she went there to tell him she was pregnant. She reasoned it wasn't Chaka's child, so it had to be his. That was the reason he threw the drink at her trick ass. He also gave Chaka the receipt for the abortion Eve had a few days after the drink incident. After all the drama that silly, evil bitch caused, Chaka still carried her. She was his woman. I tried to convince him he was making a huge mistake and that Eve's games were going to get one of us killed, but he never listened to me. You remember how they got back together on New Year's that year?"

Anissa watched Quinton's face turn to pure bitterness as he told her almost everything. Suddenly she regretted ever asking him to tell her the truth. Now she had to examine the things Quinton had shared with her. She had to try not to harbor ill feelings for Eve, and although Quinton didn't say it, she now knew he believed Earl had caused Chaka's death. She shifted slightly in the seat, stared at the brick walls of their home, and hoped they could somehow get past that moment.

"I know you have valid reasons for being angry with her, but Chaka forgave Eve," she said.

Quinton barked, "Anissa, don't finish that comment, please ... because you and I are still alive, and Chaka is buried in a box not far from where we're sitting right now."

The stress of the moment forced Quinton to reveal the things that gave him trouble sleeping. "The whole day he was killed, he was with Petra and kids. He told me he was in for the night, but about an hour later, he called to find out where Eve's simple ass had gone. Right then everybody's life changed. Instead of telling her ass to walk home, he went to meet her on Furman. He asked me to meet him there because her car broke down or some shit."

Anissa tried to control her breathing. She knew Quinton would kill Eve easily if he had proof she'd caused Chaka's death. She wanted to stop Quinton, who was so caught up in his version of what happened, he didn't even notice Anissa's reaction, but she let him continue.

"I didn't see Chaka's car right away, so I pulled into the station on Furman and then I thought maybe he meant Aberdeen, so I doubled back, and there was no Chaka. Eve wasn't there either. I pulled onto the sidewalk opposite the stations and waited a few minutes. I called Chaka's phone, but there was no answer. I drove to the curb on the dead end of Furman, and that was when I spotted Chaka's car. There were two people standing with him. I didn't recognize either of them, so I got ready to do battle. And then I stared in my best friend's eyes as he was shot in the chest at point-blank range."

Anissa's mouth flew open, and she palmed her forehead as she rocked back and forth.

"That one shot was all they got off before I started bucking, but it was no use. They got away. It was almost as if they were from the hood, because the niggas knew exactly how to get up the low wall without getting into the direct line of fire. They both positioned themselves in the little alcove that separated the church from the bingo hall. Worse yet, Anissa, neither nigga fired another shot. I was practically in the middle of the street. They climbed up the low concrete wall and disappeared in the park. On the ground, on him, there was blood everywhere. Since that night I haven't slept easy, knowing I could have saved Chaka had I reacted quicker."

Anissa's mind raced as she sat there helpless. She grabbed Quinton as he banged his head against the headrest and cried.

Quinton wanted to tell Anissa that, for more seconds than imaginable, he stood there frozen, watching his friend die, but his shame kept him from saying another word.

Chapter 13

EVE: ON MY OWN

The process of grieving had created a great deal of tension in the house. She blamed everyone for keeping Chaka's life a secret. She even convinced herself that Anissa was mistreating her for some unknown misery. The time had come to put an end to the drama and just move on.

Financially she was prepared to get her own home, but it nearly destroyed her to sit opposite Petra at the reading of the will and know that Chaka had taken out a policy for her. He had taken care of her separate from his two children. He had carried that bitch. She was his wife, instead of just some mistress.

The bulk of the property was distributed evenly between his children. The remaining businesses were split in thirds between Eve, Quinton, and Buck. In the aftermath of his death, Chaka had tied Eve to the unrelenting toad, Quinton, and that simpleton, Buck, for the rest of her life.

Although they were now her partners, so to speak, she was determined to get from under their controlling hands. Planning would be difficult without her safety net, but she would be free. The proverbial prison would not hold her down.

Mentally she was already out of the home, the friendship with Anissa, and the business relationships she shared with them all. The confines of these walls were too much to accept. Today she was liberating herself, and the mourning would end the moment she exited the doors.

Anissa walked into the house just as Eve slammed shut her footlocker full of clothes.

"Eve, you home?" she hollered from the foyer.

Eve wanted to be in the wind by the time Anissa came home. She raced down the steps with a backpack. "Yeah, but I'm heading out just now," she answered, slinking past her former friend.

"Every time I want to talk to you, you're never home, or you're leaving."

Eve's lack of response was bone-chilling. She opened the door and slammed it without a word.

Quinton was eavesdropping just behind the basement doors. He would have cursed Eve out, but decided it was time Anissa and Eve dealt with their own battles.

Several months had passed since he'd confided in Anissa regarding the real reason he loathed Eve's very being. Since that time, he had noticed a change in Anissa's behavior, almost as if she knew something and chose not to share it.

He opened the basement door as Anissa moved past it. "Hey, babe. You just getting home?"

Anissa didn't trust herself not to break down and tell him what just happened, so she retraced her steps and headed to their bedroom. Standing near Quinton and the I-told-you-so look on his face made her tired of the entire ordeal. "Yes, but I'm tired. I'm going to lie down for a while."

Hours later Quinton was in the kitchen cooking pasta and sauce when Eve sauntered by. She waltzed straight to the kitchen, opened the fridge, grabbed an apple, and slammed the door. He wouldn't respond to her antics. An attention hog, she'd been trying to start a fight for some time, and he wasn't about to be caught up in that drama.

They stepped around each other, and no words left their lips. Eve rinsed her apple. He stirred his sauce.

She glared at him from the corner of her eyes. Then she slammed her hand on the marble countertop and declared, "I'm moving out."

Quinton's answer was patent rude boy. "I'll try to miss you, Evil."

Quinton called Buck as soon as Eve left the kitchen. "Jahson, get over here now," he said. "Eve is about to pull some shit."

Buck had long ago tired of Eve's rude manners and told her as much. He had held her with the same regard he would a long-lost cousin. They didn't exist, and neither did she. He sighed. "Give me ten minutes."

Anissa woke to Eve dragging things across the floor and slamming doors. Rarely did she go upstairs uninvited, especially since Eve seemed to be distancing herself, but she had to find out what the real problem was.

Anissa walked into a mess of boxes and clothes scattered everywhere. "What's up, girl? You spring cleaning?" she joked.

Eve stared at Anissa and decided her exit should at least be cordial, since they had been through so much together. "No, I'm moving out. It's about time we all got our own space and lived our own lives."

The painful look on Anissa's face made Eve ashamed at her nasty attitude.

"You're just moving in the middle of the night? You planned this. Knowing your conniving ass, you were not going to say a word. It's just like you to up and leave without so much as a good-bye, or nice knowing you."

"Shit! Nice knowing you," she hollered. "I can't say it has been a pleasure. Between you and the beast, I've had more than I can stand. At least, now I know how you really feel about my conniving ass."

Eve's attitude didn't impress Anissa. "Your shouting hasn't moved me. Eve, you have always been prone to drama, so I guess expecting anything else is my fault. It is not our fault that you're feeling miserable. The truth is, you create every bit of drama that comes your way. Good riddance," she yelled, "you self-serving drama addict. You wouldn't appreciate a good friend if she bit you in the ass!"

Quinton did not bother to referee the confrontation. For years his woman had campaigned for Eve. Now she had to accept that her pleas for peace were all in vain.

Buck came through the door in the middle of Anissa's tirade. He didn't bother looking for Quinton. He knew where he was after smelling the sausage cooking. He raced up the stairs until he was in the thick of the drama.

"OK, Anissa. You have had your say." Eve yelled, "Now get the fuck out of my face before I whip your fat ass!"

Anissa's chuckle startled both Buck and Eve.

Buck wanted to see Anissa beat the hell out of Eve, knowing that whatever caused this battle was Eve's fault one hundred percent. He quickly stepped out of the way.

"You would rather slap Buck's big ass than tangle with me right now," Anissa snarled. "Good-bye, bitch."

Eve's cell phone jingled, saving her from having to put up or shut up.

Buck laughed when Anissa marched down the steps. He couldn't help adding his two cents before doubling back down the steps. "All these years, Eve, I thought you had some heart, but you were just perpetrating."

Eve yelled after him, "Whatever, you big, burly bastard! Try and answer the door," she said, knowing the person on the phone had arrived.

Quinton went to the door. "Who the hell are you?"

That was easy for Pop. He was nobody right now, but soon enough he planned to make the hood familiar with his presence. "Forgive my manners, partner. My name is Pop." He extended his hand like a true businessman.

Buck caught the fever that claimed Quinton. "Nah, nigga," he barked. "Where I know you from?"

"I hustle with some dudes on the dark side," he answered, a little intimidated.

The dark side was an invisible line from Moffat and Knickerbocker, all the way down to Linden Street.

"How you know Eve?" Anissa asked, blocking Buck's path.

"I met her about eight months ago at a party in the Village," he lied.

Stunned, the trio yelled, "Eight months ago!"

Eve claimed Pop's arm, slammed the keys on the kitchen counter, and they left the house without further fanfare.

Anissa was beyond angry and would have gladly whipped Eve's ass if Quinton would let her.

The energy in the house changed once Eve moved. Instead of being relieved, Anissa worried more. Quinton became more distant, coming home with just enough time to sleep, claiming he was out all times of day and night making a better life for them. In front of her eyes, he had turned into Chaka.

Ranting and raving was the couple's only form of communication. Quinton's insults were vicious, but Anissa's was lethal. During one of their shouting matches, he yelled, "You need to get a life."

In the beginning, she would cry and hide from the hurtful words, but on this day Anissa finally found her voice. "Muthafucka, I had a life, one that included a loving relationship, but I guess my lover is still trying to impress a nigga that's dead and buried."

Quinton would have responded, but he knew the sting was long overdue.

Meanwhile, Quinton and Buck were heading two rising empires. Every precaution had to be established, especially now that they would be targets for anyone with the heart to challenge the crew. The first step included them hiring a staff that could maintain the legal businesses and properties, freeing them to manage their illegal enterprises. The Dirty Dozen and their shifting responsibilities were the first items on their agenda.

Chapter 14

The Dirty Dozen showed resistance in the beginning to Buck and Quinton's leadership. They didn't believe that Buck and Quinton had Chaka's business savvy, and they began talking about dismantling the crew. Buck was clearly not entertaining the idea. He stood his ground, knowing Dave, Danny, and Quinton would lay down the life of any nigga in the room dumb enough to test him. That wasn't his concern. Buck's real concern was that one or more of these fake-ass busters could have killed his partner. Judging from the way they were behaving, the killer may have been in their midst.

Sparks flew when money came up short for the legit businesses, but Quinton was a tyrant when the illegal kitty started taking losses. It was now a matter of getting to each man, ensuring that the plan was still intact and they were on board. The buzzards were hovering, but the Baker Boys 5 weren't taking one short lightly.

The annual barbecue that the Baker Boys 5 held was the meeting place to get things in order. Niggas were walking on grass in dress socks, knee shorts, and gators, like they didn't own sneakers and play clothes. Buck reminded each man of the real reason they were able to stunt so wonderfully.

"This thing got started because, collectively, we put our heads together and made it work," Buck said. "You can pretend this is your thing and Chaka was repaid, but you muthafuckas are committed to the bigger picture."

Danny and Dave stood vigil next to a picnic table, listening and watching the reactions of each man, hoping for a negative response.

"No one wants a nigga here, if he really wants to leave. That's not what this was about, but every man here still owes for the initial venture capital that started this shit. You niggas ready to settle your debt now and walk?" Buck asked. True, Buck was a brute, but he had more sense than they'd all given him credit for. "The rules haven't changed," he continued, "just some of the faces. Each man that wants to leave owes an exit fee. The fee is the same for every man, whether he earned it or not, so I want to know if there's any man here ready to pay."

Danny almost laughed as he watched a few of his comrades' faces drop. Dave didn't waste time holding in his laughter. He didn't give a damn. Quinton was impressed as Buck waited and watched for anyone of them who was tired of living the good life.

Most of the niggas sitting on the benches were walking investments. They had credit cards, beautiful homes, fancy cars, and a number of businesses, but they all had hella spending habits. Only six men could say that they could pay the exit fee right then, four of whom were the original members of the Dirty Dozen. The other two dudes were from Jersey and Philadelphia. They were located close enough to the city to reap the knowledge Chaka had been trying to bestow. They had learned the lessons, and Chaka had claimed their loyalties, despite all the rumors of a takeover.

Buck now knew he had six men in his camp for sure. No one's books or accounts were a secret, and he knew six men could have bought their way out if they so chose. They were a conglomerate, in every sense of the word. They paid taxes and such on their legal businesses, hired lawyers, and gave to charity. He waited a little longer until a few others became restless with the silence.

"Any man wanting to leave is more than welcome to do so. Just make sure you can settle your debt. There will be no hard feelings. Enjoy the barbecue," he said as casually as he could muster.

In the park the deal was sealed. Buck, Quinton, Danny, and Dave all cleared up any misunderstandings. Business would go on as usual. They had to keep on top of the game, search for Chaka's killers, and keep the extension of their success in line.

A few weeks after the barbecue, another bit of drama had begun to unfold. Earl was back from hell with his bullshit. He had a crew of niggas hustling and making a name from nothing. Soon enough they knew that situation would not be ignored. The ruler that was used to measure others was no longer in effect. And it was becoming clearer each day that Eve might have helped Earl kill him, so the time had come to move against them both.

The potential to get sidetracked was high, especially now with all the responsibility of running the Dirty Dozen on Buck and Quinton, since Danny and Dave had moved to the Carolinas and were carving out their fortune there. But Buck and Quinton knew now was the time to focus and take action against Chaka's killers.

As Quinton and Buck spent more and more time in the streets, trying to get to the bottom of Chaka's murder, Anissa became angry with Quinton's long days and longer nights away from home, accusing him of being more loyal to Chaka's grave than her.

Quinton tried to understand her anger, but he didn't know how to explain his side of things. His lack of communication was a breeding ground for more drama. He was offended that Anissa didn't support him after he had always encouraged her to pursue whatever she needed to do, and so the tension grew between the couple.

"You're more loyal to your boys than me," Anissa shouted at him one night. "But at night when you're too tired to take off your shoe, I do it for you. When you need me to listen to your plans and fears, I'm right here for you. Muthafucka, who's gonna be here for me when they run you in the ground?"

Quinton was tired of her tirades. He had learned to just sit quietly and let her vent. It was easier than responding.

"What are you going to do if you never find out why Chaka was killed, let alone find out *who* killed him?"

The question slid from her lips with more compassion than she wanted to convey. Her plan was to make a point and get Quinton to see it was time to move on with their lives, but Quinton stormed from the house, leaving her there alone to wonder if he would return.

The thought had never occurred to Quinton that he might never find the answers to the questions that drove him day and night. He had to find Buck, who would help him make sense of it all. Anissa was right. He didn't know what would happen if he never learned the truth.

Chapter 15

ACCEPTANCE AND MOVING FORWARD

Buck heard his car alarm go off twice before he made his way to the window. Just as he pulled on his pants, he heard the annoying shrill again. He was mad as hell when he realized it was Quinton setting off the alarm. That could only mean a couple things—Anissa had chased his ass from home again, or he was stressing over some shit that couldn't wait until morning.

"Nigga, you could have used the phone instead of coming out, setting off alarms," Buck yelled.

Quinton smiled. "Nigga, stop talking shit and let's go for a ride."

Buck hung his head, knowing that it didn't matter to Quinton what Buck was doing before he got there. He could never send Quinton away. It was his responsibility to take care of his brother.

"You mind if I go get a shirt?" Buck asked, as they laughed together.

"Yeah, just make sure a shirt is all you get while you in there."

Buck smirked and walked back into the house to find Sasha waiting by the door, redder than a chili pepper, but she didn't say a word about him leaving, even though he had just gotten there.

She tossed his shirt at him and threw some socks across the room. Before Buck could say good-bye, she was slamming her bedroom door.

Seconds later, Buck was slamming the front door. "You know you can fuck up a good thing when your ass is stressing."

Quinton groaned at his friend and laughed. "You six feet tall, the size of a double-wide trailer, and you complain like a bitch."

Buck couldn't help but chuckle. Quinton was clowning, so Buck knew he was trying to take the edge off whatever was bothering him. "That's all right, because I hit like a semi-tractor trailer, muthafucka." Buck pounded his fist.

"Yeah, and after that you sit down and cry like a baby for knocking a nigga out."

Buck only nodded to cease any further banter, because whatever had Q in the streets at this hour had to be serious.

After driving for about a half-hour and bobbing their heads to music, Q finally said, "Anissa asked me what I would do if I didn't find out who killed Chaka. I didn't know how to answer, so I left the house. It never occurred to me that I might not ever know the truth." Quinton sighed and lowered his head.

Buck leaned back. He hadn't thought about that either. Now he was searching his mind to find an answer for his friend. It was like coming face to face with the limitations they never accepted. Every time any one of them felt boxed in, they redirected their strengths and pushed uphill. Buck swallowed hard, hoping the lump in his throat would disappear, wondering when life would get easier, or if anyone ever really found happiness. The farce they had been living was closing in around them.

When Q stopped driving, they were sitting in front of their old junior high school. They got out and sat on the steps in front of the school.

Buck's grandmother had been dead for years, but he heard her speaking as if she were sitting on the cold concrete steps next to him, instead of Quinton. *"You cannot start accepting failures now, because you fought so hard to achieve your goals. This is no different, Jahson. Press on."* As easily as Buck heard the words, he repeated them, thanking his grand for always being there even when he could not see it.

"There are two men in my life I would have killed and died for," Quinton said. "One is dead, and you are the other."

Buck understood exactly what Quinton meant. However, the recent turmoil in their lives had Buck wondering if he was placing his trust in an illusion. Chaka's death still had them in mourning. The culprit was still walking around and probably plotting his next move. The thought enraged Buck. He had to do something with that energy, or he would probably wake up in jail tomorrow. He convinced Quinton it was time to take a ride.

Atlantic City, with its ringing machines, bright overhead lights, and free drinks flowing like a river bright lights, was as good a place as any to take off the edge. They bounced from one casino to the next.

With their meager winnings, they got a two-bedroom suite and went to the club. Before the night's end, they were celebrating life instead of mourning it. Quinton wanted to be devoted to their cause, but he understood the importance of letting up just enough to see past the drama.

Later that night Quinton and Buck were sitting in a little cheese steak restaurant about twenty minutes from the casino when this cute dealer they had seen earlier walked in. Buck had flirted with her, but she explained it was against company policy for her to associate with the clientele, and he'd left it at that.

She looked even better without her uniform. Her hair was resting on her shoulders, instead of pulled back in a ponytail. It took her all of two seconds to notice them.

She walked over to their table and sat next to Q, smiling. "Mister," she said to Q, "you should be careful of the company you keep. He looks like a tease." She winked.

Being shy was never Buck's way. He knew if she was sitting there, then she was interested in him too. "Latisha, right?" Buck asked as if he didn't already know the answer.

She nodded, looking shocked that he'd actually remembered.

Quinton excused himself and headed to the restroom while they got to know one another. By the time Q came back to the table, they had exchanged numbers.

Latisha invited them to a party the next night, and they both agreed to go.

The following morning, Q called Anissa to tell her that he needed to relax, and he would see her in a couple days. She wasn't too happy about him leaving without saying good-bye, but Q knew he needed this time.

Latisha called later that day to remind them that the party was by invite only, and they had to pick her and her girlfriend up to make sure they got in.

At twelve thirty, the ladies climbed into the rear of the white stretch limo. Quinton rented it, so they could really enjoy the night. Buck's date brought her friend Brenda, who reminded both Quinton and Buck of Ms. Sadie because of the way she talked. She spoke plainly, yet she had an easygoing manner.

From the minute Brenda got into the car, she hugged them both as part of her greeting. Buck got the feeling that was just her way. She made everyone feel good about their choice of outfits and promised them they were definitely going to enjoy the party. Brenda explained that she was playing host tonight for the record company she worked with. They had signed a deal with a local artist, and this was part of welcoming him to the family.

During the course of the night Latisha went missing, and Buck ended up hanging out with Brenda. Quinton had collected a fan club, and the women were taking turns dancing with him. Judging from the permanent smile on his face, he loved all the attention.

When Latisha finally resurfaced, it was too late. Buck wanted to stay with Brenda. Besides, Latisha was a mess, her curls were limp, her lipstick was gone, and she was drunk as hell.

Brenda felt responsible and excused herself to help her friend to the limo. She was the only one to come back to the table, saying Latisha went home early.

It was all right by Buck. He wasn't missing anything. When the night ended, Quinton had company, and Brenda was still at Buck's side.

The next morning Brenda slid from beneath the covers and raced across the room, straight for the bathroom. She came back with her hair less disheveled, smelling like toothpaste, and wearing one of Buck's T-shirts, which hung off her like a tent. "I'm starving," she said.

Buck had been trained to be a man by every woman he'd ever dated, so complying with Brenda's big hint was as easy as picking up the phone. He got up and tapped softly on Quinton's bedroom door to see if he was awake.

Just as Buck headed toward the menus in the sitting area, Quinton opened the door, crust still clumped in his eyes. He looked behind him and stepped into the sitting area.

"Yo, kid, what you getting ready to do?"

Buck raised the menu.

Quinton smiled. "I can always count on your ass to want to eat. Order enough for everybody," he said, heading back into his room.

Brenda called Buck into the room to see if he had found the menus. Buck smiled at hearing her say his name. No one had called him Jahson in a long time, except for Quinton when he was confused or upset. He still hadn't figured out why he'd told her his real name. It just rolled off his tongue during the introductions, and now hearing it from her mouth almost made him feel like he was human again. He took the menu into the bedroom and climbed back in bed.

Brenda snatched the menu from across his lap and read the items on the breakfast list. He tried reminding her it was lunchtime, but she kept right on reading.

"I want an open turkey sandwich with cheese, extra cranberry sauce, and a pitcher of iced tea," Buck announced.

By the time she put down the phone, they were laughing about how much food she had ordered.

She appeared comfortable in her own skin as she walked back to the bathroom and turned on the shower. He told her she could have another one of his T-shirts after her shower.

She stuck her head out the doorway. "Jahson, you planning to lie around dirty all day, or are you coming?"

Buck was too excited and certainly too much of a man to tell her no. He almost tripped over his feet, trying to get in there with her. The only sound he heard besides the shower running was the sound of the door locking behind him.

Standing inside the enclosed glass was the prettiest set of tits Buck had ever seen. Her breasts weren't as perky as he originally thought, but they were all one even color, including her nipples. He was transfixed. Last night, they'd both been pretty tipsy when they came into the room, and lights weren't a concern as they quickly disrobed and got right to satisfying their desires.

Staring at the water bouncing off her shoulders and rolling down her back, Buck was hard as hell. It was mesmerizing to watch this woman do the most natural things. He wondered if he was somewhat a voyeur. Sitting on the marble stool inside the shower and watching Brenda cover her body in soap and then rinse clean was mind-altering. During the act, they touched each other with their eyes. Buck had experienced many levels of sex, but this was the first time he had experienced this.

"Wash my back, please."

Buck couldn't do anything else but comply. He wasn't ashamed of his large body or shy about his manhood. He lathered her entire body from shoulder to butt, tracing letters in her back and daring her to try to decipher the message. By the time they left the bathroom they had written some vulgar messages on each other and promised to act out a few of those messages after they had eaten.

Brenda wasn't shy either. She was a real woman. She enjoyed a good meal, good laughter, and great sex. Buck promised to provide all three by the time they said good-bye.

Their food was waiting for them when they came out of the bathroom. Quinton, his date, Buck, and Brenda sat in silence, except for the smacking sounds of eating and occasional burps.

"I think Buck's finally found a girl that likes to eat just as much as he does," Quinton said.

Brenda couldn't reply, though, because she had a mouthful of food and didn't plan on wasting one second unnecessarily.

After they ate, they all went back to bed. Hours later, Buck woke up to go to the bathroom. When he returned to the bed, Brenda was lying in his spot. As he pushed her so he could get in, she woke up.

Brenda slid from his embrace to lie beside him and stroke his dick. Feeling mischievous, she asked, "Why does Quinton keep calling you Buck?"

Buck, a sly grin plastered on his face, flipped her from her back onto her stomach. "I can show you better than I could ever explain."

"How would he know?" Brenda laughed. She got on all fours and braced herself for a good pounding, arching her back. With every deep breath, she jerked to meet his pleasure. She turned her head slightly to get his attention.

Buck raised his eyebrows and smiled. Using his body language to answer Brenda's question, he locked his fingers in her locks, gripped them, and used them for leverage.

"Damn! Right there," Brenda said, panting.

Buck hoisted her legs, sending her upper body crashing into the bed. He squared his knees slightly and dipped into the pounding.

Two thrusts later and Brenda was climaxing all over the place with a muffled plea. "Don't stop. Please, don't stop."

Buck was on fire. He wanted her to continue talking that shit to him. After allowing Brenda's orgasm to subside, he went after his own. The headboard pounded against the wall as he continued to stab at her.

As an afterthought, he flipped her onto her back again. With her legs still hoisted, he pounded, and the sweat poured off him like he was running on a treadmill.

Brenda felt the moisture before she opened her eyes to see the rain falling from his face. Down the path of his neck and back, the sweat was definite evidence that he was throwing down the gauntlet, so to speak. She used her pelvic muscles to stroke him while he crushed her. Tightening and releasing, she had him timed completely. He bucked, she double-clinched and then released, letting him know that she had a trick or two of her own. It was a challenge that could only last as long as he didn't erupt.

"Not yet, not yet," he said. Holding on to the headboard for support, he allowed her legs to slide to the floor.

Brenda smiled wickedly.

When his heartbeat returned to normal, he collapsed in her arms. He coiled one of her locks around his finger, playing with the coarse feel, and the lovers drifted into a quiet sleep for all of twenty minutes.

Buck and Brenda recognized the primitive sounds and laughed, knowing they had probably inspired all of the noise because of the fireworks set off on their side of the wall. So as not to feel like peeping toms, they headed into the bathroom to shower.

Half an hour later, Buck could still hear slight sounds and decided it was time to leave the room before he and Brenda ended up back in bed. Together the couple exited the room and headed for the casino.

"Are you hungry?"

Buck laughed and nodded like a little kid.

The days in AC had gone by quickly, and now it was time to return home. Quinton was the first to speak once they got back on the road.

"Thanks, kid, for taking me out to have a good time," he said. "With everything that's been going on at home, I never get the chance to just relax and have a good time anymore."

Buck was concentrating on driving in the heavy rains, so he offered little verbal response. The bow of his head expressed every word he could have spoken.

As they got closer to home, the dreadful feelings began to return.

Together they entered Quinton's home through the garage and found the house empty. Buck headed straight to the phone to let Brenda know they had returned home safely.

Quinton walked about the house, wondering where Anissa had gone. Most Sunday evenings she was perched in front of the television in the bedroom, watching some sappy movie. He tossed his bags in the bottom of the closet and didn't give it another thought.

When Anissa stumbled into the house around eight o'clock with an armful of shopping bags, Buck rushed to meet her at the door.

"Always the gentleman, huh, Buck?" She smiled.

In his deepest Southern drawl, Buck answered, "I aim to please, ma'am."

The giggling caught Quinton's attention. He came out of the kitchen with a sandwich in one hand and a glass of juice in the other.

Anissa leaned her body into him. As angry as she was just two days ago, the anger had now subsided.

The small gesture made Quinton smile. He leaned down and kissed her. In his mind their relationship was a representation of what life-lasting love should be, if there was such a thing. "I see you been out spending money again," Q said, motioning his head toward the bags.

Anissa flashed a smile. "Yeah. Just enough to make you wish you had been home for the last three days."

Quinton groaned, and Buck laughed.

Anissa raced up the steps, leaned over the banister, and yelled, "Buck, Sasha called this morning. She said if you don't move your car by the time she has to go to work tomorrow, she gonna have it towed."

"Oh shit! I forgot I left my car in her parking lot." Buck laughed.

Quinton yelled up at Anissa, "Don't take off your clothes. I want you to take a ride with me."

Buck climbed from the back seat of Q's car to see Sasha standing in the doorway, wagging her finger at him. He hunched his shoulders to offer an apology, and Sasha hoisted her middle finger. He looked back at his friends, only to see them laughing.

He hung his head real low and slowly walked up to an angry Sasha. The rage was still in her eyes as he leaned her back and kissed her hard on the mouth. He opened his jacket and pulled out a teddy bear with the words My MAN WENT TO ATLANTIC CITY, AND ALL HE BROUGHT ME BACK WAS THIS STINKING TEDDY BEAR scrolled across the stomach.

Sasha accepted the gift, pushed him away from the door, and slammed it in his face.

Anissa burst out laughing.

Buck had done all he could to make peace. The purring of his engine made him feel at home.

After Quinton and Anissa left, he pulled into traffic and headed home.

Chapter 16

EVE: TAKING CHANCES

Monday morning arrived to find Buck and Quinton looking over paperwork in the real estate office. It was a rare occasion when the two were there together.

The doors swung open, and in walked Eve with a briefcase and a smile.

Quinton was the first to leap from his seat as Buck just sat there dumbfounded.

"What the fuck you doing here?" Quinton bellowed.

Eve flashed her winning smile and sauntered to an empty chair. "I'm here to make a proposal," she said. She sat opposite the mahogany desk, folding her hands in her lap. She waited for Quinton to take a seat. "I've found a property that needs rehabbing. It's in a great place." She opened the briefcase and presented some information for them to look at, and they glanced at the papers.

"The estimated cost is far more than I can stand on my own, but I thought maybe we could split the cost and make some money, once everything is complete."

Buck said, "Eve, you must have fell down and bumped your fucking head. You walk in here, talking about going into a joint venture for a piece of property. First, if we do any business, it would still be part of this company's portfolio. Secondly, we could probably pay you a finder's fee for bringing the property to our attention, but most importantly in my book, I don't want to do business with a snake. You are about as trustworthy as a bank robber in a vault full of money. Now having said that, thank you for stopping by. It's a pleasure to see you leave."

Eve sat stunned for a full sixty seconds.

No words ever left Quinton's mouth. He couldn't fathom what she had been thinking when she walked into the office. He would have laughed had he not been in total shock, but he just sat there instead.

Slowly she got up from her position and turned medieval. "So be it. You don't have to do business with me, but I promise, soon enough you'll wish you had accepted my offer." She stalked out of the office, slamming the door in her wake.

Storming to her car, Eve cursed underneath her breath. She wasn't watching where she was walking and slammed into someone. "Watch where the fuck you going, asshole!" she growled before looking up.

If Eve wasn't so absorbed in her own drama, she might have had the good sense to be a bit leery of Earl's presence outside the real estate office. Instead, she opened her arms, welcoming him as if he were a long-lost friend. "Oh my God! It's so great to see you," she yelled. "What have you been up to lately?"

Earl pretended to be as excited to see her as she was to see him. Had he not been angry with her for betraying his trust so long ago, he might have been more sincere in offering her the same warm reception. Together they stood chatting about old times and long-forgotten promises.

Earl suddenly had the most brilliant idea. "Come, let me take you to lunch," he offered.

Quickly Eve glanced at her watch and seemed mildly interested in accepting his offer.

He whispered, "It's been too long since we've really talked." Smoothly he draped his arm across her shoulder and led her in the direction of his Mercedes.

Eve examined the ice blue big body with bug-eyed headlights and nodded her approval.

Earl tried to suppress the anger that seemed to rise whenever he was around Eve. Catering to her whims had been his life's mission, until he realized that Eve always had an agenda, and her top priority was Eve. Ushering her to the passenger door, he waited until she was comfortable before sliding into the driver's seat.

By the time the waiter had taken their orders, Eve was in flirting mode. She positioned her seat as close as she could, without actually sitting in Earl's lap, batting her eyes, touching his arm or hand at every opportunity, and giggling at all his corny jokes. She even seemed to be hanging on to his every word. Slowly she was disarming him of his guarded manner. Like old times, they were slipping from one topic to the next without a hitch. Lunch had been more than two friends catching up on lost times. It was a mating call of some sort.

As weird as it seemed, Earl was enjoying the flirtations with Eve. When Eve excused herself to go to the restroom, he watched her ass sway. While she was in the bathroom, he settled the check and decided this was as good a time as any to position himself next to her. Now that Chaka was dead, he knew she was probably looking for someone to fill the void. Earl imagined that, with the right amount of pressure, she would run to him the way she always did when Chaka dismissed or disrespected her.

As Eve sauntered back to the table, Earl rose from his seat to meet her halfway. Claiming her hand, he led her out of the restaurant and across the street to the parking lot.

Eve wanted to touch Earl, but she wanted it to be subtle. She had batted her eyes and wiggled her ass, and now all she needed was to add the crowning piece. As they waited for the valet to bring the car around, she pretended there were crumbs in his goatee and stroked his face.

The gesture, small as it was, aroused Earl. He pulled Eve into his arms, his large hands holding the small of her back.

Eve leaned into his embrace, standing just inches shorter than him. As the car pulled into view, she turned and offered him the sweetest kiss.

The game had definitely begun, but Earl knew he needed to measure his steps carefully. He drove her directly to her car tonight. Tomorrow might hold a new experience. He secured Eve in her car and handed her a card with his name and telephone number on it.

Eve searched her bag and discovered she didn't have any cards, so she wrote her number in his palm.

Eve drove to her home, a beautiful rehabbed brownstone in Park Slope. The money Chaka had left her was enough to live better than all right, but of course she couldn't live off it forever. Eventually she had to make some sound investments or get a job. No way in hell was she ever going to let another man keep her locked under his wing just for his money.

She kept wondering why Earl didn't try to follow her, but after listening to her messages when she got home, any ideas she had that he was no longer interested were dispelled. The message on the machine was from the melodic voice of Earl, inviting her to dinner the next night. He promised to cook and be a gentleman as long as she graced his home with her presence, offering to pick her up, if she preferred.

Eve was giddy with anticipation and had to control her breathing as she waited for him to answer her return call.

"Yes," she uttered seconds after he answered the phone.

After ending the brief conversation, she wondered if Earl would be investing in her project. Then the thought occurred to her that he might not be financially capable of investing the amount of money she would need. Further contemplation of the situation left her thinking, if he could afford his Benz, then there was no way he couldn't put up a little of the capital for her investment.

Eve's one-track mind would probably get her in trouble with Earl if she didn't handle things properly. She decided she wouldn't tell him about the tenement until she had a full picture of his finances. Once she had confirmed that he really could afford to invest, she would then woo him out of his hard-earned revenue. She planned on returning it handsomely, though, once she was able to turn a profit.

The next night when Eve arrived at the old apartment Earl had shared with his father, she was pleasantly relieved to find it completely revamped. Instead of the six apartments in the building from back in the day, there were now four. On the upper floors, there were duplex apartments.

Earl welcomed his visitor into the lounge area, taking her coat and greeting her with a glass of wine.

The aroma wafting through the place tickled Eve's nose and made her stomach growl. Just past the threshold, she looked around at the abstract paintings hanging along the walls. Stepping into the kitchen, she was stunned by the island with a prep sink, all the stainless steel appliances, and the breakfast nook. She leaned against the counter, watching Earl sauté vegetables and add last-minute touches to the meal.

"Look around, woman," Earl said. "Don't be shy."

Eve stepped into the living room, impressed by the creative décor. The large black leather sofa was flanked by a white armchair and chaise. A red portrait graced the walls, adding drama to the room, but the real attraction was the sparkling parquet floors. Outside the bay window she could see the moon shining brightly and stars twinkling. Soft music purred through the speakers, setting the right mood for the night.

By the time dinner was ready, Eve had explored the entire first floor, marveling at the amount of work Earl had done.

Earl called to her from the living room, "Pretty lady, dinner is ready." He had laid out a blanket in the center of the floor, lit two candles, and placed the meals out as if they were at a picnic.

Eve could not contain her excitement. She leaned into him and kissed him passionately. "Thank you for making everything so perfect. I can tell you took your time to make tonight special."

Earl didn't say anything. He seemed to be blushing. He raised the fork to Eve's mouth and watched as she chewed. Earl was turned on the moment her pink tongue darted out of her mouth to catch the juices that dripped on her lips. She definitely knew how to turn him on.

Eve slowly found out he wasn't at all interested in an affair. He wanted the only link she could give him, and that was the connection to the Dirty Dozen.

Earl didn't pull any punches, appealing to her sense of greed and her emotional vendetta against everything Chaka had built. She had all but told him she was ready to get every dollar that the companies still owed her either by fair and square measures or by taking it to them through other means.

"What are your terms, Eve?"

"For every dollar you make, I want fifteen percent from the top. I don't want my name implicated in anyway, if this shit goes sour, because I still have to eat. But, in one year, I want you to double the interest on my accounts today."

Earl smiled at the idea that Eve's only interest was the money. He'd also realized she'd definitely learned something from Chaka's death. She was securing her future.

Chapter 17

CHANGING PLACES, FALL 2004

It had been a year since Chaka's death, and Eve had planned a memorial service to remember Chaka. At the cemetery she had placed all kinds of white orchids and roses alongside his grave. And she rented a dining hall, where everyone could go afterward to celebrate his life.

Eve had called Buck and asked him to help her with this, knowing he wouldn't turn her down, if it had anything to do with Chaka. She had extended invitations to everyone, including Petra and the children. Petra chose to come alone.

Although Buck had reservations about Eve's real motives, he couldn't decline her request for help. Maybe after all this time she realized that she did love Chaka and missed him as much as they all did.

Quinton, however, was neither as forgiving nor trusting. He knew Eve could be charming and calculating when she wanted something. Now it was just a matter of waiting to find out what she wanted.

The service had gone well. People from all over turned out to offer their condolences, offering funny stories about their times with Chaka.

Although Eve's gesture was never heartfelt, it was an opportunity for Earl to gain necessary knowledge about the Dirty Dozen. During the years, all the members of the Dirty Dozen camp had been somewhat of a well-kept secret, but today everyone had come out to honor their brother. The crew moved about the dining hall, sparking blunts, pouring out liquor in Chaka's memory, introducing loved ones, or just clinging to the loss of their comrade.

During the planning stages of this event, Eve never once had regrets about betraying the Dirty Dozen, but as she weaved her way among some of the familiar faces, she wished she hadn't made this deal. Earl had even promised to triple her money, if she took one step further into his plan. For him it was revenge, and for her it was supposed to be an investment.

"The smart thing to do will be to ask them to buy you out," he told her when she complained about how her money was tied to the crew. "You'll get a lump sum and walk away. When things go haywire, those niggas are gonna want to stash every dollar for their families. If you get yours now, you won't have to worry about taking a loss for the team."

Eve couldn't help thinking he had a convincing argument. The Dirty Dozen had shunned her after Chaka's death. She calculated that she probably would never get the full amount she deserved if she took a buyout, but money in her purse was far better than money promised. She also made a pact with the devil when Earl promised to help her if she helped him. His most convincing argument for her was simply this—if the Dirty Dozen were on the run from the feds, or had somehow fallen from the perch, she might not get the chance to get any of the money off the investments Chaka had made before he died.

Outside, in an old, beat-up black-paneled van, Earl sat with Pop, clicking pictures of all those in attendance.

Pop marveled at the number of heavy hitters who rolled through the place in their Sunday best, outshining the sun, and flossing to no end. "I wonder how many millions we could walk away with if we just rolled up in that bitch and robbed them muthafuckas?"

Earl laughed at his protégé. "There's no needed to rob niggas' pants pockets when you could walk away with the entire bank. That's why we out here snapping pictures, because when the sun sets on those frontin'-ass big willies, we gonna have their entire operation for our own."

Six rolls of film later, they had captured the entire event—the Dirty Dozen, their cars, and the women of the hour.

The reality of what Eve had done was grating on her nerves. She had called Earl and told him she'd changed her mind.

She heard the buzzing sound that indicated Earl was indeed at the door.

With photos in hand, Earl strolled through the door straight to the kitchen. He was ecstatic. Eve's less than jovial mood didn't concern him. Pretending had long ago been her claim to fame, and today was no different.

She took a seat opposite Earl and easily sorted out the puzzle of pictures. The first image was of Quinton and Anissa standing next to a cranberry-colored Jaguar. The image caught Anissa at an angle, making her belly appear slightly rounder than Eve remembered. Then there was a photo of Quinton alone. All the pictures of the remaining members of the Dirty Dozen were similar. Eve almost couldn't stomach the giddiness of Earl as he took notes. She hated herself for being a part of it all. *These people used to mean something to me. Don't get sidetracked by fucked-up emotions. It's all about the money.*

The master conniver in Earl did not care how Eve would feel when he finished using her, but he did wonder how she would manage when he moved against her. As quickly as the thought had formed, he dismissed it from growing wings and clouding his judgment.

Eve, up to her elbows with guilt, couldn't turn back now. "Earl, you weren't the first man to try to stand against the Dirty Dozen. Certainly if you fail, I will be sending your body back to Jamaica for your father to bury. Don't misunderstand . . . I'm committed to our plan, but be careful. One wrong move"—The sob that escaped her throat stopped her from continuing.

Earl hugged Eve tightly. "Baby girl, you never thought I had the means to be the man. That is the reason you ended up with Chaka in the first place. Don't worry, I'ma show better than I can tell you." Then he went off to fine-tune his plan.

Eve had a backup plan in case Earl failed. With the exception of Quinton and Buck, the others would pledge allegiances to whoever could turn them a profit. If Earl failed, she would help him recover from his mistake, and he would be indebted to her.

Earl sat starry-eyed in his basement as he looked over the photos of the fourteen rich men doing business across eleven states. He took a long toke of his blunt and grinned. He stood and began talking to himself, saying he would take away everything.

The original remaining members of the Bakers Boys 5 were the brains, heart, and soul of the Dirty Dozen. Eliminating them wouldn't be easy, but he knew their weaknesses. He planned to extort Quinton. From the pictures, it looked like Anissa was pregnant, and there was no way he would allow his pregnant girlfriend to remain in the hands of a kidnapper. Quinton would see the cost as minuscule, compared to the life of his family.

Buck would rot in prison for the rest of his miserable life, though he hadn't decided what he'd be in jail for. The twins would be victims of a robbery gone bad, and would pay with their lives.

The ringing of the phone interrupted Earl's thoughts. He couldn't afford to miss this call. Ian was on the line, greeting him and hoping to hear good news. Earl reassured his cousin that everything was being handled according to the original agreements. He also felt contempt that Ian had the audacity to call with his foolish worries.

Before Ian could fully work on Earl's nerves, he cut the conversation short, saying he had a few last-minute things to deal with. Earl surmised he would kill Ian as soon as he got the first chance and envisioned himself the king of everything.

Across town Pop lay in Sasha's bed, waiting for her to come back and clean up the mess they'd made. She waltzed into the room, naked as the day she was born, a hot towel in her hand. Sasha was sprung over Pop and his masterful tongue. Never before him had she felt the throes of an orgasm by the stroke of a man's tongue. She would turn her mind inside out to please him, as long as he promised to do the trick with his tongue.

Sasha was a victim of Pop's insanely jealous attitude toward Buck and her having once been a couple. She thought it was cute, until Pop blacked her eye after finding a pair of underwear that Buck had left at her place so many months ago. Through all Pop's fits, he had never once taken her outside the confines of her home. She was his dirty little secret, and she had no problem with it, as long as he continued to love her.

"I don't know what your obsession is with Buck, but our relationship was over months ago," she whimpered after he threatened to kill her if he ever saw her talking to him.

"Fuck that! You and that nigga had something going, and I don't want him anywhere near my woman," he yelled, pretending to really care. "Besides, don't ever fucking question me. I'm in control of this shit. Just do what I tell you to do, and I won't have to fuck you up."

Sasha wished she'd never told him she had a relationship with Buck. The little trust Buck had given to her, she was willing to betray for a little lust. Now, whenever Pop was around, everything was about him.

Sasha didn't have a clue that she was living on borrowed time. She was Pop's plaything for only as long as he needed to get enough information on Buck and his whereabouts. So far, she had been useful in telling him about a few places she believed Buck housed his drugs and some pocket change, but he hadn't hit the mother lode yet. Slowly he questioned her until she told him things even she wasn't sure were completely true.

Chapter 18

PHASE 1: TESTING THE STRENGTH

Several weeks had passed, and the groundwork for Earl's plans had been laid. Two of his soldiers, on loan from Ian, had gone to North Carolina, where the twins lived, to scope out the operation they had established. The first thing that became evident was that the twins had capital everywhere. The big investment was the split-level strip club that opened every day of the week except Sunday. There was also a strip mall and several real estate offices, not to mention the illegal money they were making on the side.

Dave had become lax in his routine. He was living well for so long, he forgot that envy's arm could be as long as NYC to North Carolina.

Saturday night's profits had been counted and ready for depositing, but Dave decided that he would handle it on Monday morning. He turned out the lights and stumbled down the steps, headed for his car in the parking lot. The bouncers were still lingering around, so he felt at ease.

The hair on the back of his neck bristled as he stood near his car and searched the darkness for an intruder. He shook off the eerie feeling, hoping to dispel the thought that maybe he really was under scrutiny.

Like a true general, he released the safety on his firearm and tucked it between his legs as he drove home. The dreadful feeling still was with him when he secured his home and climbed the steps to his bedroom, where his young, beautiful wife had been asleep for hours, and didn't move an inch when he climbed into bed.

After lying silently for five minutes, he finally fell asleep.

Outside Dave's home, two males in a pewter Saturn contemplated their next move. The lanky driver decided it was best that they go back to the motel and wait until the wee hours of Monday morning to pick up the trail. They had discovered that Dave was a family man on Sundays. He went to church, came home, and played with his children. The duo joked that he probably fucked his wife only on Sunday nights too, after the kids were asleep.

On Monday, Dave climbed into his Range Rover, the deposits by his side and the gun between his legs. The ride was as ordinary as any Monday morning, but he was always on point.

In true gentlemanly fashion, he held the door open for two women and a kid to enter the bank before him. Despite the early hour, the bank was crowded, leaving him no choice but to stand in line.

Suddenly his eerie feelings from Saturday returned. He turned to get a clear picture of his surroundings, and like a bright light, it hit him all at once. The young'un at the desk filling out a bank slip had been in that same spot way too long. He glanced at the kid in his peripheral vision and began to observe him. The lanky boy was dressed in New York fashion, no doubt about that, but his clothes were ill-fitting, catching Dave's eye. His designer shirt barely covered his long arms, and the too-big jeans sagged. Besides, New York thugs didn't tie their Timberlands, and old boy had his tied tightly around his ankles. Even the jewels he wore suggested he was a hustler. So why was the young'un standing in the bank?

As quickly as Dave assessed the situation, he decided to eliminate his problem, without alerting his stalker. Finally Dave was at the teller's window, and the opportunity presented itself.

The young'un held his head down just long enough, and Dave left out the side door. He doubled back to his car and positioned himself to see the young'un come out of the bank, confused. The look confirmed Dave's feelings that the boy was following him.

The stalker climbed into his Saturn with New York tags and sped off.

Dave watched his rearview mirror every few seconds for his company, but saw no one. The moment he pulled into the strip mall to open the sneaker store, he spied the familiar car. The fact that the young'un knew his next stop angered Dave, but if he didn't control himself, he might alert his stalker.

Dave climbed from the Rover and greeted his waiting staff with smiles and his usual pleasant manner. The aroma of freshly brewed coffee caught his attention. Dave found humor in the situation. Did his shadow take sugar or honey with his tea? The day was as normal as any other, and since the young'un seemed to know his routine, Dave went about his day.

That night, however, was another matter entirely. The strip club was hosting an invite-only party for the most exclusive patrons on this side of the Mason-Dixon Line. The usual patrons were scheduled to attend, along with a few up-and-coming ballers. Danny had been at the club all day, ensuring everything was ready. From the sound system to the dancers' costumes, no detail was too small for Danny's attention.

Dave ambled through the double doors close to ten o'clock, irate as he could ever remember being. He stormed up the steps heading to the hidden offices, searching for Danny.

Danny sat behind the massive desk staring at numerous closed-circuit cameras. He raised his eyebrows as he felt the negative energy ooze from his twin's pores.

"Yo, Danny, I was right all this time. Some young'un with New York plates been following me, and I got proof."

"OK. Well, why the hell is he following you? If it was for the money, he had ample opportunity to snatch the money bag."

"Yeah, and if he was after drugs, he would have learned, after following me all this time, that I never move near those circles in North Carolina."

Suddenly the New York plates rang a bell. Together the brothers yelled, "Earl!"

The answer was clearer than the brightly shining moon and the twinkling stars outside. Earl had finally grown a dick.

Danny picked up the walkie-talkie and told the burly bouncer at the door that they would be making an allowance for a special guest. He would let him know when the gentleman arrived.

There were at least one hundred men in the club watching the show by midnight. Just like they had expected, the young'un arrived without an invite, but Danny's voice alerted the bouncer that he was indeed the special guest, and the bouncer let him inside.

Dave, feeling at the top of his game, yelled, "That nigga trying to represent the NY, but his bop ain't even right."

Danny laughed. "Only you would declare that the Rotten Apple has its own walk."

Neither man took his eyes off the security monitors as they trailed the young'un's every move. His first stop was the men's room. Next he visited the circular bar just off the DJ's booth. And finally he claimed a table that gave him access to the comings and goings of the patrons.

The anger that filled the office was barely contained as the twins decided they would have the chance to deal with the stalker soon.

Two men standing in the center of the club were having a very loud argument. The twins determined the time had come to confront the stalker.

While the young'un was caught up in the drama on the floor, the twins closed in on him from both sides. Danny traveled left down the spiral stairs, and Dave went right. The young'un eyes bulged as he felt steel pressed into his back.

Everyone was watching the bouncers do their thing, so nobody noticed the twins on the floor, let alone that they'd jacked up the young'un and Danny was leading him down the stairs to the hidden basement.

Fear motivated the young'un to move quickly before the door slammed and sealed his fate. His heart lodged in his throat, he remembered the box cutter under his sleeve.

When the trio was a few steps from the bottom, he reached out with the sharp razor and tore into Dave's neck. The gush of blood frightened him more than it affected Dave.

Dave's retaliation was swift. A series of punches to the back of the young'un's head sent him sailing down the remaining steps.

Danny found the common ground to reason with Dave. "Let one of the girls take you to the hospital. I'll stay here with ole boy and work out whatever I find out. I'll even save some for you."

Dave smiled at his twin, knowing he meant every word. The young'un's sprawled-out body enraged him. He secretly wished he could wake him up so he could kick the bone right out of his ass.

Shortly after Dave left, the stalker's moans alerted Danny that he was finally coming to life.

"The pain," Danny said, "lets you know you're still among the living. However, I would like to tell you some things. Either you are the dumbest nigga alive for walking up in my house, or you are the realest nigga Earl ever had in his camp. One thing is certain, though—you're about to be the realest dead nigga Earl once knew."

The urine that leaked out of the stalker betrayed his killer instinct.

Danny decided to exploit his fear. "Save yourself, kid. Tell me what Earl is planning."

Although the young'un was eager to live, he didn't speak.

Danny switched gears. He needed to get him to talk, and fast. There were lives at stake. "What's your name, young'un?"

The boy whispered, struggling to say his name through the pain. "Mac . . . Jaime McMillan."

Danny realized that Mac just might black out again soon, so he quickly fired another question. "You dress like you from the NY, but where you from, kid?"

"I'm from Virginia." His voice quivered as he tried to breathe and talk at the same time.

Danny was having problems figuring things out. He began to analyze the situation aloud. "Virginia? We don't run with them boys," he reasoned softly.

Mac thought he had a bargaining chip. "I run with a hustler named Ian. He and Earl are first cousins. I can help you out if you let me live."

Danny pretended to be contemplating the offer then feigned acceptance with a nod of his head.

Mac's breathing was ragged, but if he was going to live, he would write the words to save himself. Before he could speak, he passed out.

In frustration, Danny rushed to his office to make a quick phone call.

The tension on the line wasn't missed by Quinton or Buck when they heard the dreaded words—"We have a red-eye situation."

Quinton said, "We on our way."

When Danny returned to the basement, he was shocked to see Dave back and already talking with their prisoner. "In your absence our friend told me some things," Dave told his twin. "It seems Earl has this diabolical plan to kill you and me. He wants to take over our world. So, our young'un has been following us with another young'un for about three weeks now. He said that you agreed to let him live for some big secret."

Danny nodded.

"Earl is on his way here," Mac confessed. "He's driving with that chick,

Eve. She helped him set up everybody. He and Pop were at the memorial services, taking flicks of the Dirty Dozen, and they came up with the plan to kill you and your brother."

"Y'all was gonna kill the entire Dirty Dozen?" Danny asked. "Who you s'pose to be? The Mafia?"

"Only the remaining members of the Baker Boys 5."

"I may die tomorrow," Dave told him, "but not before I kill you tonight."

The twins figured they only had a small window of time to get this shit right. If they miscalculated even one step, there would be unnecessary casualties. Mac's Saturn had to be removed from the club's parking lot. As luck would have it, he had parked on the side of the lot that was not well lit.

The twins helped him through the back panel in the basement and out a hidden door, into the parking lot.

Danny asked Mac, "Soldier, you all right to drive?"

Mac answered feebly, "I can try." The pain in his ribs, the throbbing of his head, and his will to live kept him awake at the wheel.

"Follow that truck in front of you," Danny said, pointing to the truck Dave was driving.

A few feet away, Mac saw a construction site and knew his death was inevitable. He began to sob like a little girl as Danny sat in the passenger seat watching him.

When the Saturn and the truck reached the construction site, Dave got out of the truck and climbed into the back seat of the Saturn.

"You lied to me, man!" Mac screamed. "You said if I told you everything, you'd let me go."

The brothers looked at one another and hunched their shoulders.

Dave wrapped an extension cord around the young'un's neck until he was still. He then went to get the gasoline from his truck, while Danny tore rags to ignite a fuse.

Orange flames flashed in their rearview mirror as they left the car to burn.

It only took Danny and Dave a couple days to find Mac's partner in crime. After a little research and some stalking of their own, ol' boy was right where they expected, waiting for his comrade to return in a seedy motel room.

Porky sat in the room, chain-smoking cigarettes, wondering where Mac could be. Twice he had tried to reach Earl, but to no avail. Ian wasn't an option, so he waited and worried.

As Porky watched the battered TV in the motel room, a reporter appeared on the screen, standing outside a construction site where a body had been found burned inside a sedan. The police believed the victim had been strangled and then burned.

After hearing the report, Porky became even more nervous. This wasn't rocket science. The twins had murdered his friend. He wasn't going to wait around for his turn, so he quickly left the room.

As he headed for the front desk, he noticed an imposing familiar figure. From this distance, he thought it might be Buck. At that point the only sane thought Porky had was to run. He turned and took two steps before he recognized Quinton standing behind him.

Porky couldn't fathom dying without putting up a fight. He took a fighting stance and waited for someone to make the first move.

"I ain't here for that," Quinton said calmly. "Let's go back to your room and talk."

"Nah."

Suddenly Porky felt a fierce pain in his back. Then his legs went numb, and he fell face down on the ground.

Buck was angry, but he was trying to save his venom for the true culprit— Earl.

The twins laughed, thinking it was just like Buck to render a nigga unconscious before he could say a word.

Together they took Porky back to the room and left him lying on the floor just inside the door.

Finally Porky started to move. The image of death and Mac being burned alive clouded his judgment. "What the fuck you want?" he asked with false bravado.

There was no response. They had what they needed, and Porky knew it by the smiling faces. "Just kill me, muthafucka," he spat.

Dave raised the gun and shot Porky in the leg.

"You can die slowly or quickly, based on what you have to say," Quinton offered.

Porky smirked. "You ain't giving me shit. Death is death, so do what you do, bitch!"

Dave eagerly obliged their victim. "We ain't here to break a soldier, just to get some information. See you in hell." He saluted before firing the weapon at Porky's head.

Together the brothers walked out of the room. It didn't matter what happened from this moment on, as long as Earl understood once and forever that life would be a series of ducks, dodges, and bullets flying.

Chapter 19

THE LAST STRAW

Earl tried to convince Eve that they needed a well-deserved vacation, some time to talk about their future together.

Eve, not the least bit fooled by the gesture, knew this was about the twins. She'd been awake half the night, rehearsing the words to get Earl to confess to killing Chaka. All her life she had lived in a bubble, on a need-to-know basis. She needed to know why he had decided at that precise moment that Chaka had to die. She decided she would ride with Earl to get whatever information she could from him about Chaka's death. Suddenly it seemed important to know the truth.

A silk scarf, wide sunglasses, and earplugs gave Eve the look of a traveling jetsetter, despite her hateful mood. The morning skies were dreary-looking as Earl loaded Eve's travel bags into the trunk of the luxury sports utility vehicle.

Two hours into the drive, Earl asked Eve to get him a water bottle from the cooler beside her feet.

Eve didn't notice there was a cooler filled to the brim with everything for a road trip. Snacks were in a bag too, perched on the back seat, along with a bunch of CD's.

She punched him when she saw a battered Volkswagen Beetle. "Punch buggy," she yelled playfully.

He could not help but laugh. "You're still one silly-ass woman."

While on I-95 South, Eve decided it was safe to begin a dialogue. Shifting in her seat, she asked him, "What attracted you to me?"

"Who the hell told you I was attracted to you?" he teased.

"Stop playing and answer me, man."

Earl tried to search his mind for the first thing that caught his eye about her. "That big pretty ass."

Eve feigned shock, but thought his honesty was a good start. "Did you ever think we would be hanging out again?"

"Nah. Not as long as Chaka was alive."

Eve didn't mean to have him bring up Chaka, at least not until she asked a few more questions, but since he did, the time had come to ask. Plus, the sign ahead said REST STOP TWO MILES. She figured she could walk two miles if he tossed her out of the car.

"Why did you kill Chaka?"

Earl swerved the car across two lanes without hitting a brake or even looking behind him when he heard the words. He repeated Eve's question. The rest stop was less than one hundred feet away, and Earl needed to rest for this conversation. He pulled into the parking lot and parked in a somewhat deserted area.

"You think I had Chaka killed?" he bellowed. The incredulous look plastered on Eve's face answered his question.

Earl took a deep breath between mumbling curses and threats. "You are a crazy bitch, but here's a news flash for your ass. I never laid one hand on Chaka, or commissioned anyone to kill him. He was probably killed by the niggas in his camp, and that's just the truth."

Eve was angry that Earl had the nerve to treat her like some lame dummy.

Before she could say a word, Earl added, "He had all y'all fooled as to what kinda person he really was, but since you want to have this conversation, let's do it."

"You don't have to lie to me anymore, stupid. I am here with you, regardless of the outcome."

Earl's wicked laugh left Eve feeling threatened.

"Eve, this was never about you. You were just a carefully placed pawn in this bullshit. Chaka shocked me when he claimed you as his woman, because he only started fucking with you to create a war. The moment I conceded, that ended that bullshit. I always knew what Chaka never figured out about you. You were going to run and fuck because you could, so don't even entertain the idea that you were the reason for our battles. The main reason I never bothered to go after Chaka was because of Ms. Sadie. When my pops was locked down, her generosity kept me alive. For that reason alone, I didn't do any real harm to him."

Eve wasn't convinced just yet that Earl was being completely honest, but she didn't protest. The silence and suspicious look in her eyes said the words she held from her mouth.

"Did it ever occur to you that Chaka never did anything to me either?"

Eve shook her head.

The slight movement enraged him. Now that he was baring his soul, he may as well tell her everything. He charged forward and told her some other things that she hadn't been privy to before.

"My pops liked Chaka," he said. "He had faith that one day Chaka would make him a rich man. But all that praise ended when my dad got knocked in the apartment with enough drugs and shit to get him sent away for a long time. Anyway, the detectives kept coming around, trying to get information on my pop's connections. Since I never dealt in the business, I didn't have any idea about the people involved. As a favor to my pops, Ms. Sadie made sure I went to school, and was clean and well fed. Meanwhile, Chaka welcomed me to the fold.

"I was down with them, hustling a little bit, when Chaka decided I could take over where my father left off, but I had to get the DT's off my back, and quick. Chaka hatched a plan. I would give the DT's a name, and they would leave me alone. But we couldn't just choose anybody, or we might be fucked in the end. So Buck got caught holding the bag."

Eve started to hyperventilate.

"Yeah, the sacrificial lamb was Buck. According to Chaka, and I quote, 'Nobody expected Buck to do much with his life,' so he was the best choice. Besides, his big ass could probably survive prison better than any of us."

"Did the others know?"

Earl didn't answer her question. He just kept telling his story.

"At the time I thought they all agreed, including Buck. But, later, when everyone was labeling me a snitch, I knew better. By then it was too late to tell anyone. Chaka had already ousted me from the clique. Shit, I even became the scapegoat for a plan that he'd hatched. I was afraid and alone, with no friends and no family.

"It might sound dumb, but I trusted Chaka, just like the rest of the crew. He convinced me to stay away for a while, and he would make sure I didn't suffer too much from the drama. To survive, I got out on my own and started making a little bit of money. Nothing major, just enough to eat and pay the rent on the ragged tenement apartment. My pops had gone back to Jamaica, but he had a few friends, and they took me under their wings. Ms. Maddy had bonded my dad out, and before his feet could hit New York City pavement, she had him back in Jamaica sitting by her side.

"Anyway, when crack began to really make an appearance, I was bubbling, making money. Chaka once again came up with this plan. It was a moneymaking idea, so I ran with it. I was no longer in need of friends, and my naïveté was long gone. I understood the meaning of money. Chaka's money spent like any other man's, so I took it. I went from small-time hustler to supplier for him and his boys."

Eve was stupefied by Earl's story. By the time Earl had made all his declarations, she was ready to run.

"I told you Chaka was a self-serving bastard," Earl said in response to her look of horror. "My biggest downfall, when it came to him, was that I was always just a means to an end. When the drama came about because of you, he had already outgrown my minor racket and was doing big things, but that was OK. I was still eating, until he started eliminating all competition. He offered any local trafficker a chance to live by getting down with him, but that offer was never extended to me. I was the fuel that kept his crew earning like mad. They needed someone to do better than, and I was it."

The tears rolled down Eve's face, angering Earl. He wondered if they were out of pity for him or out of some perverse love for Chaka's corpse. "Those fucking tears are just wasted emotions. Shit, the next time you ask a question, remember it's all about the money, Eve, never about feelings. Isn't that what you like to say when shit gets thick?"

Eve was exhausted thinking about everything. Sitting there with Earl not saying a word and the miles creeping along, she wondered if he was just being brutally honest about everything, or telling a lie to keep her in his good graces.

Four hours later Earl decided he had had enough of driving. It was time to find a place to lie down and contemplate his next course of action.

As a peace offering, Eve clung to Earl as they watched the highways and byways interchange.

Suddenly, she blurted out the question that had been weighing heavily on her mind since Earl's earlier revelations. "If you didn't kill him, who did?"

Earl cleared his throat. "I've had my thoughts about that for some time, and each time I come back to Quinton and Buck."

Eve's laughter filled the car like music bouncing off the ceiling and floors.

"Quinton would probably stab Anissa and bury her in the back yard before turning sides against Chaka. If Buck found out about Chaka setting him up to go to jail, chances are, he would kill Chaka, but I still can't see him going through with it and not revealing any clues that he did it after so much time has passed."

"Financially, they both had the most to gain, from the legit business to the street traffic. Besides, I always thought Chaka was the most conniving of the group, but Quinton was the smartest by far. He just let everyone think Chaka was the brains of the operation."

By the time the pair got to North Carolina, they had come up with multiple theories about Chaka's killer, but nothing seemed to fit. No closer to finding out who Chaka's real killer was, they headed straight for the posh Marriott Hotel to check in and rest before Earl went about his duties.

Chapter 20

ALL ABOUT THE MONEY

Pop was impulsive, irrational, and greedy. He decided that, if Earl was the reigning king, his chance to get at Buck might not ever come. He planned to secure a few investments on his own. He decided to break into Buck's apartment in Sasha's building, where he knew Buck stashed his drugs and money. The longer Pop thought about the burglary, the more elaborate his plans became.

He was stunned at how easily he got past Buck's steel door with a power drill and instructions from a bootleg mechanic. Carefully he searched the place and found two portable safes, one digital, the other an old-time dial. Pop wasn't the least bit nervous. He was just eager to see his pockets filled to the brim and then some.

In the bedroom there was an average-sized bed and all the furnishings of a home, but the footlocker seemed out of place. Just as a crackhead could smell his next hit long before he saw the crack, well, a nigga like Pop could smell money. At first glance he saw a bunch of sweaters neatly packed inside the locker, but underneath, there was a mother lode of crisp, neatly wrapped hundred-dollar bills.

After careful consideration, Pop took all ten packages of money and placed them in his waistband. Next, he hoisted the two safes into separate duffel bags and quickly abandoned the mess he had made.

In Sasha's attempts to please Pop, she had given him a key to her place, hoping he would use it. Today he had good reason to climb the steps to her apartment, where he hid all his newfound fortunes. He placed both safes into one bag, and quickly peeled the money from his body. Afterward he placed the cash into the other bag, deciding to leave it behind until it was safe to move it.

He used her closet as hiding place. It was as good a place as any, especially since she had an array of shit cluttering the space. She wouldn't even know he'd been there.

During his swindling, Pop didn't figure that his men were watching his every move. They wanted in on the pie too, and if they couldn't get some, he would have none. They had a meeting without him to discuss the best way to make him understand that the trickle-down theory applied in their case.

Pop wasn't a master manipulator. He was straight hood. If he couldn't verbally convince you to do things his way, then next came the threats. Followed by death. In this case, he was one young'un in a camp of strength. They would as soon see him dead on the sidewalk rather than let him run rampant without repercussions.

Three men from Pop's camp were posted by the lamppost as Pop turned the corner, smiling. They greeted him with the usual dap, keeping things simple.

"Yo, kid, what you come off with?" Patchy questioned, his country drawl catching Pop off guard.

Pop soon realized that every man standing there wanted a cut of whatever he had. "Not much. Just two safes, and that's it," he lied.

The other two guys rocked on their toes as they asked for the take.

"I couldn't walk out with it in broad daylight, so I left it at the chick's house that lives in his building."

"All right, we want to see what *we* got to work with," Patchy said, emphasizing the word *we*, to indicate this was a joint effort

"True dat," was all Pop said.

Later that night Sasha watched as Pop searched her closet and came out with the two duffel bags. She felt the urge to question him because she certainly didn't intend to be the fall girl if the cops ever rolled up on her. Prison separated lovers, and if she had to choose between his dick and jail, she could live without his abusive ass. If she was in prison, he couldn't give her any dick anyway.

Of course when Sasha questioned Pop about the bags, he slapped her across the face. The blood that dripped from her lip was enough to shut her up until Pop left to go wherever with his bullshit. Her first thought was to ask for her keys back, but he would probably really kick her ass if she tried a move like that. The decision she made had to be final, or she would just be subjected to more abuse. Changing the locks was a better idea than having a confrontation.

As Sasha sat crying on her bed, Pop hoisted a duffel bag on his shoulder. "Don't go a fucking place until I get back. I told your silly ass, don't ever question anything I do or say. Just follow orders." He head for the door and slammed it as he left.

Pop's boys were all sitting in the apartment that Earl had given them when they'd arrived in town. Each man was trying to find a way to crack the safes without damaging the contents. They thought up everything from liquid nitroglycerin to just straight dynamite.

The laughter at the dilemma left everyone feeling better about the caper—everyone except Pop. He wanted his fortune free and clear.

Chapter 21

WHEN IT ALL GOES TO HELL

Earl went to the motel just off I-95 in search of his boys, only to find police and ambulances everywhere. The place was roped off, and the sheriff was questioning some of the customers brave enough to stand around. Earl practically ran back to the Marriott. The truth was he was not certain of the events, but he knew, whatever happened, the twins probably knew he was coming.

Eve left the hotel, hoping to get in some shopping, but she never made it.

Danny and Dave spied her coming out of the side entrance, and neither of them intended to play games.

"Hey, Ms. Eve. What you doing down here in my neck of the woods," Danny said, his words dripping with sarcasm.

Eve could have jumped out her skin as a cold chill race through her body. The look of hate in Dave's eyes almost matched the disgust on Quinton's face.

Quietly she fell in step with the twins, hoping they'd give her a chance to explain if she went peacefully. *Fuck!* For all she knew Earl could have been heading back to New York and left her here to die at the hands of the men she betrayed.

She climbed into the rear of the van, too afraid to look anywhere but at the palm of her hands. Of all the ways to die, she'd never imagined it to be in the back of a dirty van heading to no place. Instead of surrendering to her fears, Eve convinced herself being on the defensive was better than waiting to die, so she allowed herself to think of all the reasons she'd betrayed them. One by one she recited them as if they were the gospel.

As they pulled up to the club, Eve had run out of excuses.

Danny ushered her out of the truck.

Dave ground his teeth as he stared at her, wondering how she could have been so deceptive, pretending to mourn Chaka even after she had probably been the reason he was killed.

Danny asked, "Why would you help him, after all he did to us? Even you?"

Shame forced Eve to drop her head. She could have told them that Chaka wasn't everything they believed him to be, but she didn't have any proof of that, except for Earl's words. She clamped down on her lips and silently prayed they would just kill her quickly.

By the time Buck and Quinton came into the office, the twins were frustrated beyond belief.

Eve attempted to square her shoulders and prepare herself for the worst, but her false bravery was wasted.

Quinton charged at her, snatching the chair from beneath her while she still sat perched on it, sending her legs in one direction and the rest of her body in another. "Bitches belong on the floor!" he spat.

Buck rescued her from the floor and put her back on the chair.

"It's this simple, nigga," Buck told Q. "I'm not going to harm a hair on her head in memory of Chaka, and I can't watch you do anything dumb either." Buck was thinking that her punishment was best left for a later date when the misery she caused surfaced, and she would have to live with it. "If she dies now, it would be too easy."

The tension in the room was heavy, but the twins understood Buck's reasoning and nodded in agreement.

Quinton, however, felt like they were betraying Chaka. "Let's just kill this bitch," he said, "and then go get Earl's treacherous ass before he can dip."

Silent tears streamed a path down Eve's face as the men discussed her fate. She decided she'd shut up Quinton's ass for good, or make him kill her.

When she began speaking her voice shook with emotion, but as the words flowed, she became stronger. Her only regret was that the truth would destroy Buck, but she wanted to make it clear that Chaka was no saint.

"Why did Chaka wage death on anybody else in his path, but allow Earl to live?" she began. "Earl created the most drama. He was always trying to find a way to get back at Chaka, even using me to make him jealous. So why didn't he just rid himself of his biggest nemesis?"

They were stumped for a brief moment, but Quinton wasn't there to debate why. He was there to fix who.

"I'll tell you why—Because Earl knew that Chaka planned the setup that sent Buck to jail all those years ago, just so the Baker Boys Five could continue doing what they were doing without being bothered by the cops."

Everyone was speechless after her announcement.

Though Buck was generous enough to spare her moments ago, he was now ready to kill her. He drew his weapon from its holster and pointed at her head in a flash.

Danny and Dave each stepped away from her and watched in horror as Buck's hand shook.

Quinton reacted slowly, not wanting Buck to turn at the slightest movement and fire. He placed a hand on top of Buck's and twisted the gun from his hand. The gesture wasn't made to save Eve's miserable life, but to save Buck. Quinton wouldn't be able to live with himself if he allowed his friend to kill her, and Buck would probably become the pawn Chaka had made him out to be.

The angry glow of Buck's eyes scared everyone, and they all stood still. He went to the mahogany desk and flipped the massive furniture over, sending the computer and papers flying everywhere.

The noise must have alerted security, because Danny saw them on the closed-circuit monitors all heading in the direction of the office.

Six hulking men stood in the hallway outside the office, trying to decide the best way to get inside. Shooting the door might injure the wrong person.

Finally Dave opened the door and tried to squash the situation, but before he could say anything, the security team was heading for Buck.

The first body to rush in caught a quick blow to the throat. The next man ducked, but wasn't ready for the crushing blow of Buck's knee to his face.

The third man entered the room but didn't go any farther. He prevented the other bouncers from entering and explained that it was all just a misunderstanding.

The injured pair on the floor collected themselves and exited the club, headed straight to the hospital.

The physical battle helped calm only a small portion of Buck's rage. He really wished he could prove the hateful things Eve had uttered were false. Defeated, he plopped himself into a seat and stared at her for any evidence that she was lying. Had Chaka not been dead and buried, Buck would have killed him slowly.

Danny and Dave truly didn't know what to make of the situation. Quinton, however, knew Eve's words were true. He now understood why Chaka never seemed to care when Buck shunned them after he got out of jail.

After about four hours of waiting for Eve at the hotel, Earl was suspicious when she didn't return. The phone startled him from his thoughts. "Hello," he answered.

"Listen, I got your girl. I'll trade you her life for yours," the caller said, not introducing himself.

"You can keep that bitch." Earl's laughter could be heard clear across the room. "I was done anyway."

The line went dead.

Buck was the first to express his resentment, foam collecting at the corners of his mouth, his arms flailing above his head as he said, "Eve, a bitch like you don't understand the true impact of the shit they do until they have to live through it. If I thought killing you would make me feel better, I would pump you full of so many bullets, your body would end up looking like a thousand-piece jigsaw puzzle together. But the greatest punishment for you is survival. When the world is on your shoulders, you're going to wonder why terrible things keep happening to you, and the answer is going to be all the misery you caused. I won't promise after today I'll be so generous with your life, so I strongly suggest you stay the fuck out of my path."

Eve couldn't believe they were going to let her live.

Earl marched past the front desk, claimed his vehicle, and kept driving south. He figured that the twins would expect him to head back home to a trap waiting for him, courtesy of Buck and Quinton. They had managed to foil this plan, but there were many others in the works.

Earl was exhausted when he reached Atlanta. He didn't feel like talking to anyone, but decided it was in his best interest to find out how things were working back at home. The moment he spoke with Pop, the knot that had formed in the base of his neck eased. For the first time in a long time, he was able to sleep without nightmares.

The morning light brought with it the truth of where his life really was. Earl had mostly lived in the gutter. It was his way of life, but he always managed to climb out squeaky clean. He knew there was a way to fix his problem with

Danny and Dave and save Eve.

His feelings had changed quickly with a good night's sleep. She at least deserved the chance to change her life and become a better person. He needed to speak with someone who might lead him in the right direction, so he decided to call his father.

The island dialect poured through the phone lines as if his father was sitting next to him, and not back home in Jamaica.

Earl explained the dilemma he had created and the emotions that had brought him to this point in his life.

His father listened intently, unsure at first what to say to his son. It suddenly occurred to him that Earl had called him for help. Rootsman's voice was filled with concern as he begged his son's pardon for not being there at a crucial time in his life, and Earl accepted the apology, for what it was worth.

"Can you live with yourself if you walk away?" Rootsman questioned.

Earl thought briefly. "Yes. But if I walk, where can I go? This drama been brewing for a long time. Chaka used me, and I was dumb enough to allow it. Now they think I killed him. Eve accused me too, until I was able to explain."

"You have to understand that I failed to give you the things you needed to make you stronger. From the beginning, you had to make your own way. Earl, do things the way you see fit. I promise to stand by you when it matters."

His father's speech hadn't done anything to help him make a decision, but he had to do something. He laid out his options. He could take his chances and, no doubt, come up on a short end of a hot-ass bullet. The odds of winning were slim, especially since they knew he was coming. He could choose to run away, but running like a coward wouldn't ensure someone wouldn't put two in his head just because he was hiding. He thought, however, that a combination of both might turn things in his favor.

"Fuck it!" he yelled. "I'm gonna see this to the end, however it might turn out."

The drive back to New York was tedious. Earl needed to rethink Chaka's position. If the universal rule was true that if you killed the head, the body must crumble, then Chaka wasn't the head. His death didn't cause the slightest ripple in the Dirty Dozen's operations. In fact, they seemed to be doing just as well, if not better, since the tragedy. It was plausible that Quinton had finally gotten tired of everyone praising Chaka's greatness while he did all the work.

Eve had confided to Earl that Quinton had come home hours before the officers who came to the house on the day of Chaka's murder. For some reason, she'd even remembered that he smelled like gunpowder. He never mentioned how he knew about Chaka's death, and he damn sure never told anyone where he was coming from while Chaka was dying.

People judge you by the company you keep, Earl kept thinking repeatedly.

Chaka was definitely selfish and conniving, and his loyalty was about as strong as a cheap garbage bag. None of the things Earl had learned about Quinton suggested that he was like that, but Earl hadn't been the greatest judge of character in the past.

Suppose Eve was really responsible for Chaka's death and decided to accuse him, to divert attention from her. Although Eve and Chaka's relationship had been dysfunctional, they were both selfish as hell, so he knew he could dismiss Eve as the culprit. Eve had confessed to him already that she wanted out of the relationship, but her lack of courage and her greed kept her bound to the misery.

Anissa couldn't be ruled out of the equation either. Living with Chaka couldn't have been easy. Eve bragged that Quinton took his cues from Chaka on how to treat a woman. Most nights if Chaka stayed out, then he wouldn't come home, and for a while, Anissa tried to deal with the disrespect, but Eve told Earl that one night Anissa blew up. Chaka told Anissa that he was Q's boss, and she had better fall in line, or she could find herself another man.

Anissa made it clear that the blatant disrespect would not continue, and didn't give a shit that he was the boss. She even went so far as to point out to Chaka that he had gotten away with so much because the men around him were willing to tolerate his rude manners.

Anissa didn't have a problem explaining to Chaka that she took care of herself, so if he thought she needed any man, he could kiss her natural black ass. She related all the reasons why Chaka should want his friend to be in a productive relationship, since he himself didn't have one with Eve.

Chaka, of course, didn't like that, and Eve said that he tried to drive a wedge between the couple after that argument, trying to cause fights between the happy couple, but soon Quinton began to see the light.

Anissa definitely didn't have any love lost for Chaka, so she could have set up his murder.

The twins, Earl decided rather quickly, had no reason to kill Chaka. Going away to college had taken care of their day-to-day interactions with Chaka, so if there was any resentment, distance and time took care of that.

Earl knew he didn't have all the information regarding Chaka's murder, especially since everyone suspected him. Once again, he felt that he was a patsy for the excitement someone else had caused.

Twelve hours later, after arriving back in New York, Earl was climbing the steps to his home. He didn't bother to alert anyone of his presence, thinking it was better that he rest and have a clear head for the drama that would soon unfold.

The nagging ring of his cell phone would not stop. It seemed suddenly everyone wanted to talk with him, yet no one left a message.

Standing in his shower, he allowed the water to beat against his aching shoulder blades as he pondered his next steps. Pop, he figured, was the safest route for now.

After exiting the shower, he punched in the telephone number and waited to hear the familiar voice.

After several rings he heard, "Yo."

"All right, nigga, I see you still alive." Earl laughed in Pop's ear.

Pop was giving Earl all the usual lines about everything being normal and the crew keeping low profiles, but Earl didn't feel comfortable telling Pop he was back in town so soon.

"All right, it's good to hear all is well. I should see you soon."

Pop didn't give a damn about Earl, so long as he didn't get in his way. His concern was the safes in the living room. One of his homies had opened the digital safe. The shouting stopped the moment they stared at its contents.

Inside the safe there were several stacks of money, a baggie filled with a white powder, and two large silver handguns. The look on Pop's face was pure shock as he drooled over the contents. Pops quickly tasted the powder, and his tongue went completely numb. The wide grin on his face told the story. He wondered if his crew understood the real meaning of this situation.

Everyone tried to talk at once, but Busta won the battle for who would talk first. "I heard about shit like this," he said, "but I ain't never seen nothing like it. That nigga Buck gonna come back here and turn this fucking city upside down for this shit! It probably costs a fortune, and we in here laughing like we hit the jackpot. The worst thing is, we don't even know how to cut this shit and make it marketable on the streets. Nobody has seen that dude Quinton or Buck since Earl left this bitch, so for all we know, that nigga Earl might be dead."

Pop knew if he told them everything they would go ballistic. His intentions were to use their fear to keep them in line and loyal, but he hadn't given any thought to the fact that they were really strangers trying to get on in a new place.

The mutiny was in full swing, and it wouldn't be long before every nigga broke camp to save himself. Pop could probably hush the noise for a minute, but they needed someone to confirm that this coke was indeed what they thought it was.

Chapter 22

FAMILY SECRETS

Petra sat on the sofa staring at her daughter, wondering how one person could influence the look of someone so greatly. Chanice had her father's big head, freckles, deep-set eyes, and long, curly eyelashes. Sadly, she realized her daughter's butter complexion and quick wit were even influenced by Chaka.

"You're doing it again, Mom," Chanice said, annoyed.

Petra offered a weak apology for making her uncomfortable. "I miss your dad so much. When I look at you, it's like seeing him."

"But, Mommy, I'm not Daddy. I'm Chanice," she said with a nervous smile.

Petra's mother had moved with her daughter for a while, since she seemed to be having such a hard time. Earlier in the day, she had explained to Chanice that her father's death was sudden, and it saddened her mother. The reason might have made sense to the adults, but to Chanice, she only wondered whether her mom had died too.

CJ wasn't fazed by his mother's confusion, since he didn't resemble his dad as much as his sister did.

"My grandchildren aren't going to suffer the loss of two parents because you can't function. Grieving is a process just like anything else in life, but you must remember you cannot mourn him for the rest of your life. These babies need you," she told Petra.

Petra said, "Mama, why did he have to be like that? Why didn't he just stay with me and let me love and care for him?" The unbridled tears streamed down her face.

"Baby, you talk like you are guilty of not protecting him from his decision to leave. Chaka was a man. He was responsible for his actions, not you."

Petra's labored breathing caught her mother's attention. She thought, maybe, she'd said the wrong thing.

"Mama, you don't understand. From the beginning of our relationship, we were responsible for each other. Whatever he needed, I provided. When I wasn't taking my studies seriously before I found out I was pregnant, Chaka would threaten not to see me until I got my head back in the books. I was going to run away when I found out I was pregnant, but he promised he would provide everything I needed, as long as I stayed on course and got my degree. In return, I didn't complain when he didn't come home or came in late, because I knew he was out there working for me. I didn't fight back when I discovered that Eve existed. I just accepted it. But I couldn't accept when he promised to marry her. That was more than I was willing to deal with. I worked hard to maintain a home he could be proud of, and he was planning to marry her.

"The night he was killed, it was CJ's birthday. I cooked and baked a cake. We were all having a good time when the phone went off. When Chaka returned the call, I knew he would be leaving soon, but I didn't expect to be so angry about it. I could hear the girl yelling, saying he was spending too much time out, and telling him to come to her. At first he dismissed her, and we carried on like nothing had happened, until the beeping began again. Mama, I couldn't deal with it, so I took the thing and smashed it against the wall. Chaka didn't say a word. He just got up and went to bed. For the briefest of moments, I had his full attention. That night I told him I was angry that she was still able to create so much tension between us."

The wailing sounds of Chanice interrupted the women's conversation and forced them into the living room, where they found the child on her back. The footprints on the bookshelf indicated that Chanice had tried to climb up the shelf and had fallen.

CJ stood back in horror as he watched his sister lying there. He ran from the room the second his mother began yelling, because he knew he would get a beating too for being in the vicinity of trouble. Luckily, his grandmother was there, or they might have been beaten something fierce.

Petra's mother helped Chanice to her feet, checking her for any serious damage. "I bet you won't try that anymore." She gave her granddaughter a stern look.

The sniffling and whimpering softened Petra's heart. Her daughter could have really been injured, all because she was crying over Chaka. The sadness turned to anger as she accepted Chaka was already all right. She needed to be sure her children would be all right. She held Chanice in her arms and softly chastised her for trying such a stunt.

"What did you want from up there anyway?" Petra asked.

"Daddy gave me a necklace, and I remembered you put it on the top shelf. That was the day you and Daddy had that big fight."

Petra remembered the necklace, but she hadn't seen it in a while. She searched the top shelf until her hands felt the coarse metal. "I got it," she yelled. "It's right here."

The smile on Chanice's face could have brightened the room, and CJ slid back into the room just as Chanice hugged her mom.

The sight and feel of the necklace left Petra feeling hollow, like there was something she should remember, but because of her new determination to move on with life, she refused to allow the feeling to linger.

As the children slept soundly that night, Petra walked about the house, trying to decide what her first step should be, moving forward.

The bedroom closet still held many of Chaka's things. After a year, she was still holding on to them as if he would return one day. Hoisting the sweaters from the overhead shelf, she refused to get caught up in the scent that permeated the room. She pushed her things to the side and began pulling down all the hangers that held his pants.

The next stop was the dresser that contained his underwear and T-shirts. She removed all the things that held her captive in her home.

Her mother heard the moving about and decided that Petra needed the time alone.

By the time Petra made her way to his socks, her eyes were clouded, but the tears wouldn't fall. She began speaking to his memory as if he was sitting at the foot of her bed.

"Chaka, there were things in our relationship that just were never going to be perfect. It didn't matter that I was willing to sacrifice everything to make you happy, that I accepted all the misery that was yours, that I let you come into my life and take over. You were never going to do the right thing by me. Here I was living in this house with two children, waiting for you, and you had another woman. She was everything you claimed you hated, but you still were promising her things that should've been meant for me.

"I begged you to tell me why you raced home to her. You never said a word. I wondered if she was smarter, and you laughed like I was telling jokes. I needed to know what she had that made you love her more than me and our two children."

Slowly Petra's mother climbed the steps, hoping she could get to her daughter before Petra completely lost her mind, but it was too late.

Petra was cutting item after item of Chaka's clothing as she talked to him. The hatred in her eyes blazed like wildfire. She turned toward her mother just as she entered the door. A wicked smile crossed her face as she raised the scissors and brought them down hard on the mattress she shared with Chaka.

The blind fury in Petra's eyes frightened her mother. She never would have believed her child was capable of such a violent display. She prayed that Petra would calm herself.

The silent prayer appeared to work, because Petra began to lose momentum. The hysterics subsided, and just as suddenly as the outburst started, it was ending.

Petra surveyed the damage surrounding her and instantly felt a rush of shame. Turning her back to the mess, she lowered her body to the floor.

Fear held her mother just beyond the doorway. "Petra," she called and received no response. In a more demanding voice, she called out again, this time getting acknowledgment from Petra. "Reasoning hasn't worked for you," her mother said, "and allowing you to work through this has only made the situation worse, so I am just going to be brutally honest with you."

Petra sat transfixed by the stern look in her mother's eyes. Nothing could have been more embarrassing than sitting on the floor in a heap of damaged clothes, listening to her mother chastise her as if she were a child again.

"You have been behaving as if he was your entire life. Your children should be your world, and that is the truth. Now I won't take away that you are angry with him for the decisions he made, but you chose to stay and accept your lot in this life. You could have left and lived a different life without him, but you wouldn't hear any of that. Honestly, you're acting as though he is alive and is rejecting you for some woman. Chaka is dead. He won't and can't come back, so move on. Judging by the turmoil displayed in this room, if he had chosen her over you, you would have probably killed him anyway." Petra's mother glanced about the room and wondered if her daughter could have done just that. *Could she have killed Chaka?* She wondered if her daughter had that kind of hate in her heart, especially after watching her all day behave like a hateful bitch, instead of a lovesick widow.

Chapter 23

FACE TO FACE

Earl had created a simple plan that would give him all the power, money, and respect he deserved, but it had somehow been twisted into a bunch of mess. Porky and Mac had gotten themselves killed before he could even get to South Carolina, and Eve, the most dangerous of the lot, was probably saving her soul by telling them his entire plan. But none of that mattered now. He was certain the Baker Boys were gunning for him.

"Dammit! I can't lie down now."

If he didn't do anything else, he decided he'd chip at the Dozen's fortune one spot at a time, until niggas in the street were scared to hustle. "Fuck it, by any means," became his new oath. Earl was hustling to pull in the reins of his spiraling plan, but he believed there was still one part that was salvageable. Sasha had been Buck's last girlfriend, and since there would be no way to get to him, he decided murdering her would put Buck on the defensive. It stood to reason, if Buck was crying over his woman, there would be no room for him to hunt her killer. Only, Earl didn't expect to walk into another ring of deception.

No one had heard Earl come in through the back of house. Pop and the boys were too busy celebrating and acting up over the little bit of wealth from Buck's apartment. One by one they posed for pictures to preserve the moment. Earl almost flipped out when he noticed the coke sitting on the table.

"What the fuck? You niggas getting high now? And where the hell did all this shit come from?" he hollered.

No one was in a rush to speak, and Busta had all but found a corner to hide in while Earl blew up. Earl didn't bother to look in anyone else's direction but Pop's, knowing he had to be the one to have set things in motion, and the rest of them followed like peons.

Pop stared back at Earl with a look of contempt and didn't say a word.

"Pop, I'm asking you, where you got this shit?"

Pop hunched his shoulder before he spoke. "I came across it," he answered with a smirk."

Earl snatched a package of coke off the table. "Muthafucka, you came across this shit, my ass! This is Buck's shit. I know that D-12 stamp, because I designed it. I suggest you take these drugs back to where you came across it because when that muthafucka find out it's gone he gonna chase you to hell to get it back.

Pop's eyes flashed with hate. "Nigga, you stupid. I ain't taking shit back. As far as I'm concerned, you been living in that nigga shadow too long to see the treasure in this free shit, or maybe you're just embarrassed I did something you could never have done."

Earl smiled before his first step. "You did it, young'un, but how long you think you gonna live with it? I'll tell you what—if you found this, then you found the money. What you do with that? Did you share it with your boys, or are you holding out on them?"

Pop saw through Earl's ploy to oust him. "Nigga, you the outsider. Everybody in this room is here because of Ian and his plans. It's all about the money. Once we get this shit clicking, you will be obsolete like Betamax, nigga."

Earl prepared to leave the house. "Well, let Ian get your ass out the hole Buck's gonna bury you in once he realizes you stole his shit." Earl walked out the door. He couldn't believe he'd been dumb enough to put any trust in Ian or his crew. "Dammit, I gotta step up my game before these niggas pull us all down."

Pop was fronting big time. As soon as Earl walked out the door, he walked over to the table weak-kneed and examined the package, wondering, how was he going to get rid of this shit.

Busta said, "Yo, Pop, were you just teasing us with these safes, or was there more money?"

Pop turned his full attention on Busta. "The entire time that nigga Earl was in here hollering like a bitch, you didn't say a fucking word, but now you got the courage to question me. What you see is what there is," he lied with a straight face.

❖❖❖❖❖

Pop couldn't sleep as he thought about the bullshit he'd gotten himself caught up in. If Earl was home, then where the hell was Eve, he wondered. They'd been fucking around too long behind Earl's back for her to flip on him now, especially when he was so close to running shit. Everything was in place, and now that he'd come up on the drugs he knew he could work it off in no time. All he had to do was keep his homies in line.

Before he drifted to sleep, he decided tomorrow he would go see Sasha one last time to pick up the bag filled with money and then he'd ditch her weak ass. After that he'd tell Earl to suck his dick because he was lame. Pop had no clue his plan was way too simple for real life.

❖❖❖❖❖

Sasha had mentally prepared the items she would need for her stay at her sister's house. The suitcase lay on the bed, open for the garments of her choice. Quickly she waltzed back and forth, examining one outfit after the next before making all her selections. Suddenly it occurred to her that she hadn't chosen one pair of shoes for her pilgrimage.

As she contemplated the appropriate shoes for her outfits, she heard a knock. The interruption made her stand still and hold her breath. She figured if she didn't respond, maybe the uninvited visitor would go away.

The light taps became loud banging, and she knew it was Pop. She decided she wouldn't open the door. No matter how much he banged, she would just wait him out.

Silently she prayed Ms. Jones, her next-door neighbor, would hear the ruckus and call the police, because Pop didn't seem like he had any intentions of leaving without getting in.

Pop began kicking the door and calling her name. All he wanted was the duffel bag full of cash he'd left on the shelf in her closet.

His persistence unraveled Sasha, making her hand tremble and numbing her body. She tiptoed to the door. "I called the police. Please leave," she said.

Pop didn't believe her right away, but he had to make her think she was safe. He pretended he was leaving, but quietly stood on the side of the door and waited.

The constant noise stopped and gave her a false sense of safety. With the speed of a cat, she slammed the suitcase shut and forgot about any shoes. Slowly she tiptoed back to the door and listened, hoping Pop had gotten the message and gone away. As a safety precaution, she looked through the peephole and felt comforted that he wasn't there.

With the suitcase at her side, Sasha quietly opened her top lock and turned the knob, releasing the latch that secured her inside. When the door creaked opened slightly, Pop burst in, and the heavy steel door flew into her chest, sending the suitcase flying behind her.

As she fought to maintain her balance, Pop stepped past the threshold. Sasha tried to move, but shock held her down. As he advanced toward her, she backpedaled, trying to get away. Pop, tired with the cat-and-mouse game, offered her his hand to help her up from the floor, betraying the threat of a serious ass-kicking.

Feeling cornered, Sasha allowed him to help her up.

As she stood, Pop struck her with a right across her head and sent her sailing across the room and into the wall. The force of the blow and Sasha's feeble attempt to stand excited Pop. He whispered, "My dick is hard right now."

The next punch was timed perfectly as she struggled to raise her throbbing head. He slammed his fist into her eye. The cracking sound made Pop feel like he might cum. Her whimpering made him angrier.

"Stop crying! You fucking up my shit!"

The next jab to Sasha's stomach made her double over, and her nose made contact with his raised knee, forcing her to see stars. She crumbled to the floor, unconscious.

The sound of sirens stopped Pop from delivering another blow, and stopped him from getting the money, his real reason for being there. He didn't have time to look left or right. He didn't even bother to close the apartment door all the way as he rushed down the steps to freedom. He figured the neighbors had heard him banging and kicking the door and decided to call the police.

If he'd taken a moment, he would have seen that the sirens were coming from an ambulance, and not a police car. His feet couldn't carry him fast enough as he headed to the phone, hoping to find Eve.

"Hello," she whispered, wondering who the hell knew she was home. As far as Earl was concerned, she was dead.

Pop didn't waste words. "How long you been home?"

Just as she was going to answer, he stopped her.

"Fuck all that! I need you to meet me over here now. Don't ask any questions. I'll explain everything when you get here."

Eve didn't have a chance to respond, because Pop had already hung up.

She cursed the entire ride across town. "Damn! If I haven't learned my lesson … Once again I'm chasing behind a nigga, his dream and some money. Didn't your dumb ass almost die behind this same shit? You one simple bitch, but at least this time I running with a thoroughbred." She laughed, trying to make light of her situation, which could've been avoided, had she just let the damn phone ring.

Eve couldn't believe Pop wanted her to go in Sasha's house. Didn't he understand they'd been in the same parties together? It wasn't like she was a complete stranger. Shit, she only hoped no one noticed her walking out of this girl's house with a duffel bag, especially if Pop had kicked her ass the way he'd claimed.

He tiptoed to the door and tapped lightly, pretending to be on a friendly visit. "Hey, Sasha, girl, you left your door unlock."

Eve slid past the doorway and saw Sasha lying unconscious on the floor, her face disfigured. "Oh shit!" She realized Pop had really fucked up her face. Eve wanted to turn back, but something told her Pop might fuck her up if she didn't come back with that duffel bag.

Just as she got up the nerve to step farther into the bedroom, Sasha moaned and scared the hell out of her. "Fuck this!" Eve whimpered, trying to back out of the doorway.

Sasha grabbed the hem of her pants.

Eve almost leaped off the floor. "Let me go," she whispered loudly. Eve jerked her leg, and Sasha slumped back into a twisted position. Eve rushed into the bedroom before she lost her nerve. Just as she pulled down the duffel bag, she thought she heard someone entering in the apartment. She slid under the bed.

Earl stood over Sasha confused as to what happened to her. Quickly he leaned closer to her. "Girl, what the fuck happened to you? Someone beat your pretty face badly."

Sasha was trying to plead for help, but Earl didn't seem interested in helping her either. He whispered, "Don't worry, I'll get you some help, so you don't have to suffer anymore."

Sasha was relieved, until she saw the gun in his hand. She lifted her arm to shield her face seconds before Earl fired the bullet in her chest. Eve literally, vomited under the bed.

Earl walked away without a glance backwards.

Eve scrambled from beneath the bed and almost ran past Pop, who was waiting for her two floors down in the stairwell. She threw the money and didn't stop running until she was sitting in her car.

"What the fuck up there that got you so scared?"

Eve rolled her eyes and didn't say a word. Pop could think whatever he wanted, but she wasn't about to implicate herself in Sasha's murder. Fuck that! He could keep the money and carry his ass back to Virginia, for all she cared. She hadn't bargained for this.

Pop interrupted Eve's thoughts. "Eve, take this money with you, count and then put it away, until I tell you what to do with it."

Eve gave him a look of death.

"I'll see you tonight, and I promise to fill you in on everything." Pop got out the car a few blocks from the house where he'd been staying since coming to New York.

Eve only had a chance to nod, and she drove off, reliving everything that happened in the forty-five minutes from the time Pop had called her.

Chapter 24

VALUED FRIENDS

As they drove back to New York, Buck didn't have time to think about his own safety. He was too busy reliving the old feeling of resentment. Angela's death had left him angry and bitter with the two people he trusted most. Oftentimes, he believed that those two men were betraying him, but he would just as easily accept the thought as paranoia. Now he knew for sure that Chaka didn't care about Buck or his ability to be a friend, and the madness began again.

Could Q have been a part of the plan to set him up? Just as the thought rolled around in his head, he began to have trouble breathing. Quinton sat in the driver's seat while Buck, in the passenger's seat, seemed to be hyperventilating. Quinton navigated the truck to the shoulder of the road to check on his friend.

As the car pulled slowly to a stop, Buck raised his head. There was no question, something was torturing Buck. His eyes were red, and his chest was heaving.

Q tried to make his voice light, in case Buck was angry with him. "You all right, man? You seem to be having trouble over there."

Buck turned his glare to Quinton, as if seeing him for the very first time.

"Nah, nigga, I ain't all right. You let me go to jail for some shit we were all down with. You and that sorry son of a bitch used me to take the fall. I lost everything that year—my chance at life, a decent girl, my freedom, and more importantly, I destroyed my grandma's dreams for me."

Q allowed Buck to air out his anger, hoping that when it was time to defend his actions, Buck would believe him. But he lost his patience just as Buck got to Ms. Sadie.

"I wonder if she was down with the plan to fuck me over—the stupid football star— because she didn't think I was worth anything."

"Yo, Jahson, you reaching now. Chaka did some fucked-up shit, and I'm as angry as you are, but I wonder how else he used us all. But if you asking me whether I knew about the plan to send you up, my answer is emphatically no. I would not have gone along with that shit, and I hope all these years as friends have proved that to you. Granted, we were all guilty, but I like to think, had things worked out differently, I could have dealt with my punishment."

Buck lost control of his emotions. He leaped from the truck and slammed the door.

Quinton recognized Buck's frustration, but was helpless to make things better. For his fallen friend, he harbored a new sense of pity. Chaka must have been desperate, to use his oldest friend just to fill his greed. Buck had always been the most loyal of them all, and he'd proved it every time one of them needed him. It didn't matter if it was in the middle of the night for bullshit or if it was real beef. *How could he have been so wicked*?

A sense of dread came over Q as he accepted that this might be the end of their friendship. All the years the crew had been together, Buck had become his confidante, and he still believed that if he lost his brother, it would be like losing a lung. The will to hold on to outdated shit in the name of Chaka lost its luster. All Quinton wanted to do now was mend the fences between him and Jahson.

Buck leaned against the truck, working out the bullshit in his head. He even threw up his hands, as if surrendering to some unknown thing.

Quinton climbed from the truck slowly, walking toward him, hoping to make heads or tails of the faraway look in Buck's eyes.

As he got closer, Buck's anger boiled over. The first punch landed square on Quinton's jaw, rattling his teeth. The next was a left to his right eye, and the last was an uppercut that landed Q on his back. Buck's knuckles split, and the shooting pain in his hand left him a little less aggressive.

The attack happened so quickly, Quinton didn't have time to recover and fight back. He could only cover up and hope the damage wouldn't continue for too long. He rose off the ground and yelled, "You stupid muthafucka! You feel better now? What you want to do? Kill me?"

Buck turned his back as Quinton walked toward him. The force of the blow from being rushed from behind sent Buck face first into the dirt. Two grown men, worth millions of dollars, rolled around on the side of the road like children wrestling.

Finally out of breath, Quinton went back to the car, climbed into the driver's seat, and drove off, leaving Buck sitting on the side of the road.

Twenty minutes later, the truck came back, stopping just in front of Buck. Neither man had the courage to say anything, for fear they might start fighting again.

The rest stops were becoming fewer and fewer with each mile. Quinton couldn't wait any longer to eat, so he pulled into a restaurant, leaving Buck sitting in the car.

Buck's impatience got the better of him. He wandered into the diner and found Quinton sitting at a booth with a menu held up to his face. The aroma of grilled onions carried Buck to the booth, where he claimed his own menu. The anger was still fresh as the waitress took their order and left.

Buck finally spoke. "You OK?" he asked with a slight smile on his face.

"Yeah, muthafucka, in your old age you hit like a girl. All ain't forgiven, though. When I get home and Anissa sees my face, I'm gonna let her beat your ass."

Buck couldn't laugh at the threat. Anissa had been taking karate classes for years, and even in her pregnant state, he feared her. She was the only chick he knew with a black belt. The expression on Buck's face made Q laugh as much as his jaw would allow.

Together the duo ate in silence, both deep in their thoughts. Q prayed they had gotten over the hurdle of betrayal Chaka had caused. Buck hoped Q would understand that there was no way to be certain that the twins and even Q hadn't been a part of the drama that got him locked down. He needed to put some space between the things he called his life and the drama from yesteryear.

Rolling back into the city had Buck contemplating if he was even going to go back to the places that once held so much joy and pain for him. Anything left behind he could definitely live without. He clicked off the things he would be leaving behind—money, drugs, women, and even the cars. The only person he owed an explanation was Angela's mother, who he had been visiting at least twice a week since he got out of jail. She had become his surrogate mother when things got rough. He didn't want her to worry about him, and he needed to tell her that he loved her. The thought of leaving her behind made his heart ache, but he knew he had to go or he would only lose himself in more drama.

Quinton pulled into his driveway with Buck asleep in the passenger's seat. He tapped him and told him to get the hell out.

Anissa was waiting in the kitchen when Q swaggered through the door. The horrified look on her face made him wince.

"Nissa, I'm OK. Everything is fine. It looks worse than it really is."

Before she could form the words, a tired Buck stormed into the kitchen with just a little skin missing from his nose, forehead, and chin. Anissa looked back and forth between Buck and Quinton. "OK, what the fuck was it over this time? What the hell did Chaka do that you two can't get over now? Or were you fighting over which one of you dumb fuckers miss him the most?" Her slippers slapped across the floor as she searched for her first-aid kit. "I get so tired of patching you two up, like y'all some little kids. This some bullshit! Next time, take your asses to the emergency room."

Neither Buck nor Quinton offered an explanation, fearing they'd have to tell her everything, and Quinton didn't want to listen to her rant all night.

"Oh, by the way, Buck, I am not your secretary. You left this number for your latest little girlfriend. Well, she called and left this number." Anissa flashed the piece of paper in his face, but she snatched it out of reach just as he tried to touch it. "I'll give it to you if you promise to keep those big-ass mitts you call hands off my man. Either we got a deal, or I'm throwing it away—going once . . ." She laughed as Buck nodded.

Buck hadn't been home two hours before word of Sasha's death was brought to his attention.

Dana Richard had been calling Buck half the night and was relieved when he finally answered the phone. Tearfully, she told him everything, from the beatings Sasha had been suffering to her decision to get away for a while. Dana had mentioned Pop's name several times, but he wasn't registering to Buck as someone that ran in their circles. However, when Dana told him Sasha thought Pop might be out to hurt him and his friends, Buck couldn't make sense of it, and it frustrated him.

"Why would he hurt Sasha, if he was really after us? I mean, she wasn't a part of the street. What could he stand to gain by killing her?"

"Sasha said he stash some stuff in her house, but the night before she decided to change her locks, he took everything. So he didn't have a reason to come back, unless he thought she might tell you."

Buck hung up the phone and decided he wanted out. He was tired of people dying around him. He just wanted to be normal and not be responsible for everything and everyone else. Sasha was innocent, and her only fault was that she'd chosen to get involved with him.

Sasha's funeral left everyone wondering how this could happen to such a nice person. Buck offered the usual support to her family when the arrangements were being made, and he and Quinton purchased all of the flowers for the service.

The church was packed with friends and family. Even coworkers from Sasha's job had come to offer support.

Petra walked into the room wearing a black pantsuit and dark sunglasses. At her side were two men that seemed vaguely familiar to Quinton. She nodded to him, and he returned the gesture.

During the service, Quinton pulled Buck's coat to point out the duo sitting at Petra's elbow. Buck couldn't place them either.

Suddenly, like a flash of lightning, Quinton remembered where he'd seen these men before. The smirk on the face of the man to the right let Quinton know he was on target with his remembrance. Quinton would have lost his everloving mind right at that moment if Dana didn't start screaming at the top of her lungs.

Pop, donned in a black Italian suit and shoes, sauntered into the church and took a seat opposite the deceased family. Though Dana had never met Pop, based on her sister's description, the chocolate face, green eyes, and his ever-present waves gave him away. There wasn't going to be anything refined about her behavior.

Dana called him a murderer in front of everyone. In three-and-a-half-inch heels, she tackled the man she believed responsible for Sasha's death. Dana was showing out to the fullest. Pop was stomped, kicked, spat on, and beaten until he ran from the church.

In one afternoon Quinton and Buck had managed to fill in all the pieces. Pop was a flunky for Earl and Eve. Eve even had the audacity to bring Pop into Chaka's home after they'd murdered him. Sasha was probably just a means to an end and didn't deserve to die just because she knew them.

Calmness enveloped Buck as he thought about the war he planned to wage against everyone remotely connected to Eve and Earl. It was only a matter of time.

Quinton was sorry he'd allowed Eve to live. Instead, he wished they'd left her in a garbage bag along the highway. Quinton had been friends with Buck long enough to know his look of war, and knew they were beyond caring about rules or laws. This was personal, and no amount of patience could stop Buck.

The twins walked into the sanctuary just as the service was beginning.

Quinton was walking back up the aisle when he noticed Petra sitting with two men. His breathing slowed, but his mind sped up as he relived every second of Chaka's murder. He could hear the shot fired and see Chaka's body falling to the ground. He could even see the two men standing over the body watching Chaka bleeding to death. *Damn!* Quinton couldn't believe he was so blind.

As they exited the church, Quinton blurted out, "The two men sitting with Petra killed Chaka."

Buck and the twins looked at Quinton as if he had sprouted a second head.

"You mean to tell me that Petra had Chaka killed?" Danny asked.

Quinton nodded, leaving Buck confused.

"You sure?" Buck asked. "That doesn't make sense. She was in love with that nigga."

Quinton was just as dumbfounded as they were, but he knew what he saw that day. "I don't know why. I guess we're going to have to ask her."

Buck shook his head. "The reason doesn't matter to me. They did me a favor." Buck wanted to hear Petra's reasons, and he vowed not to participate in the revenge, no matter how the crew felt. Chaka had betrayed him, and he wouldn't help avenge his death. Buck had been confused about so much, but he was adamant about this.

Quinton opened and closed his mouth without saying a word to Buck. However, he felt the tingle building in his core. He knew Chaka had betrayed Buck, and even understood Buck's reaction, but he wouldn't accept Buck walking away from this fight. Unwilling to let things rest, he turned to speak just as the mourners exited the church.

When Petra stepped onto the sidewalk, she was alone. Her eyes were covered by dark shades, hiding the look of scorn in her heart.

Quinton went to her side, and she looped her arm through his elbow, speaking softly.

The melody of her voice could have soothed a raging bull, but it was having the opposite effect on Quinton. *Incredible,* Q thought. *This bitch is really playing with my intelligence.*

Quinton drew his gun, but the smooth movement didn't stop Petra from her close contact with him. She wasn't afraid. Somewhere in her mind, she wanted him to kill her. It would end the guilt and the hate. Unmoved she never slowed her step.

"I know you recognized my brothers," Petra said as she took a step. "Now you know the truth about who killed Chaka. The only thing you aren't certain about is why." She said the words as if they were talking about a recipe, not the death of her children's father.

They found themselves positioned between two benches, and Petra took a seat, waiting for Quinton to understand that she was going to tell him everything he desperately needed to know.

With reluctance, Quinton sat in the seat farthest from her, furious that she'd played them. Fixated on Petra and the pain she had caused, his resentment left him completely unaware of Buck's presence behind Petra.

Buck called to Petra, forcing her to acknowledge that he had followed them.

Petra turned to the waiting arms of the man she considered the most special man out of the entire crew. From the moment Buck found out about her children, he sheltered them. Uncle Jah, as the kids screamed every time he walked through the doors, was a good-time uncle. He played on the floor or chased them around in the yard. If there was a movie out for kids, he was the first to mention it and promised to take them or buy the video. Never once in their short lives had he broke a promise to them.

After Chaka's death, Buck became the mentor they needed to get through the pain of missing a father. Before her mother came to help her out, Buck had taken the kids off her hands, prepared their lunches for school, and even helped them with homework. No matter how things turned out, she knew Buck would care for her children until his last breath, not just because they were Chaka's, but because he loved them genuinely. Somehow they allowed him the chance to be a kid again.

Quinton watched the exchange and understood that Buck had taken his stance. He was going to be on Petra's side, no matter the outcome. He finally understood the meaning of betrayal and disloyalty. Watching Buck holding Petra left Q bitter.

Chapter 25

THE TRUTH

Petra, debating on the best place to start her story, decided that the beginning was as good a place as any.

"I met Chaka hanging out with Sasha at school during my second semester. We hit it off, and before long, we were spending a lot of time together. Despite the fact that he had business in the streets and I was supposed to be in class, I don't know what did it for me, but I was in love. The first thing Chaka forced me to accept was that school had to be my first priority, especially when my grades came in and my average had dropped a whole grade point. He stayed away for a while and made me promise that I would do the right thing while he was gone. When he came back, everything was back to normal for us, except I was more in love because of his sacrifice.

"The first year we were together, I got pregnant, but I didn't have a clue as to how I was going to raise a child on a student's salary, let alone go to school. Chaka convinced me that he would do whatever it took to for me to continue with my education. Never once did he offer me marriage or a serious commitment. He just promised to provide. That was enough back then, but as time went on, there were still no promises of commitment.

"CJ was on the way by this time, and suddenly this bitch Eve became a real factor in my relationship. I mean, she was claiming my place in his life."

Quinton didn't give a fuck about the way they met, or why they were together. The more she talked, the more his anger grew.

"Chaka was coming to me complaining that he wished he had done things differently," Petra continued, "but he had to live with the shit he created. Then Eve claimed she was pregnant or some shit. Things were only getting harder for us to be happy. They were living together, and the last straw was hearing him tell her he would come home to her forever."

The fire in her Petra's eyes matched Quinton's.

"Hell no!" she yelled. "I had played mistress long enough. I was either going to be the woman he would spend the rest of his life with, or I would see him buried in the ground. I didn't have the courage at first to see him dead, but then he did the unthinkable. He bought Eve a platinum chain with a medallion that declared her his baby girl. Well, that night I snatched it and refused to give it back. I wasn't going to step away from the pain he had caused anymore."

Both Q and Buck were stunned.

"I couldn't smother the feelings of betrayal, hatred, or even jealousy. This woman had claimed the heart of the one man I would have died for. That night I put my children to sleep, and we followed his cocky ass to the gas station where my brothers waited. I knew that if I did not cast some shadows somewhere, you would have turned the world upside down trying to find his killers. But, thank God, you didn't get caught up. By the time you arrived, you only saw the end results of the pain that muthafucka caused. My only regret is that I still feel the effects of his blatant disregard for the woman I was to him."

Quinton's arm shook as he felt the weight of the gun in his sweating palm. *Is this bitch serious? She killed Chaka because he was having an affair?* The snort that left his nostrils stopped Petra for a brief second.

"He cried to me at night about the lives he ruined. Because of it, I became his cheerleader, encouraging him to do the best things for the family. He confided in me about causing Buck to be locked up. He told me all his little insecurities, and I held it all to my chest like a fucking therapist, when the reality was, I was his woman, the mother of his children, and I was not good enough still." As Petra spoke, raw hurt was in her voice. It seemed to build into hate without a second beat. "One of them had to go. Since she was just as much a victim as I was, he was the only answer."

Quinton sat speechless as Petra held her head ramrod straight. He attempted several times to speak, but the words were stuck in his throat.

"Every now and again I wondered when I would have to tell you both what I had done before an innocent person suffered as a result of the murder. Nothing came to mind, except hoping you would recognize my brothers if you saw them, Quinton. The guilt has been riding me lately, and this is my solution to ridding myself of that useless feeling."

Tears stung the back of Quinton's eyes, and the gun in his hand shook. He found the words, but didn't know exactly how to make them come from his mouth.

Buck moved first to embrace Petra and offer his support for her pain, and she returned the gesture.

"You had other choices, Petra," Quinton told her. "Now, look . . . your children will have to live without their father."

Petra, unimpressed, shot the same venom back at him. "And you will have to live without a friend. Is that it? Chaka was going to have to make a decision soon enough about my children and that bitch. Well, I made the decision for us all. Don't expect me to apologize, because I would do it again if given the chance."

The rise of her head and the strength of her words were stronger than Quinton could stand. Silently, he prayed before he accepted his decision to kill her. He wouldn't live with regrets. He was going to take action and fuck the rest. His mind told him to run, but the heavy burden in his heart kept him rooted to the bench. Confusion finally lifted, and a trail of anger stood in its wake.

"How could you do something so wrong?" Quinton asked.

Buck leaned forward and stared at Quinton. The look was an attempt to make him surrender, but Q's rushing tears and his empty stare made Buck and Petra nervous.

Quinton raised the gun to her side. Through blurry tears, he waited for her to move or even scream.

Petra smiled, daring him to pull the trigger. "Buck might have suffered jail, but, Quinton, you were supposed to pay the ultimate price," she spewed.

Buck continued to listen attentively as she weaved a tale for them both.

"Chaka was convinced you wanted his position, Quinton. The plan was to kill you, but he didn't have the heart to make it happen."

Most, if not all, of the last-minute mourners had gone. And Danny and Dave were the only two still sitting on the church step when things quickly heated up. The bright sun cast a shadow on the sidewalk at the side of the building.

Danny immediately recognized the threat and warned his brother with a quick head nod in the direction of one of Chaka's killers.

"Shit!" Dave hissed the moment he saw the barrel of the gun coming around the corner in full view.

Danny had anticipated the movement, and by the time dude came around the corner, Danny had let off one shot, hitting his target's center of mass.

The rest was a blurring change of events that sent passersby fleeing for safety.

The other killer had come out from hiding, but instead of running in the direction of his brother, he ran toward Petra, hoping to protect her. He didn't realize the danger was behind him.

Danny and Dave were too far away to get a good shot, but Quinton had stood with his gun aimed at the open space behind them the moment the first shot rang out. A rapid succession of shots rang out as Quinton hit his target three or four times before the body dropped.

Buck had pushed Petra to the ground, but now she was fighting to get out from beneath him as she saw her brother's body falling.

Petra opened her mouth to scream, but the words were lost as she realized Quinton had killed her brother. She sprinted across to him as he walked away with the gun still in his hand.

Danny and Dave weren't too far behind, and Buck had already rushed to his car and pulled off, heading in Quinton's direction, hoping to get him off the streets before the police arrived.

Chapter 26

Later that week, Buck was ready to throw in the towel and move on from the drama. He saw the broad shoulders and wide-open strides of Pop marching toward him. Buck watched the movement of his prey. Judging from the way he held his head, down to the lazy way his arms swung back and forth, Pop wasn't prepared for an attack.

Finding Pop was easy, especially after Buck realized Eve was up to her old tricks again, trading in or up, whichever suited her needs. As he sat in the darkness waiting to kill Pop, he realized that too many things had been left to chance in the past. They had allowed their own loyalty, fears, and even greed to make them patsies in another man's twisted war. From Chaka to Earl, they were still running and gunning after the illusion of freedom. Buck was more determined to pull together any strings that threatened to come loose.

Some men were born to the paths they had chosen. Buck, however, had decided he was forced on this path, and he would die trying to destroy it. After he killed Pop, Earl was next. The thought was as simple as waking up in the morning. And he decided that killing Eve was a string that had dangled long enough.

Evil had awakened in Buck, and he was making no effort to quiet it. He was feeding it, as he imagined himself luring Pop toward his car.

Pop saw movement and got suspicious. Tilting his head downward, he recognized the imposing figure. Fear crept up his back as he accepted that he should have taken Earl's advice. Pop quickly assessed his chances. Backing out of the block was his only option.

Buck leaped from the vehicle with death and destruction on his mind. Pop reasoned he could probably outrun the burly bastard, so he set out on his trek. Buck was on his heels, running low with his weapons drawn and ready to fire. Pop's arrogance had once again placed him in a bind. He wished he had a better hold on his surroundings. Surprise was the only element he had left.

Buck had always been a smart killer. He knew that darkness covered his tracks, but the sound of one wasted shot could claim an innocent life.

Pop, nearly as savvy, tugged at his weapon, hoping to slow down his stalker.

The first shot rang out and told Buck exactly where Pop was heading. Buck marveled at how easy this would be.

As Pop ran, he lost his bearings. Instead of taking the ramp that led him to the alley, he found himself trapped in a yard that led to a dead end and realized he was cornered. In an attempt to come down the ramp, he fired several shots.

Buck was certain of his enemy's position now, but he wasn't sure if he could let himself relax before he killed his prey. No more shots rang out.

There it was—Pop's head slid from around the brick wall. Buck was elated. *Easy,* Buck declared to himself seconds before he opened fire. The beast had come face to face with the lamb. Taking a deep breath, he leveled his gun at the sparkle of Pop's gold rope chain and fired one shot.

Pop's body slumped against the wall with the impact of the first shot.

Buck whispered in his ear, "I know you stole from me, and now I'm getting even with you for killing a friend." The last shot was in Pop's face, to ensure a closed casket.

Buck didn't look back as he sauntered away to the alleyway Pop had managed to miss, walking out on the other side. The two cannon-like sounds from Buck's gun had rattled windows and set off almost every car alarm on the block. Yet he still calmly walked away, as if out for a stroll.

Time wouldn't take care of the pain Earl had caused. Buck had to see him and pass judgment on his soul. The thought that Earl was a victim too never occurred to Buck, and he refused to let go of the hatred he harbored, now that he was forced to face the next truth. Earl and Chaka had set him up from the word go.

Earl had witnessed the entire ordeal from a distance, but nothing compelled him to help Pop. The will to be great without work and effort had made Pop think he was invincible. The thought that he could waltz in and steal somebody's hard-earned fortune and cause tragedy in their lives was enough for him to sit back and allow Pop his opportunity to rise or fall. He secretly wished that Pop had the balls it took to rise, but seeing Buck walking away unharmed confirmed his worst fear—he had backed the wrong horse once again.

Earl convinced himself he could kill Buck at that moment as he raised his gun to Buck's back. Sweat fell into his eyes as he tried desperately to take aim. Unconsciously he held his breath and placed his finger on the trigger. Fear gripped him as he dropped the gun into his lap. He realized he still had too much loyalty to a false memory, the memory of teenage boys talking about girls, sharing *Right On!* magazine, or claiming the fly cars as they drove through the block.

During the last few weeks, Earl had to deal with the man he was, and not the man he wished to be. He had set out to do so many great things now that Chaka was dead, but the ugly truth was, he lacked the ruthless manner it took to be "the man."

As for Eve, she would always manage to go where the money was. Even after everything they'd gone through, there seemed to be so much unfinished business between them.

The constant ringing of her phone made Eve angry. She hoped that whoever was calling had something important to say. Hearing the husky baritone voice on the phone made her sit straight up in bed. He didn't ask her to get up; he demanded that she get up and open the door. He'd be there in ten minutes.

Eve leaped from her platform bed and scrambled about, trying to bring order to her space. Quickly, she changed from the ordinary T-shirt and sweatpants into his favorite teddy. She lit candles and sprayed herself with her favorite scent.

An hour later Pop still had not shown up. Normal, she rationalized, but his absence made her angry. Before long she was sound asleep on her huge bed.

Two hours into her dream, the annoying buzz of the doorbell woke her. She was really pissed that he could make her wait this long. She contemplated not letting him in at all. That would make him think twice about keeping her waiting around.

She slowly opened the door without asking any questions, and was astonished to find Earl on the other side. He pushed past her and strolled in as if he'd been invited. *The nerve,* she thought. "What do you want, Earl?" she asked with more attitude than was called for.

Earl waited for Eve to look in his direction before he spoke to her. "How long did you think you could hide that you and Pop were sneaking behind my back? Did you really think I wouldn't figure out that you were fucking him too?" he yelled at the top of his lungs.

Eve tried her best to look bored by his one-man act, but she feared that he might really know her secret. Eve had become good at bluffing, but she decided Earl didn't matter anymore. She folded her arms. "You come up in here, yelling about the man I'm fucking, but the truth is, it isn't any of your business."

As long as Earl wasn't interrupting, Eve thought she was telling him how it was going down. "You have always been second fiddle, so it shouldn't bother you now. Why are you angry? Is it because Pop is a soldier in the general's army?" Eve was proud of her affair.

The anger boiled over inside Earl. Eve saw the change in his demeanor and had the right sense to be afraid.

He wrapped his hands around her neck, squeezing until he felt her going limp. She clawed at his hands, hoping they would let up and give her some air. No relief came.

Eve was giving up on life when Earl heard her slight whimper and finally let her go. She dropped to the floor on all fours, coughing and trying to catch her breath.

With the immediate intake of oxygen, she began to change back to her normal coloring.

She crawled away from the door over to an overstuffed chair, climbed into the seat, and curled up into a ball.

Earl didn't leave. He sat across from her and delivered the news of Pop's demise.

She refused to believe him at first, but something in his smirk told her all she needed to know. Although Earl had released her, she now felt as if she was being strangled again.

The pasty look returned to her face and Earl laughed. "Don't look so happy to be stuck with me," he taunted.

Eve whispered the words, "Fuck you," and lowered her head to cry. "Why did you kill him over me? Shit, you left me for dead in North Carolina. Why did you do this?"

"First, you simple bitch, I didn't do shit to him. Buck got hold of him for stealing some valuables from his home, not to mention, Pop killed Sasha."

Eve's emotions were all over the place. She couldn't accept that yet another man who promised to be there for her had been killed.

"Earl, you're going to get yours. That, I am sure of. No way are the twins, Quinton, and Buck going to let you walk away from the shit you set in motion. If, by some sheer miracle, they let your ass live, Ian is going to come for you with both barrels."

Earl had long ago accepted his fate, but he wouldn't allow her to see his fear.

"Besides, you simple bastard, I know for a fact that it wasn't Pop who killed Sasha."

Earl felt like ice water had been poured into his veins. His hands were clammy, and his eyes glazed over. He slowly spun back to her with fire in his eyes, asking her to repeat what she had said. The look on Eve's face said she knew that he was the person who shot Sasha.

"Pop may have beaten her near to death, but it was someone else that put the bullet in her skull."

"Whatever you think you know, bitch, you better keep to yourself. It don't much matter anyway, 'cause I figured your ass is about dead too." Earl leaned close to her and, as a warning, slapped her in the mouth. He left the house without a backward glance at the imp that still seemed to be the cause of most of his drama.

"You like hitting women, you bitch," Eve yelled after him. "But I didn't see you hitting them niggas when they were herbin' you. Now you a fucking tough guy! I wish I could be there when they catch up with you, you punk-ass muthafucka!"

The first law of nature was self-preservation. There was no way in hell Earl was going to lie down and die. He felt like prey in the middle of an unknown land, waiting for someone to pick him off. As he hiked away from Eve's door, his mind raced over all the time he had wasted. His heart pounded with each step, alerting him that danger was definitely in the air. If the twins were waiting for him to return, right now he was a sitting duck. Feeling vulnerable, he palmed his .44 Magnum and prayed that the police weren't on the prowl.

A cat leaped from a nearby porch, making him jump off the ground. Seconds before he fired a shot, he realized it was just a feline scurrying across his path.

He was done being afraid. If he died tonight, it wouldn't matter to anyone, so he might as well fight to live.

Earl recognized every car on the block, except the black Lincoln sat four houses away from his home. He figured it was the twins. He didn't slow his strides. Using all his senses, he marched at an angle past the car and saw the twins sleeping inside.

The headlights turned on suddenly, startling Earl from taking any further action. The occupants of the Lincoln didn't move, but the headlights forced Earl inside his home.

Pacing, Earl chastised himself for not taking Buck's life when he had the chance, and now he was even angrier that he could have made a bigger mistake by trying to kill the twins right in front of his home.

Lying in the darkness, Earl realized his memories and loyalty were a major hindrance to his next breath. The proof that he was a target sat just inches from his home. Only strength could get him to the next level of this game. Outnumbered, he cleared his mind and made a plan.

He peered through the blinds and noticed that the car was no longer there. He opened the window for a better glimpse of the area. The twins had left. It was time to begin the next phase of his plan.

The dawning of a new day brought on new convictions for Earl. Earl knew he could eliminate his mishaps by getting rid of some deadweight. Three of the six men Ian had sent to New York were still alive, and Earl didn't want to be responsible for their well-being. They were the first order of business. It was time to send them home.

Next, he planned to deal with Ian and his unreal demands on an unseen fortune. The best way to deal with the likes of a man like Ian was to make him an offer he couldn't refuse, which Earl intended to do in person.

After that, he was going to see the twins wherever they were, and either he was going to buy his freedom from this nasty business, or he was going to blast his way from the bullshit. He would be free from running, or he could be dead.

Finally he had to deal with Eve. Her breathing might cost him his life, if he managed to get out from under all the rest of his circumstances. He couldn't have her blackmailing him over Sasha's murder.

Later that day three men, looking fashionable in their New York clothes, marched into LaGuardia Airport, leaving richer than when they arrived. They were heading home with laced pockets and lies to tell about the Big Apple.

Earl, however, decided he was going to drive south to see his favorite cousin.

Six hours after he hit the highway, he pulled into Ian's circular driveway. Earl actually believed Ian had bigger dream than he did, but none of that mattered now.

Ian's girlfriend opened the door and headed to her car as Earl walked up to knock. She pointed into the house and said, "He's in the basement. Go on in."

Earl looked around to discover Ian was alone in the house, making for a better discussion.

The coke Pop stole from Buck, Earl was going to use it to his advantage. Four of the six bundles Pop stole were now in a duffel bag that he would present to Ian. Earl had come ready for battle. Hidden underneath his colorful sweater was a bulletproof vest, and the two Magnums holstered at his side were barely hidden by the short leather jacket he wore.

Ian was watching television when he noticed Earl coming down the steps. His fake smile made Earl angry.

Without warm greetings, Earl got down to the reason he was there. He said, "As payment for your loan, I personally came here to give you this. It should settle our debt, but if it doesn't, we can talk." He slid the duffel bag across the floor to his cousin.

The smile on Ian's face broadened when he looked inside. He could barely contain his excitement. Desperately he tried to control the muscles in his face, but to no avail. His eyes danced, and he nodded.

While Ian was drooling, Earl slid both guns into his palms and kept his hands hidden behind his back.

Ian looked from Earl to the contents in the bag. With a serious face, he told Earl, "Bring me four or five more packs like this, and we're even."

"Cousin, I'm really sorry you said that, because what you have there is all I'm offering."

The wide grin slowly faded from Ian's face as he stared, confused. Suddenly the light went on, and Ian stood from the chair, only to come face to face with Earl's midnight-black firepower.

He quickly reclaimed his seat and started talking. The stuttering was enough to make Earl cry with laughter.

Ian said, "This is good enough. Don't worry, this'll do."

Earl knew that Ian had probably shit his drawers. He had to have understood now that Earl wasn't to be fucked with. Going home would be the hardest thing he'd done, but he had to face the pressure he left behind.

After a few months of relaxing and thinking in Miami, Earl knew it was time to head home. The ride back to New York was about Earl's unwillingness to let go of a vendetta that made no sense. It was about getting even with the ghost of Chaka and accepting he could never get even with Chaka himself.

For two states, he tried to decide whether it was all worth it.

Finally, just outside the toll on the outskirts of New York, he decided the money, the countless women was worth it.

A wide grin etched across his face as he decided he could rise above the Baker Boys 5. All he needed was the right amount of money. He would rock them to sleep, pay for his freedom, and make them believe they had won. And then he would kill them all.

Chapter 27

HOMECOMING SURPRISES

The tenants in Earl's building had moved without much prompting. For months the rent had gone uncollected, but they didn't complain. He hadn't given them any notice on his intentions to tear down the property. But the first signs of the coming demolition work convinced them that the absentee landlord was a snake. Earl was known for his disappearances, but he always came back expecting every nickel owed from the time he was gone.

Plywood had been in place for weeks where the windows were removed from the frames. The decorative doors were replaced with steel. Furnishings were tossed into the rented Dumpster as the fake construction crew cleared out the place. The neighbors passing by didn't give a second glance to the crew, knowing that the owner of the place hadn't been around for months. They figured he'd either sold the property or the city had condemned it.

Buck watched the activities from the concrete mixing machine, laughing at his own genius until his sides hurt. The plan was to level Earl's home, but instead they were illegally confiscating it and leaving him with the shell. The floors had been ripped up and the walls were nothing but exposed beams and hollow brick. All the clothes that had been discovered inside were neatly collected and delivered anonymously to the local thrift store. The gators, the fine watches, nice minks, silk shirts, and tailored suits were going to grace the backs of those in need. The pennies the poor would pay to look good made Buck feel like he was giving back to the community on Earl's dime. The Italian couch was sitting along the curb when some local crackheads picked it up and carted it off. The sight of the huge couch resting on two shopping carts rolling down the hill would have caused someone somewhere else to talk shit, but this was the hood. Living on the edge was as ridiculous and normal as a circus act.

Lounging back in the cut, the crew laughed as they watched the crackheads stop passersby, trying to sell the treasure they had just acquired. Tears sprang from Dave's and Danny's eyes as they marveled at Buck's commitment to getting even. Each man would pay to see Earl's face the moment he realized what had happened to his home. Buck had basically stripped the entire house from the first exposed brick to the last electrical wire on the inside.

Quinton was barely in New York between the day of Sasha's funeral and the day his daughter Mifaith was born. The guilt and shame were running him more than he even imagined. Anissa's disappointed looks and lack of interest in him made the pressure worse. Every passing day he kept expecting the police to come to his home and arrest him, and he decided he didn't have the courage to stand.

One night, after a huge argument with Anissa, he left the home and headed south to visit relatives in Mississippi he hadn't seen since he was a small child.

The heat had forced people outside. Kids were running about laughing and having a good time when they saw the car. The black Jaguar rolled into the block as if it was part of the street. Its dark tint hid the driver, but the loud bass of the music caught their attention. The slow roll of the chrome rims shined against the smooth tires. Earl had bought the car as his coming-home gift to himself. During his absence, he'd missed the comforts of his luxuries, and the Jag put him in the right frame of mind. Short of yelling, "I'm back, muthafuckas," he sat back and grinned at the success he had achieved in such a short time.

Pulling into the first empty parking space he found, he sat bobbing his head to the sounds of Wu-Tang. He wasn't paying attention to his surroundings. He was too busy living in the moment of his achievements.

After a few moments the neighbors recognized Earl.

"Astounding," Ms. Harding said and laughed as she watched the slow, fluid motion of the young man she thought was dead.

The people sitting in front of her door playing cards and dominoes were just as shocked to see him come out of the car.

Earl knew the car would cause whispers, but the angry glares he received were uncalled for. Still, he hadn't noticed that his home was merely a shell now. Instead of allowing the jealous faces of his neighbors to bother him, he raised his hand in an attempt to say hello. He walked past all the homes he had been passing for years before he realized the beautiful home he had remodeled and invested in was gone.

"What the fuck?" he whispered as he looked at the two homes that sat on either side of his property.

The look on his face was one of confusion, which turned into angry frustration, and the bellow that escaped his voice left the neighbors snickering.

Earl turned toward the stoop where the people were sitting and headed in their direction. "What the fuck?" he demanded, as if they owed him an explanation.

Mr. Harding stepped off the stoop. He shrugged his shoulders and offered what he knew.

Earl couldn't believe this shit. He had come home to a shell of what he once called home. Tracing his steps back to his structure, he lost his mind.

"I'm gonna kill them bitches," he yelled as he walked back to his car.

As he sat in his car, he didn't feel the same pride for the vehicle he felt only moments earlier. He banged on the steering wheel and allowed his tears to flow. Tears of anger and frustration clouded his judgment as he tried to make sense of the bullshit. Buck, Dave, Danny, and Quinton were walking corpses.

Recklessly Earl pulled away from the curb, heading toward the real estate agency that had been part of the Baker Boys 5 portfolio for a very long time.

The neighbors watched in amusement as the Jaguar left the block. They laughed and told jokes all night, thinking that Earl was crazy for coming back here, knowing he was a wanted man.

Dusk was setting as Earl waited outside the agency, hoping one of the crew would come out. So far he had been there for more than two hours, and the door hadn't even opened. He pulled his gun from beneath the hidden compartment in the door panel and leaped out. Stomping across traffic, he decided he wasn't going to wait to get at these niggas. Either they would die, or he would, but he was prepared.

The door swung open, and Earl raised his gun at the pretty young woman sitting at the receptionist's desk.

"There is no money here on the premises," she said when she saw the gun.

"Shhhhh," he whispered as she began to speak.

"The safe is locked, and I just work here. Please don't kill me," she begged.

"Are they here?" he demanded.

"Yes, Mr. Holden is here in his office," she answered nervously.

Earl placed the gun to the forehead of the receptionist and ordered her to get up. Just as she stood, her bladder gave up. She walked toward the office as Earl commanded, praying the stranger wouldn't kill her.

Buck was sitting at his desk when he heard the knock. Slowly he turned as the door opened. The fear in his receptionist's wide eyes was a testament to her fate. The silenced gun barely made a sound as the bullets entered through her back and she fell forward. Earl was just inches from entering Buck's office when the young woman hit the floor.

The hate in Buck's eyes radiated as contempt oozed from Earl's eyes.

Earl wanted to see fear. He wanted Buck to beg for his life, especially since his ass was as good as dead anyway. The gun hissed again, and Buck fell backward, his hand covering his stomach where the bullet had entered.

In Earl's excitement or confusion, he didn't fire a second shot. He turned and quickly walked away, leaving Buck there, bleeding.

Back in the safety of his car, he laughed. "I killed you, you stupid muthafucka. After all this time I finally killed your slow ass. Yes!" He pumped his fist in the air.

Buck growled as he felt the pain in the pit of his stomach. He had to trip the alarm and alert the alarm company he needed an ambulance before he passed out again. Struggling to get to his feet was harder than it looked. Slowly he crawled on the floor until he was able to pull the handle of the hidden safe beneath his desk.

The silent alarm did its job, but Buck wasn't sure he would live to receive the help that was on its way. The room spun around him as he lay motionless on the floor. Darkness took over as his eyes drifted closed and he struggled to catch his breath. He desperately tried to hear the sounds of the ambulance, but all he heard was the sound of his own ragged breathing.

Forty-five minutes later the police arrived and found the receptionist lying face down in her own blood. The attendants from the ambulance found Buck lying face up just inches from the woman. The EMT yelled that Buck was breathing, causing the rest of the attendants to rush to his aid.

PART 2

Chapter 28

"Circumstance can change the perception of things, especially when the facts are far more ridiculous than a boldfaced lie. No one here is pretending to be a victim. Everything ever said against the defendant in the last couple of years is the truth."

The defense attorney hesitated briefly, watching the jurors as they listened. He remembered to pace himself, for dramatic effect.

"If you believe that editors don't sensationalize to sell more papers, then we are done here. If you believe that the police have never planted evidence or lied under oath to protect their case, then convict the defendant. At this moment, however, I have confidence in every one of you sitting here that when the facts are clear you won't be able to accept a lie. You won't accept it, because a lie would seem too embarrassing when compared to the truth."

The defense attorney decided that he had the jurors hanging on to his every word. They wanted to hear the fantastic truth against the unbelievable lie that came with this case. He spoke with purpose and conviction as he ended his opening statement.

"My client, Mr. Earl Clement, promised me he couldn't lie to me during our first meeting, because the truth was far more fascinating. He will admit to being a drug dealer. He will admit to trafficking guns and drugs. He will admit to being the pawn for some very bad men. In the light of all I've said, you will see that circumstance can change the perception of things. The prosecutor won't tell you they've shackled my client with these charges because they are afraid to go after the real culprits. They don't want you to even know that half of the witnesses they parade through this court are part of a larger conspiracy. The only question left unanswered in this case is simply: Who should be sitting in that chair, instead of the defendant?"

Earl sat in the courtroom, shackled to his chair, listening to his attorney, Brian Hopewell, try to convince the jury of his innocence. Despite Hopewell's earlier protests, the judge granted the prosecutor's request to have Earl restrained in the courtroom during his trial. Judge Clayton Dawson, like most other people, believed the sensational media coverage that painted him as a monster.

Earl began to come undone. It was harder to keep the tremors in his hands at bay while trying to hide the weakness in his eyes. Gone was the confidence of the man he had emerged into just two years before this trial. Gone was the larger-than-life ego he thought would coast him above the sinking ship. Instead he sat humiliated and defeated before the first witness could appear. Conceding the loss, he decided death by lethal injection was the only thing he had to gain if this trial continued, especially with this judge.

For the briefest moment Earl wanted to accept the prosecutor's earlier offer of a plea. It could save him the trouble of facing the jurors. If he hadn't been a coward, he could have held court in the streets. He could have fired the first shot and allowed his body to be ripped to pieces by the police officers' bullets. Quietly, he realized it was too late for any other outcome than the one he was already facing.

Slow panic rolled over in his mind, and his body began to react. Gritting his teeth, he fought the tears that stung the back of his eyes. He struggled to control his breathing as he allowed his head to fall forward.

The slight shift in his body language caught the attention of the court officer. Quickly the guard stood erect, glaring at Earl. The camera operators even responded to the slight movement, zooming in on his side profile.

"Hold it together," Hopewell whispered to his client. "This is only the beginning. If you lose faith now, then we lose the war."

With his eyes still closed, Earl lifted his head, flexed his muscles, and attempted a quick head nod. It took a moment for him to completely trust he had his emotions back in check. Finally he inhaled deeply and let the air slowly escape his lungs.

And the day ended pretty much same way it had started.

Chapter 29

GETTING EVEN, 2004

Buck's mind was wide-awake, but his body was asleep. He could hear the annoying sound of hissing machines and beeping, but he couldn't see. He felt a cold draft, but his arms weren't strong enough to pull the thin cotton sheet over him. Struggling against himself, he tried to move the burden on his chest. Even his eyes wouldn't cooperate. They were glued shut. The panic of being alive and dead at the same time rose up in him, and he began to moan.

"Stop all that whimpering. If you can feel pain, you know you still among the living. Now quit it 'fore I give you something to cry for," the woman yelled.

Buck knew he had to be dreaming. His Grand Bea never spoke above a whisper, except when she was angry.

"Open your eyes, baby, and take a look at the world around you."

Suddenly he could feel her hands on his face and the sadness in her voice. There was no more fight left. He was resigned to dying. "Grand Bea," he whimpered, "I can't. They won't open."

Quickly he felt himself fading away from the dream. His heart slowed, and his mind went blank.

Brenda walked into the house to a symphony of ringing phones. Too exhausted to answer, she sank into the lounger with one shoe lying by the door and the other dangling from her foot.

Finally the noise stopped.

The peace and quiet didn't last, though. She heard another familiar jingling sound coming from her purse that hung at her wrist.

"Hey, girl," Brenda whined. "You know I did it again. I'm tired as hell. I skipped lunch, and Buck ain't here to cook. Damn, that man loves me right on Monday and Tuesday, but leaves me to fend for myself the rest of the week." She giggled.

"Brenda, Buck could have been hurt tonight. It's on the news right now," Anissa cried out.

"Girl, ain't a dang thing wrong with him. I spoke to him when I was on the parkway heading home. He's fine."

"I don't give a damn when you talked to him. I'm telling you it happened sometime this evening, and the news is all over it. They're showing the real estate office, and a newsperson is confirming that at least one person is dead. I'm ten minutes away."

Brenda nearly fell flat on her face as she tripped over her shoe and purse trying to get to the remote. "Oh my God," she screamed at the top of lungs. "I can't go through this, Lord. What have I done to deserve this?"

She was pleading as she watched the recording of the paramedics bringing someone out of the door with a sheet covering the body from head to toe. She recognized the storefront and accepted that it was the right building, but she couldn't believe Buck was inside.

Quickly she tracked down her phone and began dialing the office. The line rang until a message began. Still, she wasn't convinced, so she pressed the speed button that took her straight to his private phone. Brenda's fears were starting to sink in. Maybe she was right, and Buck was hurt.

When Anissa arrived at the house, Brenda turned into her arms and collapsed. "Why isn't he answering the phone?" she wailed.

"I don't know, but I do know how we're going to find out. Get your shit and let's go. We're headed to Brooklyn." Anissa didn't stop moving. Even with Mifaith on her hip, she hurried to the car and ushered Brenda into the passenger seat.

"No, let me sit in the back with Mifaith. She'll help keep me calm."

"Whatever. Is she strapped in the car seat properly? Oh, and don't be back there tearing up, 'cause I don't want to listen to her whine all the way to Brooklyn." Anissa was nervous, but she hid it behind her take-care-of-business attitude.

"Anissa, if he's hurt"—she paused—"what am I supposed to do?"

Anissa peered in the rearview mirror and locked eyes with her friend. "Bitch, we going to get through it one day at a time. When Quinton decided he wanted to run from his responsibility, I almost gave up, but you held me and let me cry. I'll do the same for you, but first, let's be sure there's something to cry about."

Brenda nodded and then closed her eyes in silent prayer against what she knew was the truth. "At least you know Quinton is alive and well," she stated as an afterthought.

"I do? Have you heard from him? I haven't. For all I know, he could be in a ditch somewhere, and if I have to find him, he'll have to wait for hell to freeze."

Brenda lowered her eyes and felt ashamed that she had actually caused her friend so much frustration. She knew it had to be hard to accept Quinton's choice to leave.

Anissa needed to pull Brenda from the place she'd descended to. She decided to tell her friend a little about how the crew first got together.

"You know, Brenda, there used to be five of these boys who were close. Chaka—God bless the dead—was the ringleader, or at least his little ass thought he was. They started selling baked goods to their classmates for change."

Brenda smiled. She had heard some of this story before, but Anissa had a way of making it sound funny.

"Buck was big from birth, but in the second grade that nigga was a jolly green giant compared to the rest of the kids. His grandmother used to dress him in striped shirts, and the kids in class used to tease him, calling him Spanky."

"Stop lying, girl. Ain't nobody ever called that boy Spanky." Brenda laughed.

"Yes, we did, till that nigga learned to fight. Then we started calling his ass Killer. Anyway, Chaka used to get beat up for his money, so Buck made a deal with him. It was all about the money. For a fee he protected Chaka and got to eat all the brownies his big ass could stomach."

Brenda was laughing so hard, she forgot about her sadness.

"The business was a hit by the time they got to junior high. Quinton, with his moneymaking ass, convinced Chaka to try adding other things to their line of sweets. Of course, with the money, drama soon followed. Girl, those Negroes been doing this thing since forever. Don't count them out just yet. Trust me, I won't."

Brenda smiled. "The other day I found a jacket that Buck won't let me throw away. It has BB5 on it. What does that mean?"

"Baby, where you been? That is for the original Baker Boys 5—Chaka, Buck, Quinton, Dave, and Danny. It's a commemorative of their first crew. It's the truth to their beginning."

Brenda was confused. "So what the hell is the D-12 jacket all about then?"

"That's who they have evolved into over the years," Anissa said sadly.

"Do you think that has anything to do with this shooting today?"

"Probably. You don't get to this level in the game without being tested, but they always seemed to come through before. Maybe it was good luck, or maybe it was just the hustler in them."

"You said don't count them out. Well, girl, I'm leaning on you and your faith. Because I don't think I could do this alone."

Their conversation died down as they arrived in Brooklyn.

Anissa didn't bother to offer Brenda any advice. She was too busy trying to find Buck. She headed for the real estate office. "You stay here with the baby," she said. "I'll go see what the fuck is going on out this bitch."

Brenda was anxious to get out of the car, but her fears kept her rooted to the seat.

All that ended quickly when she saw Anissa's head began bobbing back and forth. "Oh shit," Brenda said as she hustled from the vehicle with a sleeping Mifaith in her arms. Whatever had been said, Anissa wasn't going quietly.

A policeman in a white shirt and a bunch of gold colored bars pinned along his chest intervened. He said something, and Anissa went plain nuts, drawing the attention of anyone with a camera.

"This is my business, and whatever has happened in there, no one has had the decency to notify the families of the injured parties before allowing it to be broadcast on television," she screamed. "My husband, along with about ten other people employed here could have been hurt, and I had to witness it on the news. Who are you? And where can I find your boss?"

The media still standing around hustled trying to film the lunatic who was giving the sergeant from the 73rd precinct a good cussing in front of the world. Anissa was on fire as she told the sergeant how an officer had threatened to arrest her for identifying herself as a partner in the business.

"That worthless beet-red biscuit-eater over there called me a liar and told me to get the fuck out of here."

Less than a heartbeat later, a microphone appeared in her face as she screamed the officer's name and badge number. "He has no business in our neighborhood if he doesn't respect the people he swore to protect," Anissa yelled.

By the time Anissa pulled off, she had all the information she needed.

"Buck's been shot several times. He is alive, and he should be at the hospital now," she told Brenda. "The paramedics were working on him when they left. Mia Williams, the cute receptionist, is dead, and no one has notified her father yet."

Stress showed all over Brenda's face. She bit down on her bottom lip to keep from screaming.

"I have to tell Baldy about his daughter," Anissa said, referring to Mia's father. "If the police get there first, there's no telling what he might do to them."

Brenda wanted to haul ass away from everyone and everything associated with this mess Buck had gotten into. *What the fuck have I gotten myself into?* she wondered. *Baldy's daughter? Oh shit, Buck praised this man.* Anissa said he might go after the police, but Brenda wondered what was stopping him from killing them for bringing the bad news.

❖❖❖❖❖

Corinthian "Baldy" Williams rested in Anissa's arms, crying like a child. "She was a good girl," he said. "She wasn't in the life. Fuck! I did everything in them streets and never got a scratch. She didn't deserve to die."

Suddenly Baldy stopped crying. He was now enraged. His voice changed, and the cold in his eyes ricocheted off the walls. Anissa didn't even flinch as he began to curse and rant.

"For years my mother ran numbers, and she died an old woman. My father was a drifter, and nothing happened to him, except he became a wino and died. Now my daughter and Buck, my best friend, are dead. I feel sorry for the streets. I feel sorry for the mother of that muthafucka who killed them. I hope there's enough of him to bury when I'm done."

Brenda wasn't certain if Anissa had purposely omitted to tell Baldy that Buck was still alone, but she'd been too afraid to speak, and now all she wanted to do was find Buck.

Baldy felt shame the moment he locked eyes with Brenda. He realized she was afraid and uncomfortable. He quickly softened his tone. "Anissa, take her home. I promise, whatever needs doing, I'll give it my all. There is no fixing it." Slowly Baldy walked to Brenda and embraced her, offering her his deepest sympathy. "Buck was like my family, and I trusted him with my life many times. If there is anything you need, please don't hesitate to ask. I got your back."

Nodding, Brenda waited until Baldy was finished before she thanked him. She glanced from Anissa to Baldy, puzzled about why Anissa didn't say anything about Buck being alive. Why didn't she correct him?

Baldy stood at the door long after the car disappeared, trying to get his emotions in check. Soon the police arrived, and the drama of trying to get information began. Baldy decided nothing they had to say meant shit. He knew how to get real answers.

Anissa sat in the car as Brenda rushed into the emergency room area. Kids were crying everywhere, and nothing seemed to be moving, except the nurses as they talked amongst themselves.

Brenda was timid at first, waiting until the hospital guard stopped talking to people as they moved along. "Excuse me, can you tell me where to find someone that was brought in by ambulance?" she asked.

The guard didn't seem interested in Brenda's emergency. Lazily, he pointed to the nurses' station.

Brenda marched across the room, hoping someone could tell her where to find Buck. She ended up staring down at the top of some nurse, who was looking at a pay stub and refused to acknowledge her. She tapped the thin glass with her finger.

"Don't do that." The woman scolded her as if it was huge disturbance.

"Look, bitch, my husband came in here some time ago with several bullet wounds to his body. I don't know if he's dead or alive, but I am damn sure he is here. Tell me where he is, and I mean now."

"Ma'am, I can't give you any information. You will have to wait to speak with the administrators."

"Does it look like I give a fuck about rules right now? I am looking for my husband, Jahson Holden. He was the man brought here from the shooting that was on the news."

The security guard intervened quickly, sensing the drama that was about to unfold if someone didn't give her an answer. "Your husband is in surgery, ma'am," he said.

"Where in the hell is that?"

After the guard gave her directions, Brenda barely said thank you as she rushed to the bank of elevators to find her man.

Chapter 30

OLD FRIENDS AND NEW FRIENDS

Earl lounged across the hotel bed watching the early morning news. "The fuckin' news people are turning this into some fuckin' crusade," he yelled when he saw that they were talking about the real estate office shooting again. "They don't know that he stole my home from me. Look at this. They call me a monster. Damn you and all your opinions! Nobody can hurt me now. Fuck you. Catch me."

Seeing Anissa's angry face on TV and hearing her rant infuriated Earl. He couldn't hear a word she said, but he was certain he would have a chance to make her cry for her man too one day soon.

"Fuck you, bitch! Just wait. I ain't done yet."

Earl popped the cork from a warm bottle of champagne and watched the foam flow freely. He then lit up a blunt and took a long toke. Soon Earl was stumbling and staggering around the room, until he passed out between the double beds.

The next morning the housekeeper made her way toward Earl's room. Eddy Soto begrudged the life she lived as a housekeeper. From the early morning shift to the lousy pay, it was all a slap in the face for all her hard work.

Staying on the right side of things doesn't make life easy. It just makes you old, she thought.

Her sister Eve had made out like a bandit, pulling the top earners in the game. Chaka left her with insurance and property after he died. In addition, that pretty muthafucka Pop had left her two bags filled with money. Eddy knew better than anyone that Eve suffered greatly with all the money she had received. It didn't buy happiness or friendship, but still she wished she had a little of her sister's luck when it came to finances.

"My dumb ass scrubbing toilets and making beds while my sister is sitting on God knows how much dough and won't share," she mumbled. Pushing the cart with an attitude, she continued toward room 2210.

With the tip of the key card, she tapped lightly on the door. "Housekeeping," she yelled. "Damn! This place is a mess," she said as she entered the room. The empty champagne bottles rattled against the door as she moved inside. The bedspread was half on the floor, and the entire room smelled of weed. "Nasty bastards!" The money thrown all over the floor stopped her in her tracks.

Earl quickly awoke and turned to the door, his gun aimed and ready to shoot.

When Eddy saw the gunman, she couldn't believe it was really him. "Put that shit away before you fuck around and shoot me, Breito." She chuckled.

Earl froze when he heard the nickname that only the Soto family used for him. Only Eve's mother had called him that. It was her pet name for him.

"Damn, Eve! What happened?" he asked, assuming it had to be her. He'd heard that Mrs. Soto had died years ago. He imagined Eve's mother telling him loud from the stairwell, *"Breito, the sun has baked you well."*

"You working in house cleaning now?"

"Guess again, fool. It's not Eve. She'd die before she said one word of Spanish."

The grin said it all. He knew exactly who this was. Eve's little sister stood in the middle of his room. They were spitting images of each other, except Eddy had a mole just above her right eyebrow. To Earl she seemed to be winking when she spoke.

"Yeah, it's me," she said, seeing recognition register on his face. "I see you're still living the same," she stated, picking up a backpack filled with crack vials.

Earl looked around the room, but didn't feel a bit of shame at the mess he'd made. Seeing Eddy humbled him, though, and he stood to pick up the money from the floor. "I was celebrating," he offered.

She giggled. "Yeah? Well, help me clean this shit up, and put on some pants before you blind me with that thing," she teased.

Earl, a smirk on his face, slid into his pants.

"You still flying solo?"

"Yeah, I'm still watching my own back. Eddy, you don't have to do that. I can clean up after myself. Sit down."

Ten minutes later, they'd agreed to meet after Eddy left work, so they could really catch up.

Later, as they strolled along Forty-Second Street, they laughed about all the dumb things Eddy used to do to Eve. Eddy remembered the things Earl had done to help her family. No matter what trials Eve put him through, he was always very respectful to their mother.

"Remember the time you hid in the closet and came out screaming while Eve and I were naked?" Earl asked.

"Hell, yeah. That's around the time my mother started calling you *Breito*. I told her everything on you was burnt." (*Breito* is a Dominican slang used to describe something burnt or darkened by the sun.)

"Did you ever marry the boy from Menudo?" he teased.

"Of course. I married the one that turned out to be gay. That's the reason

I clean toilets for a living." She sucked her teeth.

"Do you have any kids, at least?"

"Are you crazy? Hell, no. It's hard enough going to school full-time, working full-time, and trying to keep a roof over my head."

Earl laughed. He couldn't see the prissy Ms. Eddy Soto struggling, especially with her beauty. "I know you got a man to help you. Where's he at?"

Eddy could have slapped Earl. He was insulting her pride. "First off, I don't see any man worth wasting my time with. I mean, my mother didn't get a winner. Eve certainly had her share, but, shit, she's still shedding tears. Better to do it by myself. At least I know it got done right."

Earl nodded. "So what? You a coochie bandit? Is that it?"

She punched him in the arm playfully and laughed. "Why do I have to be into coochie? I just don't want anyone wasting my time and taking up space on my couch."

"I see. So the answer is yes," he joked.

Eddy stopped walking until Earl turned around. She was examining him. She admired the way he'd changed from the timid man who used to sit on the stoop with Eve into this confident hustler. Eve had told her some stories about him, but none of them mattered. He was still the good man she remembered.

"Why you struggling so hard, Eddy? Tell me what you thinking."

Eddy considered the question and slowly began telling him about her life. "I'm no different than any other girl that has chosen the wrong man. It's just that I almost lost my dignity trying to chase a man that didn't want me. I worked and came home to give him my money for the bills, and he was taking it to get high. When things got rough, he offered me to the dealers, and that did it. I got smart and went home to my mother. I've been on my own ever since she died."

"What about you and Eve?"

Eddy didn't hesitate to share her opinion. "She has changed a lot, but she's still the same. Eve is about herself first, and everyone else is last. If you can't stand on your own, don't look to her for help."

Earl smiled and allowed himself the chance to think about Eve briefly. It was a wasted memory, though.

"What about you?" Eddy asked. "Why hasn't some woman captured your heart?"

"Too mean, I guess."

"I find that hard to believe. What happened to the man that would bring my mother groceries and take her to the beauty shop?"

"He died in these streets."

They'd walked for so long that they ended up back in front of the hotel. Eddy explained that she couldn't go up to his room with him. "I'm not supposed to fraternize with the guests. Sorry, Cinderella's chariot awaits me." She stepped off the curb and into the street to hail a cab.

"How about I put a hat on your head, you hide that pretty mug of yours, and we go upstairs and trash the room?"

"Fuck it! Let's do it. Maybe somebody else will have to clean that bitch tomorrow." Eddy laughed.

Hours rolled along. They laughed, drank, and smoked as if the outside world didn't matter.

Eddy was beyond intoxicated. "I am so comfortable with you," she said. "It's the best time I've allowed myself to have since my mom passed."

Earl understood and let her ramble on about the difficulty of being alone with no one to love. He felt the sadness in her and wanted to make her forget, even if it was just for this one night.

"Oh shit, that was the song," Eddy hollered when she heard the radio switch to her favorite reggae song. She jumped off the bed and started to dance and sing, *"Lonely won't leave me alone. I'm so lonely. Won't leave me alone,"* swaying to the rhythm.

"Who taught you how to dance, girl? That's not how you dub. That's some Yankee shit you Americans do."

"You got nerve. What? You think you ain't American? Bullshit. You been here so long, you sound corny when you hiss your teeth," she said, mimicking his native patois.

Earl couldn't help himself. He burst out laughing. "Gal, you got to grind your hips like this. Forget the salsa. This is a Jamaican girl dance. See, let me show you."

The weed they had been smoking almost made him fall as he tried to teach her. Eddy was on the floor crying and wooing as she watched Earl. It was a sight. His face scrunched up as if he was serious, and he closed his eyes.

"What, fool? I'm imagining my girlfriends and how they do it. Get your bent ass up and learn to dance."

The two drunken friends danced as he held her waist and slow-stroked her into a groove with the music. Finally she was able to keep the pace and grind.

"Stop concentrating so hard. Add some Eddy flavor to it. Get it, gal."

He laughed when she dipped to the sway of his rhythm.

Half the night they alternated between talking about their lives, drinking some, and just enjoying one another's company. Even the silence was comforting, Earl thought, as Eddy stretched out across the bed and bounced her feet. He realized she was so much more fun than her sister had ever been. The idea of being so at peace when her life seemed to be so shitty was an awakening.

By the time they'd fallen asleep, neither of them cared about how things might look to anyone else.

The morning came too quickly. As Eddy raised her head off the pillow, the shift in the bed forced Earl to rise up slowly also.

"My gotdamn head hurts," she complained.

"You? All I remember is teaching your klutzy ass to dance."

"Shut up. I'm trying to get up so I can take a shower and go home."

"Don't you have to work today?"

"Thank God, I don't, or I would have been late, drunk, and too sleepy to clean up anything."

Earl leaped off the bed, ready to get rid of Eddy. The clarity of morning made him realize that she brought back a side of him he wished to keep buried. Things had changed since he first knew Eddy, and he needed to stay on top of his game in order to survive.

Chapter 31

THE PLAN

Anissa hadn't used the number Quinton had left on her dresser since the day she accepted that he wasn't coming back. However, petty differences and lost love were not going to stop her from contacting him now.

First, she called the twins. Danny assured her he was on the next plane home. All she needed to do was be strong until he could get there. Dave only had time to say, "I'm coming," before he hung up the phone.

The last number took her four tries before she found the courage to let the call go through.

Quinton didn't recognize the number on his phone, but he knew the area code was from home. Only two people had this number, and neither had called him in months. Something was wrong. "Yo, what up?" he asked.

The words jumbled in her head and couldn't find their way to her mouth. She listened, hoping he would just hang up and she could pretend she never called.

"Nissa, I can hear Mifaith in the background," he whispered.

No longer shocked by his voice, she let her anger take over. "Whatever. Buck's been hurt bad, and he's in ICU," she offered before she slammed her phone shut.

Quinton leaped up from the recliner. Rubbing his head between his hands, he searched for an excuse to stay away, but nothing was good enough.

He had to go home.

Anissa had accused him of following in the demented path that Chaka had set for him. Even though he tried to explain that he was his own man, she never really believed him. He had grown tired of the fights and the disappointment in her eyes when he decided to leave.

Even Buck questioned his motives, and that alone scared him, because he and Buck could always find common ground.

Things had changed so drastically, Quinton checked out of their lives. One moment he was standing at the nursery in the hospital after Mifaith was born, promising to be a great father, and the next he was staring down at the murky waters of the Mississippi, heading home to see family he hadn't seen since his parents migrated to New York.

Almost six months later he was going home, hopefully to people that still loved him. Fear was the biggest problem he would face. Maybe they wouldn't want to see him. Maybe Anissa had moved on with her life. Mifaith probably wouldn't recognize him. And the only man he trusted in his absence needed him.

"Damn, Buck! Just hold on. I'm on my way," he whispered.

Quinton's great aunt Selma stood in the doorway with a smile on her face. She knew the moment she saw her nephew on her doorstep months ago that he needed a hug. He needed to know someone was happy to see him. In the few months he'd been there, she found reason to love and hope again. Now she had to return the gift he had given her.

"Don't you worry," Aunt Selma said. "They're still gonna love you. That doesn't change. Go home and take care of them. Just don't forget auntie when you go back. I'm going to miss you."

Quinton immediately felt the love that only family could give. He wished he could bring her with him. "Come with me, Aunt Selma, so you can meet your great-grandniece in person."

Selma understood his fear and she wanted to tell him so, but she didn't want to cause him any more hurt. Instead she smiled at her nephew and offered him a hug filled with promise.

"Your grandfather was my favorite brother. He was everything to me, and losing him was more devastating than anything I'd ever known, but I made it through. This old gal has outlived damn near all her family and most of her friends, and sometimes I wanted to give up, but you came around here and reminded me of so many wonderful things I've done in my life. Now it's time to remind you that there are too many beautiful people waiting for you. Go home and do what needs doing. Aunt Selma will be right here waiting on you when you bring back my niece."

Quinton knew his aunt was right. It was time to go home.

Chapter 32

GIVE ME WHAT YOU CAN'T GET BACK

After the happy reunion between the remaining members of the Baker Boys 5 was over, and all the hugging and joking was out of the way, the conversation turned serious. Quinton, Danny, and Dave each had a chance to reveal what they'd found out before coming home. The unanimous thought on the streets was that Buck was dead.

The police were claiming that two people died in the shooting at the real estate office. In addition, the streets had a list of its own suspects. The young gunners figured someone was trying to come up in the ranks by killing the head in order to cause the body to fall, especially since Quinton had disappeared.

The more seasoned hustlers figured it was all a misunderstanding. Buck was generous, and his kindness had got him killed. He had probably helped the wrong muthafuckas. Who else could get so close, except someone he thought was harmless?

One thing was certain, though. All debts owed were lost with Buck's death. No one was expecting Quinton, Dave, or Danny to come at them for payment. The only concern on the streets was Baldy, a wild card whose daughter had been caught in the crossfire. He might make it hard for niggas to make money.

Only one soldier knew the truth, and he wasn't talking until he was with the right set of dudes. Dirty Red was infamous for his ability to know shit others wanted to know. All he wanted was to see one of the Baker Boys, and he'd spill his guts for free.

Later that day as Quinton, Danny, and Dave walked the streets, letting everyone know they were back in town, Dirty Red spotted them.

"Yo, is it true?" Red asked. "Is that you, my nigga, big Q? What? You went to Oz on us, man?"

"I ain't been here twenty-four hours. How'd you find me?"

"Don't ever think you can sneak past me. I'm an old bloodhound, and when family comes home, he is welcomed right."

"Come on and talk to me," Quinton said. "Tell me what we've been missing."

"I'm ready when you are. You want to go say hello to the rest of the family first?"

"Nah. I'm already with family, nigga, so let's do this now."

As they walked, Quinton kept his eyes on the corners, taking in the new faces. He stopped a few times to greet niggas he hadn't seen in a while.

Danny approached things quietly, observing the body language of the hustlers. He was picking out their problems, based on the information he'd been getting while he was away.

Dave didn't give a fuck. He alternated between angry stares and disrespectful comments, his attitude saying everything his mouth didn't. No one was exempt, except family.

"Get the fuck outta here," Dave yelled at one new face. "You niggas is shaking because y'all don't know how it's coming. I'm coming, bitches, for my money and my rep."

It was the sentiment of the trio as they surveyed the area. Every now and then they exchanged knowing glances amongst themselves.

Dirty Red didn't notice the change in the wind as he walked alongside Quinton. The air was thick, and more than one hustler was trying to get his attention, hoping he didn't tell "the dirty" he'd heard them talking.

"After Rush came to tell me Earl was on the block," Red began, "I headed this way to see Buck. I missed the beef by a block at least. Dread was coming out with the burner in his hand, practically smoking. The only thing I could do was head into the joint and snatch the tape."

"Yo, Red, you need to be careful on these streets with that info," Quinton said.

Dirty Red smirked, lifting his shirt. "On my right is my American Express," he said, revealing his gun. "You know I can't leave home without it. I'm a card-carrying member since I entered these streets. On my left is the money, baby."

"Will you ever be serious, Red?" Dave asked.

"Yeah, right about the time y'all murder that twisted, backstabbing lame ass that got my man."

Quinton rolled his eyes, fighting back the emotions of having almost lost another friend. But Buck being alive would remain a secret for now. "Red, I guarantee you gonna have to lay down your toys real soon. You ready to get a job, 'cause that nigga gonna be ghost."

"What do we owe you for always taking care of us?" Danny asked.

Dirty Red hoisted his middle finger and quickly picked up his step after handing over the tape.

Chapter 33

YOU CAN'T HIDE

After business was taken care of, Quinton, Dave, and Danny entered the house from the back, trying not to wake Anissa, but their constant laughter and teasing easily woke her.

Danny heard her feet hit the floor, and Dave saw her tired eyes when she entered the kitchen.

Quinton was oblivious that she was standing two inches away from him, waiting for him to notice her as he peered into the refrigerator for something to eat. He almost leaped four feet off the floor when he heard her voice.

"What the hell? It's gonna take you all night to figure out there isn't anything in there to eat unless you cook it?" she asked.

Quinton was surprised to see the big smile on her face matched the laughter in her voice. "Y'all ain't shit," he said to his friends. "You could've warned me she was standing there."

Danny was the first to leave the room with a big mug filled with soda. Dave soon followed with two apples, a butter knife, and a block of cheese.

Quinton stared nervously at Anissa, hoping he wouldn't ruin the moment before he got the chance to hold her.

Seeing him had done something to her sensibilities. Before she could prepare herself, the tears began to flow. She wanted to kiss him, to make sure he was fine, but her feet wouldn't let her move.

Quinton couldn't take it anymore. He grabbed her and held on as tightly as he could. His heart pounded, waiting for the rejection, but she leaned into him and clung to him with all the emotions bottled up inside her. Neither of them had the courage to speak. They stood together rocking back and forth in their embrace.

Danny and Dave departed a little later, leaving Quinton and Anissa to tiptoe around one another.

"It's good to see you. I mean, alive and well."

"Same old Nissa. Get straight to it," he answered, knowing it wouldn't be easy getting back in her good graces.

"Were you hoping to find someone else? Because I'm sure she died when you left."

"No, I was hoping to find a forgiving woman that would accept my apology, but I can see that's not going to happen in this house."

"You got that half right. I'm not forgiving you. You didn't bother to offer me a choice before you left, so you will take what you can get now that you're back." She stormed from the kitchen.

Quinton stood there watching her retreat. He knew his battle in the streets would be easier than standing up to Anissa's wrath. "Oh hell," he whispered to himself. He had to beg and plead. She was the woman who possessed him every day that he'd been gone, and the one he missed the most. He had to get her to forgive him somehow.

Quinton followed in her path to the bedroom, breathing slowly and trying to think of the right way to make her understand. He decided that the truth was the only approach Anissa would accept, and that was going to be hard to tell.

"Don't come in here looking lost and hurt. *You* left me, *you* owe me, and *you* should be comforting me. I'm not going to pardon you this time."

"What do you want, Anissa? You want me to come up with some fantastic story, when all I know is, I couldn't do it anymore? I'm sorry, and I'm begging you to forgive me."

"Fuck you! You have the audacity to come into my home with an attitude after you left me. Go to hell, straight to hell with gasoline drawers on, my man, because that's not an apology. I know you knew before you opened your mouth that that shit wasn't going to work. It didn't work before you fled, and it won't work ever."

"What I gotta do? Please don't make me promise something we both know I can't keep."

"Quinton, you're sorry all right, and until you can apologize to me properly, you can say good night."

"Anissa, you just gonna turn your back on me? That's it? Good night? You don't want to talk about this?"

"Good night, Quinton. I think we both know you don't know what to say to make me listen, and I ain't listening to any bullshit."

For the first time in their relationship, Anissa wasn't going to forgive him easily. He felt a strange feeling in the pit of his stomach. With his head hung low, he tried to reason with himself. He wanted to say all the right things, but nothing came to mind. Twice he opened his mouth, but nothing came out. Finally he sat in the seat closest to the bed and stared at her back.

Anissa didn't have the courage to turn around and see if he was still in the room. Calmly she turned off the night lamp off and didn't bother to give him another thought. It was a trick she'd learned and mastered when he'd first left. She only prayed it still worked.

During the night Quinton took off his clothes and climbed into bed next to Anissa, only getting close enough to smell her hair and hold her lightly.

Chapter 34

THE ROUNDUP

The euphoric haze from the pain medication lifted all too abruptly. The intense burning in the pit of his stomach felt like hot coals. Afraid to move, he moaned, fighting each stabbing pain that danced though his body. Nothing Buck could have imagined compared to the hurt he felt.

Brenda stood at the foot of his hospital bed in shock. The horrible sounds coming from him frightened her. Watching his legs fold and flatten against the mattress was proof that he was alive, but the moans he made stole her resolve to be strong for him.

Finally Buck's eyes fluttered rapidly against his closed lids, and Brenda knew it was just a matter of time before he opened them wide enough to see her face. The thought to run was priority number one for her. She had accepted that she couldn't stand by and suffer loss. She quietly prayed he'd open his eyes and she would be able to stay.

Just as quickly, she hoped he'd keep them closed, so he wouldn't have to watch her leave. She believed she could just walk away from the love they'd shared and never look back, but first she had to be certain he would be all right.

The pain was unbearable, but Buck concentrated until his eyes popped open. The blinding light forced him to close them again. More slowly this time, he opened his eyes, willing them to focus on the things around him.

Almost immediately he saw the sadness in Brenda's face. He'd been suffering, but seeing her standing there made his pain seem trivial. He tried to smile with his eyes, but another wave of pain ripped though his body, and it was too much to hide.

Brenda suddenly became aware of the fact that she'd been holding her breath. She'd been so worried about her own emotional pain, she still hadn't acknowledged the depth of Buck's pain.

Quickly she pulled herself together and walked to the nurse's station to advise them about Buck's condition.

The nurse rose from her seat with a big smile on her face.

"Well, it's good to meet you, Mr. Holden," the nurse announced as she entered his room. The nurse chuckled as she methodically began checking Buck's condition.

Brenda, paralyzed by fear, didn't go any closer to Buck.

Buck didn't bother pretending that everything was OK. He knew something was wrong by Brenda's distance, and it hurt.

Soon a group of doctors stood at his bedside. He carefully watched as they each put on plastic gloves and talked about him as though he were a corpse.

Only one doctor, Dr. Halibash, introduced herself before she actually began her work. She explained what she was going to do, and informed him that she'd been monitoring his progress all along, and he was doing exceptionally well.

"Don't worry, Mr. Holden, you're going to be fine. I've been here with you all along. I won't let you down."

She wasn't annoyingly chipper, but she was efficient at making Buck feel that he was in capable hands.

By the time the curtains were rolled back, Buck was still taped up and attached to more beeping machines than he could count, but he was free of his breathing tube.

Dr. Halibash leaned him forward and pounded softly on his chest, asking him to cough. "Come on, Mr. Holden, you've got to do better than that."

Buck smiled because he knew his attempts were lame, but he feared the pain if he tried anything close to the roar she wanted.

"I know you're worried about the pain, but I'll take care of that in a minute. Trust me, I want you to give me something with some heart and soul behind it."

Buck didn't hold back this time. He coughed until she happily announced he'd done a good job.

Brenda had been feeling panicky since finding out Buck was alive. It was a feeling she didn't want to get accustomed to, but somehow she knew staying with Buck would probably mean living on the edge.

Losing her father had made Brenda believe there wasn't any good left to live for. Meeting Buck changed that empty pit, but when he got shot, she started to believe again that there was nothing good in the world. Good things only lasted as long as a good feeling. That feeling wasn't nearly enough to last through the pain when it was over. She was going home.

Brenda struggled with her emotions while she packed. She even considered everything she'd be losing. The truth was, she had to leave before she lost the courage to go. She thought about her pregnancy, which she had to keep a secret. If Buck knew she was having his baby, he would never stop looking for her.

While the doctors were working on Buck, she slipped out of the room, and then left the hospital. Her fears got the better of her, and she decided walking away was easier than saying good-bye.

In the parking lot she cried like a lost child. She knew leaving Buck would kill a part of who she was, but she had to leave. She didn't have the staying power Anissa possessed. She accepted that some women understood the words "stand by your man," and they didn't hesitate to do whatever was called for, but she certainly wasn't that woman, and she wouldn't pretend.

Later that day Buck heard Quinton's voice then he saw his face.

Quinton stood beside his friend, trying to mask the regret he felt for not being there to protect him.

Danny and Dave came into view only seconds after Quinton.

Dave immediately began clowning on Buck. "If you needed some time off, you didn't have to go get shot. All you had to do was take a vacation," he said.

Buck struggled to hoist his middle finger.

Danny, however, turned deadly serious before the laughter could stop. "We all home, so that could only mean the block about to get hot. If you were expecting anything else, take your pain pills now and go to sleep until it's over."

Buck still hadn't said a word. He just watched as the men before him traded places. It was a changing of the guard, so to speak. Quinton stood in the front, while Danny and Dave traded positions quite often. Dave could change his demeanor with the wind, but Danny was always lethal.

Buck was worried. For years they'd stayed under the radar. Ms. Sadie had taught them how to do it so well before her passing. She had prepared them for the times when they couldn't stand each other. She even taught them the meaning of falling apart so they could come back stronger. Buck knew these were now the times she had prepared them for, the kind of times that changed friends into enemies, if there wasn't a real bond.

Quinton had tested that bond when he'd run away from everything. He'd left behind Anissa, their new baby, and three men who depended on his friendship. None of that mattered now because when Buck needed him, he was there to stand beside him.

Quinton couldn't let Baldy continue to think Buck was dead. He knew a man like Baldy, with his reputation, was an asset to their team.

As the brothers caught up, Baldy walked through the door. He immediately flanked Buck's left side.

Buck knew that the sinister grin on Baldy's face meant death was imminent for any man dumb enough to cross his path. Earl was going to die. It was just a matter of where and how.

Each member of Buck's family promised to return the next day, but it was Baldy who stayed longer.

Over the years, Baldy had become Buck's partner in many wars, and Buck had given him true friendship, something he'd never really understood until Buck came along. The two had built a friendship stronger than life or death.

The meds were beginning to pull Buck into an abyss, but he wanted to ask Baldy about Brenda. He needed to know why she hadn't stayed, especially now when he needed her strength the most.

Struggling against the fog, he found the words to ask, but Baldy didn't have the right answers, and he wasn't gonna lie intentionally to his friend. Instead he stayed silent long enough to hear Buck's heavy snores.

Before he entered the elevator, he promised himself he would find Brenda, if only to talk with her.

Brenda wasn't ready for the angry man standing in Buck's doorway, ready to put her and her clothing on the sidewalk. Baldy's head was glistening, his eyes glowed with purpose, and he was ready to confront her best excuse.

Stepping back into the house, she offered him a seat.

"Brenda," he called softly, "why aren't you at the hospital with Buck?"

She understood the question, even respected his candor, but her guilt made her angry. "It's none of your business," she answered, surprised at her own anger.

Baldy nodded, and the snarl on his face suddenly frightened Brenda. If running was an option, she might have tried, but her own foolish pride made her stare back at the imposing figure before her.

"I've known Buck practically his entire life," Baldy began. "I've been friends with him about as long as you've been alive. He was my responsibility, until he made you part of his life. As his friend, I've asked you the same question he asked me today—Why aren't you at the hospital?"

Maybe it was the tone he used when asking the question, followed by the in-your-face glare, but Brenda couldn't compete with him. She dropped herself into a chair and bowed her head, ashamed of her behavior. "I can't do this," she answered truthfully. "I can't sit by and watch Buck's suffering, only for him to get up and go back out into those streets, and eventually not come back."

Baldy waited patiently for Brenda to work though her emotions. He sat quietly, watching her intently, searching for any untruth in her words, but he found none. That alone endeared her more to his heart. He immediately recognized the quality that attracted Buck to Brenda. She wore her heart and emotions visibly for anyone to see.

"You've got every right to your fears, but he needs you, and if you walk away now, you may not be able to come back when you realize the mistake you've made."

Without further input or fanfare, he left her with her thoughts. The next step was hers, and he prayed she made the right decision.

Brenda had heard every word Baldy said, but she was determined to protect herself.

Chapter 35

THE UGLY SIDE OF THE GAME

Word was spreading fast about Earl. The rumors were out of control. Niggas were lying, saying they'd seen him walk out the real estate office with the burner in his hand. One dude even claimed he'd sold Earl the heat to get at Buck. The only truth to the rumors was that Earl had been running up in spots and taking work from anybody still doing business with the crew, and niggas were forming coalitions to get rid of his ass, but no one was willing to get dirty.

In the ten days since he'd been home, Quinton had heard just about every version of what happened in the real estate office. Quinton stood listening to story after story as to why hustlers couldn't come up with their dough. Displaying a meek demeanor, he accepted every short, wondering how these men could be so foolish. They were a family. Baby showers, weddings, funerals, good and bad times, they were there to help carry the weight. Each loss was a personal attack on the measure of their friendships.

"Sleep, muthafuckas," he whispered every time a long tale didn't match the short stack.

Young Gotti was the worst of the bunch. He had come to the fold with his ass tucked between his legs after some no-name strays murdered his brother. He begged and pleaded to be down, and no matter how hard Buck tried to convince him to go to school, he kept saying he didn't have time to earn slow money. Now the lame ass had a lot of nerve to be standing there talking shit in the spot they paid for.

"Q, man, my bread ain't right. This nigga Earl is draining me slow. I ain't scared or nothing, but I thought you had that nigga under your thumb. Since he's been back, I haven't been able to flip a pack, let alone turn in what I owe. That nigga is a leaking faucet. What're y'all going to do? If you scared, I'll put my people on his ass for the right price."

Quinton couldn't contain himself as anger welled up in his soul. Too dumb to understand the meaning behind Q's silence, Gotti kept talking. It would have been comical to watch, if Quinton hadn't gone crazy.

"Nigga, are you the dumbest muthafucka that ever lived, or do you really believe that bullshit coming out your mouth? Bitch, please, a little over a year ago you were willing to suck a dick to get on. You seemed to have forgotten that part of the scenario."

Dave shook his head. He knew Gotti wasn't ready for the blast coming his way. Nor was Danny ready to catch the heavy beast as he fell.

Quinton raised his foot and planted it dead center in Gotti's chest.

"Don't you dare disrespect me by asking me for bread when you owe me, you ill-mannered bitch," Quinton yelled. "You know what . . . get up and run everything you got. The money in your pockets, pull 'em inside out. Give me those jewels and the keys to the Tonka truck you been bragging about. Fuck! You give me the keys to your momma's house right now, punk. And move faster, before I change my mind about letting you live. You had better go see your girl and tell her it's time to move, because I'm burning your shit down for the insurance money. That's how gully I'm getting with this shit. It ain't difficult. This is grown man's business. Now, boy, consider yourself saved."

And with that the trio walked off to collect from the next nigga.

"If you were going to kick the shit out of that muthafucka, the least you could have done was tell a brother," Danny complained later. "I could have gotten out the way and let that nigga hit the ground."

"Brother, I guess you know it's on from here on out," Quinton said. "Be ready, because I don't have a plan, except to run right at these lames."

The gossip wire was burning up. The game was over, and niggas were shaking with the thought. Anytime they saw Quinton and the twins, lames were surrendering whatever they had. There was no longer a waiting period. If you owed, you paid. If you didn't, they'd take something of value until you could make a suitable payment.

Hustlers had even shut down Earl's stick-n-trick operation. Every precaution implemented was to ensure against losing one dollar. Dudes were holding product in one hand and a burner in the other.

The remaining members of the Baker Boys had become the new fear on the streets. Quinton was seeing niggas every day, and would leave them sitting on a curb with no ride if they came up short. The real stress was having to watch a flatbed tow truck lift your shit off the ground, and there wasn't a damn thing you could do. Some folded with the mess of it all, while others robbed, tricked, or ran until they covered the debt.

Quinton didn't offer any sympathy for game. Bitterness spread like jam, and there was no love for the weak. The rule of the trade was no consignment—Don't ask, and don't get your feelings hurt. If a nigga only had enough for half, he only got half. Niggas were walking away from the game stripped naked of any rep.

Earl became better with every new precaution instituted by the hustlers. He began collecting bodies like cops were catching crooks. In the cover of the night, he'd put the burner to a fiend's back and walk right up on the dough man. If the vic pretended to hold out, Earl didn't hesitate to make him an example. He'd already shot two people, to prove his commitment to crippling Buck and anyone working with the D-12 stamp.

Even the police were looking suspiciously at the change in the guard.

They couldn't understand what was happening. The only dealers really eating stayed hidden in the background. The names of the dealers were even a mystery. Except one. "The Dread," rolled off the tongues of anybody with an open case.

Detective Stuckney thought it was time he and his men visited this dread, but no one could give more than vague information as to his whereabouts. The art to catching men like Earl was to wait until they settled and got comfortable. Right now things were still new and fresh, so Detective Stuckney and his crew decided to watch from a distance.

Chapter 36

THE PARTNER

Hoes couldn't run up on a nigga for the night and catch a "come-up." The designer tricks were back to seeing the local booster for their fashionable wear. Dudes stood on the corners holding meetings about what they used to have and what they used to push. The game was seeing the darkness, and the damage was putting Earl in a very tense place. From all the money he'd robbed and all the work he'd stolen, he could open a spot of his own, but he knew he had to be careful how he ran his shit.

Earl decided he had to re-group, and in the interim, he and Eddy became a real couple. He picked her up from school, and she went home to cook his meals and wait for him to return.

Her luck was finally changing for the better. After a few weeks, she quit her job and became whatever Earl wanted her to be.

"Breito, what are you going to do with all this shit in the closet? I can barely get to my clothes because of these damn duffel bags and knapsacks."

"Move it out the way, and put it back when you finished."

"Easy for you to say. Why don't you start selling this shit? I bet you got enough in there to take me on a cruise," she teased.

"And who am I supposed to sell it to? Your husband?"

"Sell it back to some of the niggas you got it from. You become their suppliers with their shit."

Earl smiled, knowing she meant well, but the game wasn't predictable.

Eddy turned to Earl before she went bed. "Think for a moment, Breito," she said. "This shit is just taking up space, and there are niggas out there just looking for connections. You can re-bag it with your own seal and call it Tech-9 if you want, but you could make the money. When you get the return, go see your pops and Ms. Maddy to keep the steamboat rolling."

"How long have you been meaning to have this conversation with me?" he asked innocently.

"You really want know?" She laughed. "Since the day I came to your room to clean it and saw the duffel bag."

"Ah, so that means all these weeks you haven't been after my body and sexy smile?"

Eddy, strutting toward the bed, began stripping off her clothes until she was standing there wearing only a satin and lace bustier with matching panties.

"I've always been after your body, especially when I would hide in the closet and watch you and Eve doing the nasty. It was the way your dark skin looked next to her light complexion. Right now I'm getting horny just thinking about it."

Earl waited patiently for her to get closer before he pulled the clip from her hair and watched her tresses fall neatly down her back. He loved her boldness. She didn't hide from anything, and she had no qualms with doing all the things he thought exciting.

"What's your pleasure, *mami*?"

"I haven't completely decided yet," she answered, taking off his wife-beater. "How about you lie back and I'll work it out on my own."

She pushed him gently toward the bed and began rubbing the head of his penis through his silk boxers. Then she dropped to her knees and bowed her head.

"Damn!" Earl tangled his hands in the mess of curls in his lap. For every bob of her head, he hoisted his hips to meet her stroke.

"*Mami*, stop. Please stop. I'm about to explode."

Words like that were an aphrodisiac for Eddy. She wouldn't stop, no matter how many times he cried out. She gripped his waist and held him in place until he gave her every drop of his liquid.

Relaxing in the afterglow, Earl thought about Eddy and the extent of their friendship. He really wanted to talk to her now rather than play. "What would you do if this was your shit?" he asked, gesturing toward the closet.

Eddy rolled over and sat up in bed. The smirk on her face said she'd thought about all that too. Her eyes danced as she spoke, explaining detail by detail how to work things.

"That dude, Young Gotti, he lost more than everybody when Quinton first came back. I'd be where that nigga hangs out, feeding him slowly and putting the idea in his head that we could make it happen. I'd use his resentment against Quinton to my advantage until he started badmouthing those muthafuckas too. Once he flips and niggas start to see him climb, it's over. My team of soldiers would be the niggas Quinton threw away."

"You're forgetting one thing, Edd—Those soldiers you are talking about flipping are the same ones I beat, robbed, and shot, and whose workers I murdered."

"No, I didn't. First of all, we're talking about me, and this is my operation, not The Dread's."

Eddy stopped talking long enough to let her words sink in. The light went on, and Earl understood exactly what she was saying.

"Gotti would become my point man," she continued, "especially since you never got a chance to get at him. He was just swindling from the till. I'd let his balls drop from his stomach, and then I'd steal those shits from him if he ever tried to steal from me."

Earl laughed. "Just how would you make him fear you? With your beauty?"

"No, that's how I'll get him to listen. With the heavy weight of a nickel-plated gun and one of the most dangerous natty dreads on my side, we can't lose," she whispered seriously.

Earl leaned back, giving full thought to her plan. It was good enough, but she hadn't factored the NYPD into the equation. They would certainly be up on any new superstars rising from the rubble.

"Let's say I give you a chance to make this happen. You have to think about the risk. There can't be any hesitation or second-guessing me when I tell you something. If I say run, pick up and run. Don't look back, don't stop to pack, just move. Do you understand?"

"Breito, I—"

"You will move when I say. No excuses, no explanations, just do it. Or we can forget about doing this."

Eddy was stunned. Earl had always been gentle and soft with his requests. He'd always given her a chance to voice her opinion. She just nodded.

"I'm letting you have your chance for a host of different reasons. Some are pure greed, others are because you're smart, beautifully sexy, and I believe you are a hustler waiting for your chance. Here it is. For better or worse, we're in this together."

"Thank you!" She giggled. "I can be everything you need me to be."

"Nah, *mamacita*, just be what the streets require when you're in them, and be what your man expects when we're in here like this." He pulled at the tiny fabric covering her triangle.

Gotti wanted to change his nickname to Depression. That was how bad things had gotten. No one wanted to fuck with him. He couldn't get a loan, and he couldn't get any product to hustle his way back out. He was down to the last few pieces of jewelry his girl was willing to part with to keep them afloat. He hated Q for embarrassing him and stripping him of everything. The only thing that kept him going each day was the fact that he would one day see them all cave and fold. He just wished he could be part of their destruction.

Eddy was standing next to her broken down Volkswagen Beetle, pretending to be stranded, when she spotted Gotti heading her way. *Damn,* she thought, *money must be what makes a man, 'cause he is looking worse than my car.*

Gotti no longer cared about his appearance. His hair was fuzzy and matted, his clothes looked like he'd been sleeping in them, and he smelled like a chimney.

"Excuse me, can you help me?" Eddy called. "I got a flat, no money for a tow, and no way to get home."

"Nah, baby, I ain't got no money to help, but if you got a spare, I may be able to help you out." As he worked, he tried to place her beautiful smile, but it eluded him.

Gotti made light work of changing the tire.

"Thank you so much," Eddy said. "I've been standing here for almost an hour, and it'll be dark soon. My worthless ex-boyfriend sold me this car, and I've had bad luck with it ever since. I don't have money today, but if you call me, I can give you something for your trouble, handsome."

Gotti knew he was anything but cute right then, but he accepted the compliment and the number. "No payment necessary, but maybe when things are a little better, we could get a few drinks and talk. Maybe hanging out with a beautiful woman will change my luck," he joked.

"Thanks for the compliment, but if you want drinks, there's a spot across the street. Let's meet there tomorrow about six, and I can properly thank you for your help."

"That sounds like a plan, pretty lady. I'm Gotti. And you are?" He thought she looked just like Eve, but she was younger and maybe even a little prettier.

"I'm Gotti's new lady luck. You can call me Lady *E*," she joked. "No, for real, my name is Endira."

"Well, Lady *E*, nice to meet you, and I'll see you tomorrow."

The next day, after Eddy explained her plan to Gotti, he didn't hesitate to move with her. At the least, he figured, he'd get some work and some pussy. That was until Eddy made it clear that the arrangement was pure business. The moment the smile disappeared, he knew for sure she had to be kin to Eve. She was a dead ringer for Eve. *Damn,* he thought, *down to the cold-ass stare.*

It didn't take long for the streets to notice the new-and-improved Young Gotti. In a few weeks he had turned thing into a gold factory. He was undercutting prices, offering two-for-one deals, and taking no consignment. He was back riding high in a bigger truck. The clothes and jewels he wore made many envious, but no one dared to test him. They knew the hunger it took to come back from where he'd fallen. They knew this time he was prepared to defend his success by any means necessary. He walked with a new attitude and heavily taxed niggas who laughed when he was struggling.

Earl and Eddy's intricate plan had paid off.

Chapter 37

A SUSPECT FOR AN OLD MURDER CASE

The stale smell of smoke interrupted Buck's dream.

"Mr. Holden," the raspy voiced officer called out. Leaning closer, he whispered again.

"Yes?" Buck answered groggily.

The detective didn't wait for any further acknowledgment before he spoke again.

"You are being placed in handcuffs and arrested for murder. A witness is willing to say that you and Sasha Richards were dating when she died. As a result of your medical condition, we can't transport you or put you through the system yet, but we can place cuffs on you until you're up for the transport."

The fog had lifted for Buck with the sound of metal clinking in his ears. Immediately he struggled against the restraints until it became clear that he was indeed in handcuffs. His movements were restricted, but his mouth worked fine.

"What the fuck is this?" he yelled as loud as his sore throat would allow. "What are these handcuffs for? I am the victim here. Can't you see that?"

"Are you Mr. Jahson Holden?" the shorter of the two detectives asked.

Buck didn't think it was smart to withhold that information, especially since they could look on his chart and get the answer to the question. "Yes," he answered. Carefully he watched and waited for the next question.

The officers looked at one another before continuing.

"Did you know Miss Richards very well?" the detective asked, as if he didn't already know the answer to the question.

Before Buck could respond, the door to his private room opened, and a team of doctors entered and stood around his bed. Immediately the detective asking the questions threw covers over the handcuffs, trying to hide the bulky metal.

Dr. Halibash dismissed her medical students as calmly as she could without alerting them to the madness she was about to cause. She quickly forgot about professionalism when the door slid shut behind the last pupil.

"Who the hell are you? And why do you have my patient shackled to this bed?" She got up in the detectives' faces.

Standing toe to toe with the detectives, the doctor explained that Buck couldn't get out of bed, let alone answer any questions they might have, due to the heavy dosage of meds he was being given. She demanded they hand over any written authorization they received from hospital administration giving them permission to be on the floor. When neither made a move, she firmly requested they leave the area immediately or she'd call hospital security.

The detectives all but laughed in her face, believing they had rank. They were the police and no place in the city was out of their reach. They both stood their ground, daring the doctor to follow through with her threat.

Seconds after she spoke into her phone, security was all over the place. The chief of security, a short, round, brown woman with a killer attitude, walked into the room and immediately demanded that the officers step into the hallway and away from the patient.

Dr. Halibash calmly requested that the handcuffs be removed before she called the local police captain and report the duo for jeopardizing the recovery of her patient. The detectives knew when they were outmatched. They would leave for now, at least until they collected more evidence against

Buck.

Buck decided Halibash had earned his trust in the beginning, but now she'd earned his friendship. He promised himself to thank her for her courage.

"Listen to me," she told him once the detectives were gone, "you don't answer any questions from now on. This medicine is liable to make you tell the secret to your momma's trust, so keep your mouth closed, young man." She scowled.

Buck could feel the cloud coming back faster than he was prepared for. His tongue felt heavy as he struggled to speak.

"Go back to sleep." The doctor patted away the sweat on his forehead. "I'll see you later," she whispered to him as he drifted farther into the zone.

Quinton was just returning to the hospital to visit Buck when he walked into the middle of the heated debate between hospital security and the NYPD. Quietly he hung back until he got the gist of their argument. The shit had hit the fan. Buck was a suspect in a murder, but whose murder wasn't revealed.

Danny and Dave arrived right behind Quinton, and Quinton explained to them what he had overheard.

"That means we gotta tighten up any loose ends now," Danny said. "The word in the street is Buck was killed, and that's the reason you're home. So the witness has to be someone that doesn't have an ear on the street."

Quinton nodded but didn't offer up any opinion.

Dave, however, had plenty to say. "Earl has crossed too many lines in his return. Buck's death seems to have caused a real panic. We either gonna strike back, or we gonna cut our losses."

Danny and Dave's chatter cut into Buck's drug-induced haze.

"What the fuck?" Buck asked. "Don't you niggas know that this is a hospital and I need my rest, you loud muthafuckas?" Buck's voice was filled with laughter, despite his pain.

All three men looked at Buck as if he had a second head attached to his shoulders.

"You ain't too sick, if you still managing to talk more shit than anyone else in the room," Dave said.

"Fuck you, runt. When I get out this bed I'ma run all over you on the court. You gonna cry for Danny to help you up again. Keep running your mouth."

"You're a fuckin' bully. That's all you are, the big-ass bully. Get better, nigga, so I can put your ass back in the hospital from a heart attack. All that good cooking Brenda done gave you, I know you ain't running a full court anytime soon."

Buck hoisted his middle finger as if signaling the fight was over, but Quinton wasn't about to let Buck go back to sleep without finding out more information.

Baldy came through the doors just in time to hear Buck's explanation of what happened with the detectives. Bad news turned into worse news as Baldy began talking. "Four more of our spots took hits. But that dumb Gotti is somehow gettin' back on his feet, looking sharp again. Looks to me like he may have joined forces with Earl. After Quinton put that nigga on his ass, Gotti couldn't buy a fucking vowel, and ain't nobody in the street crazy enough or got enough supply to front Gotti like he stunting."

Danny's eyes lit up after hearing that piece of information. Quinton smiled, and Dave rubbed his hands together. Baldy waited patiently for the plan he knew they were forming.

"Don't look at me," Buck said. "I'm dead. I see y'all at the after-party. Just take care of business before you head out."

Buck slid comfortably into an unconscious euphoria as he listened to the plan. Earl may have accepted he was a target. He may have known they were coming, but he wasn't ready for the devastation, determination, or heart of the men that would dig his grave. They wouldn't shy away from destroying their number one predator.

Quinton carefully explained the plan. It was perfect. Not only would Earl finally get what he deserved, but that traitor Gotti would end up where all traitors went.

Baldy was the first to leave after everyone agreed to the plan. He had his own ideas.

Meanwhile, the trio sat around Buck's bed, trying to accept the path they were yet again about to take. It was life-altering, but turning back wasn't an option.

"Does anybody feel like we've been here before," Dave asked, "in this very same place at a different time?"

"Yeah, twin, that's called *déjà vu*. The only difference is, this time we got the full story and we know exactly who we got to bury."

"I've wanted to get rid of this fool for a minute, but Buck wanted things peaceful until we made our move," Dave said.

"I've never seen a peaceful war," Danny said, "and I don't want to be the first nigga to have one."

"If we all walked away right now, we don't owe shit." Dave turned to Quinton. "It's all on you."

"There's only one way I want to walk away, and that's with my rep intact, my niggas at my side, and money in our pockets," Quinton said. "We could burn down everything, every spot, every house, and have a garage sale, but we ain't leaving shit for that bitch to live off. He gonna have to build on his own, from the dust to the bricks."

Chapter 38

PROTECTION

Detective Brice Stuckney had been on Earl's ass for weeks, watching in the shadows, waiting for the moment to catch him alone, but the chance never arrived.

"Detective Stuckney, you know breaking and entering is a crime," Detective Bubarcar warned, laughing.

"Fuck you. I'm investigating a potential dope dealer's home. I'm seeing how much he owes us for operating without our permission. Shut the fuck up. Now I lost count."

"When do you think they'll be back from their vacation?" Bubarcar asked.

Stuckney had seen Earl and his woman leave with a car packed with suitcases a couple days earlier, so he knew they were out of town for a while, and it would be safe to enter Earl's home.

"It doesn't matter when. The question is whether he will be equipped to stand the price tag it will cost him to continue to live so lavishly. The fucker got gold-plated fixtures. Tammy wants to buy these same ones. They go for almost eighteen hundred dollars. This is some bullshit."

"Let's go before you convince me we should steal them like common crooks," Bubarcar whispered.

"I should steal those shits. Maybe then I'd get some head from my wife for a change." Stuckney laughed.

Twenty minutes after the officers left, Eddy and Earl pulled into their driveway. Immediately Eddy felt a chill. Standing in the foyer, she made a sign of the cross while trying to pull her gat from the holster between her legs.

Earl followed her path, oblivious to Eddy's hunch that someone was in their home.

"Breito," she yelled from the den. "Some fucking body has been in here. Look." She pointed to the monitor on his desk.

Earl was stunned. There was home video of two men walking around their house, touching their things.

"Who in the fuck are they?" Eddy asked. "Why the hell were they in my home?" she screamed hysterically.

Earl grabbed her to silence the hysteria as he continued to stare at the monitor. Finally after the video ended, Earl said, "They're the police. They are NYPD, and they were here to get their percentage of our business. That, *mamacita*, is how we will operate outside the law but with the law."

"It doesn't bother you that they came into our home uninvited? They were going through our things, touching my personal items."

"No, it doesn't bother me, but do you want to pack up and run?"

Earl knew that everything that happened from this moment on could be the end of Eddy's innocence. He wanted Eddy to show fear. Fear would mean that she understood the path they were taking was dangerous.

"This is the next level," Earl explained. "This is what you've been nagging me about. Did you really think we'd be able to stay out of sight as the business got bigger?"

"Don't talk to me like I'm stupid, Earl," she yelled, angry at Earl for making her feel small. "I realized things would change. I just didn't expect to find my home invaded because of it."

"Eddy, you can walk away right now, and I won't hold a grudge. At this level, it only gets deadly. My love for you won't change, but if you hesitate to bust your gun, you won't live. I'm asking you, do you want to pack?"

"Why does it always come to that with you? Any time I show any signs of weakness or I think for myself, you offer me the door. When I'm ready to leave, I'll go. Does that answer your question?"

"It's a good thing you love me, because the look in your eyes is much too dangerous."

"Fuck you. I'm not giving you any pussy until you change the locks," she yelled, running by him.

Earl laughed loudly and hoped Eddy believed that he wasn't worried. The truth was, he was very upset, knowing that, at any time, the cops could come into his home and murder him or arrest him. He wasn't pleased at all.

❖❖❖❖❖

The next day, traffic was clear, and Earl decided to open up on the highway and test the horsepower beneath his ass. Suddenly, flashing red and blue lights sparkled in his rearview mirror.

"Gotdamn!" He slowed the vehicle and coasted to the shoulder of the road.

"Mr. Clement, do you know how fast you were moving?" Detective Stuckney asked after requesting Earl's license and registration. "Do you realize the speed limit on this highway is fifty-five? Please step out of the car."

Earl immediately recognized the face of one of the officers who had broken into his home. Instead of giving away his knowledge, he descended from the truck and waited for further instruction.

"Put your hands on your head, Mr. Clement."

Before Earl could comply, another vehicle pulled up and two officers got out, assisting Stuckney in his charade. "What you got here, Brice?" one officer called out.

"Mr. Clement here was driving recklessly. I clocked him doing upward of ninety miles per hour."

"So you like living in the fast lane?" Bubarcar asked with a sinister grin.

Another officer yelled for Earl to put his left arm behind his back. Earl quickly lowered his left arm and waited to feel his right arm jerked behind him.

"You ride dirty, Mr. Clement?" Bubarcar asked.

Earl didn't bother to speak as two more officers arrived and began pulling shit out the vehicle and tossing things on the ground. He hung his head, hoping they wouldn't find the money belt hidden inside the well for the spare tire.

"Ah ha! Look what I found," one of the officers yelled, showing off the belt and laughing.

Earl knew he'd never see it again.

Stuckney moved closer to Earl and whispered to him, "How much is this in here, homeboy?"

Earl glared at Stuckney, wishing he could talk shit, but things would only get worse.

"All right, monkey, since you going to make me count it, I will, but I think you know what this is. It's your first payment to continue to operate your illegal enterprise in my city. Each week you will provide me with twenty for starters, and we'll work out the rest later."

"Twenty? Are you crazy? I ain't pumping that kind of work in them streets."

"Don't be disrespectful. I expect my money on time every time. Don't make me have to pull you over again either."

As Earl drove home, he brooded over the dilemma.

"They finally fuck with me, and I feel like they raped me!" Earl screamed when he walked through the door.

"What the hell are you talking about?" Eddy asked. "Speak English and slow down. Your accent is thick when you're yelling."

"The *blodeclaat* police, the two that were in here looking around, they pulled me over for speeding. They sat me on the side of the road like a cheap criminal, called me a *blodeclaat* monkey. The *pussyclaat* had the nerve to handcuff me and come in my face like we were lovers." Earl stomped back and forth.

"What do you want to do? Do we cut our losses and run, or do we dig in and get richer? It's time we decided what we gonna do. I found this spy shop on Eighty-Sixth Street last week. It has all kinds of neat stuff. I say we need to take a trip and see what it has to offer."

"You don't trust me now? You want all kinds of gadgets? I keep telling you, you are a girl. Girls don't like gadgets," he teased.

"I am a woman—there is a difference. And I love gadgets, especially if they'll give us an advantage when Stuckney no longer wants to use you."

Later when they went to visit the shop, the clerk was too excited about his work. He showed them all kinds of tiny wireless toys that could be placed in plain sight and go undetected. The more items he showed them, the more Earl became hyped. Eddy had already decided on the things that were necessary, but she wanted Earl to be on board for the full plan. There couldn't be one doubt in his mind once she sprang all the details on him.

Earl virtually hit the roof of his truck as Eddy sat in the driver's seat explaining her plan on the way home.

"I need you to trust me the same way I trust you," she said. "Stuckney is greedy, and he's cocky. He feels he can do anything because he's the police. We need something to bargain with when the time comes, something they can't deny, and this is the only thing I could think of on short notice."

"You have lost your fucking mind. There is no way in hell I'm going to record my dealings with this cop. It could backfire. They could get the tapes and use them to fuck me. Remember, he is a cop. He'll see that shit a mile away."

Eddy nodded, but she wouldn't give up so easily. She needed to enact her plan to protect Earl, the man she loved, whether or not he knew it.

❖❖❖❖❖

Two weeks later Earl got his wish for his birthday when Eddy bought him a new truck. He was impressed with the lock boxes and false floor in the back area to hide the drugs.

He cranked up the Dolby sound system and felt the vibration of the instruments from the custom speakers. He loved his new truck.

Eddy didn't reveal all the new things she had done to the truck before pulling it into the garage.

❖❖❖❖❖

For a couple of months Earl was ignorant to the cameras inside the truck, and so was Stuckney. He'd been inside the car every week to get his money, but he'd never noticed the cameras, just as Eddy suspected he wouldn't.

One evening Eddy decided it was time to tell Earl what she had done before he found out the hard way, but she wasn't brave enough to tell him outright.

"Breito, I need to use the truck today," she told him. "I have some things to pick up, and I need the extra space," she said, lying convincingly. Earl agreed without much thought.

After Eddy left, Earl was on the couch watching TV when he heard noises coming from the computer. He didn't bother to get up at first. He figured Eddy had installed some new screen saver. But then the soft hum of music playing in the background started to annoy him, so he quickly walked over to shut down the system.

When he looked at the monitor, he realized he was practically riding in the car with Eddy. She was there on the screen, and at that moment he wanted to kill her. He realized she had installed cameras in his truck, despite him telling her not to. She waved and blew him a kiss, as if she knew he was watching.

An hour later Eddy walked through the door with grocery bags in her hand, waiting for Earl to erupt. Instead he didn't say a word. He glared at her until she broke down to explain. It was useless. He was furious, and he refused to acknowledge anything she had to say.

For two days an overly polite rudeness existed between the couple.

Finally Eddy decided to give Earl the DVDs of his recorded meetings with Stuckney, hoping seeing the evidence would convince him of the value of what she had done.

When Earl got home that night, he saw the DVDs sprawled all over the bed. Eddy was locked in the spare bedroom and wouldn't open the door, no matter how much he banged.

Earl conceded and began watching the recordings. He was surprised at the things he was seeing. Stuckney's head was huge. He became humiliated as he listened to the crooked cop refer to him as a monkey every five minutes. But he did see the value in having the DVDs. Stuckney had completely incriminated himself with his own words, clearly revealing that he was involved in the drug business, and that he was collecting fees from Earl to allow Earl to continue to operate within what Stuckney considered his territory.

Earl couldn't apologize to Eddy, though. He was afraid. This was the biggest disagreement they'd ever had, and he was scared that she would still walk away even if he apologized. He wouldn't wait for her to walk, so he decided to leave first.

Chapter 39

LOST

Eddy was standing in the foyer when Earl walked through the door the next day, looking lost. After only one night away from her, he realized he couldn't live without her.

"Hey, how was Miami?" she asked, suspecting he had flown there to see his father.

"It was Miami. Um, you were right, and I was wrong. I should have listened, and I'm sorry."

"Fuck you!" she said. "Tell me your plan for what we should do now."

"The only thing Stuckney hasn't done yet that's illegal is committed murder," Earl began. "He hasn't admitted it on any of these recordings. He has mentioned everything else—planting evidence, breaking into spots, and robbing dealers—but not murder. If I can get him to agree to kill someone on camera, I don't think the police department would be able to ignore his crimes any longer."

"He isn't going to agree, unless you sweeten the pot so much that he can't say no. He's going to get suspicious if, all of a sudden, you start asking him to eliminate competition by murder, rather than the usual way. We haven't had that kind of beef since ever."

"But watching the last few DVDs, I noticed a difference in his behavior. He's back to being an overly cocky bastard, calling me monkey every five minutes, like he knows something I don't know."

"Well, we know he isn't on to me yet. If he had any idea I was the head, he'd fuck with you about it. So we're safe there. Maybe he flipped Gotti, and is getting his money from him now too. It's worth thinking about. For our last couple of meetings, Gotti's been late, or he doesn't show. Something is going on there too."

"If he flipped Gotti, that means he thinks there is no more need for me. Gotti's business is bigger than what I do alone. He could use Gotti to pump his shit on the streets, and Gotti can't say no. Sooner or later Gotti could give you up. It's about that time for you to pack."

"Oh, nigga, please. I'm not packing shit yet. It's too early for that. Besides, if I run, you go to jail yesterday. When I go, we'll have a plan. We have too much going in our favor."

Earl lost his patience. "You one hardheaded woman, and I get tired of chasing your tail. You promised to listen and do what I said, but you do what works for Eddy, and tell Earl later."

Eddy pretended not to understand the severity of the situation. She stood behind him yelling in English and Spanish.

"I ain't going yet. We could walk away, you and me. We could go to someplace nice and live well, if that's really where we are. But when we go, there can't be any excuses. You won't sacrifice me, and I won't sacrifice you."

"What the fuck is that supposed to mean?"

"It means you still need me to put some things in place before we go. Notice I didn't say me. I said we."

"What things, Eddy? What else do I need you to do for me? Go to jail for me? That happened once in my life, and it took this long for me to realize how wrong I was to sacrifice one friend for my fears and greed."

"What the fuck are you talking about? Buck? Fuck them muffin men muthafuckas. They didn't think about you when the real money hit the table. They didn't hesitate to blame you for Chaka's murder, and we all know how that turned out. There's no room for guilty. I'm not going until I'm sure we can go without repercussions."

"A hard head makes a sore ass. You don't listen," he yelled before storming out of the room.

❖❖❖❖❖

It took Eddy five months, but everything was in place for them to leave town, and not one second too soon. Recently the news had reported that a local drug dealer was found dead in the garage of his home, killed execution-style. The entire family was found dead in various rooms of the house. Earl saw Gotti's home on TV and almost shit in his pajamas.

Eddy walked into the room just as they showed a portrait of Gotti's family. "What the fuck is that about?"

"Stuckney is making his move, or Quinton and his crew have decided they want the streets back."

"It's not Quinton. He might be mad about being forced outta his territory, but he wouldn't kill an entire family to make a point. Besides, after all this time, why would they want these streets back?"

"OK, then, we agree it's Stuckney. What point is he trying to make?" Earl asked.

"He's trying to make a point to us that he can take what he wants any time he wants it."

"Why now? He'll lose more than he can gain trying to put a new set of dudes on the block to carry his weight."

"Stuckney loves the money, but for him it's about making the streets fear him. He's becoming what you used to be. He wants the block to move 'cause he's coming through. He hasn't accepted that there's a new breed of young boys on them corners. They don't respect a badge, and they don't respect a big-ass mouth. Stuckney is mouth. Two things can happen if he makes a wrong move. They gonna pull him in so deep, he can't shake free, or they gonna murk his ass when he shows too much greed."

"Well, one thing's for sure," Earl said. "He ain't gonna get me. He's given me a reason to call him. I need to know exactly what he knows about Gotti."

"He's gonna brag. You can believe that. His entire career he's been dirty. This is probably just the next rung on the ladder for him."

"I'm still stuck on why he'd want to destroy everything now?"

"Why does the answer have to be more complicated than he's a dirty cop that wants to be a hustler?" Eddy asked.

"Seriously, maybe we need to go on vacation for a few days, watch events unfold from a distance," Earl suggested.

Eddy quickly became suspicious. If Earl was trying to play with her emotions, she'd make him pay. "Why now?" she mimicked. "Is this your way of telling me it's time to pack?"

"Yeah, except let's go lay up on a beach, drink, smoke, party, and fuck, before we have to get back on our grind."

"You're not slick, Earl Clement. If you try to leave me anywhere, I'm gonna come home and whip your ass."

"Pack light, woman, and make sure we have enough money."

Once they arrived in Jamaica, Earl couldn't force himself to relax. He could feel the pressure coming, and he didn't think he was quick enough to outrun it.

That night he dreamed that there was a storm. The crackle of thunder rocked the skies, a flash of lighting blinded him, and the rain poured down all around him, soaking his clothes. He searched for Eddy, but she was gone. He'd seen her running toward the bungalow, but he'd searched every inch of the private beach and couldn't find her anywhere.

Frightened, he called out to her, but she didn't answer. Then he felt her warm hand touching him. It was magic how she appeared from thin air to kiss him. He kissed her back with a need and ache he'd never known until that moment. He fought back the idea that she might leave him before he could tell her he loved her. The tears burned his eyes, and her scent filled him with remorse. He panted, trying to hold on to the moment, and then it all vanished.

Earl panicked. The dream was too real. He sat upright in bed, looking back and forth, until he heard Eddy's voice asking him if everything was OK. He tried to lie, but she caught the tremor in his voice.

"Was it a bad dream?"

"Is there any other kind when you wake up shaking?" he snapped.

"You want to tell me about it? It can't hurt us if you share it. We can both be on the lookout for the pain."

"It's not so much the dream. It was the feeling of loss. Everything and everyone that I loved was gone," he whispered.

"Breito, I can't change dreams, but we can create memories together. Let me love you. Let's forget about that dream and make loving memories now." She began to cry, afraid about what Earl's dream might mean for their future.

Her tears frustrated Earl. He didn't know how to respond to them. Nothing had happened yet, and she was crying. How was he supposed to fix that? "Damn it! Stop crying. I don't know what I'm supposed to do when you crying and not talking."

Eddy tried to dry her eyes, but it was a feeble attempt at stopping the floodgates. Instead, she climbed onto his lap and stripped.

"Nothing matters but now, you and me making love, laughing, and talking," she whimpered in ecstasy and fear.

"Will I ever feel this way again?" Earl wondered after they finished making love.

"You will every day for the next six days, *papi.*"

"Marry me. Let me give you something I've never given anyone else, and something I'll never take from you."

Eddy was coming down off her spin cycle of pleasure, and would have said yes to anything, but she was afraid his proposal was just a "good nut talking," so she stayed quiet, hoping he'd ask again. The few seconds she waited felt like minutes. Her eyes begged him to repeat the question, but he just looked at her.

He knew she'd heard him, and he was waiting for an answer.

Eddy slid off his lap, saddened that he wouldn't repeat his request. She wouldn't give him an answer until he did.

On the last day of their vacation, the sun was smiling and winking at pedestrians as they walked along the boardwalk. Earl had steered this vacation in all kinds of directions. They'd gone to pubs and drank until they were drunk. They danced until the lights came on, and they rode scooters all around the busy island, stopping randomly at different shops. They'd ate on the streets, in little raggedy restaurants that held lines of people waiting their turn, and the previous night Earl found a swanky little place that had beautiful tablecloths and a live jazz band that Eddy would remember for all eternity.

But none of the entertainment of the last six days had changed Eddy's one wish of hearing him ask her to marry him again.

Sitting on the beach that night, they cuddled together on a blanket. Eddy quietly watched the stars, while Earl wished he could find the words to make the night perfect.

Without warning, Eddy heard the sounds of steel drums playing "Lonely Won't Leave Me Alone."

"I used to sing this song, not understanding the meaning until I met you again," Earl said. "I didn't understand how miserable I was until you came dragging into my room with your cleaning supplies and that beautifully wicked tongue. I love you, Endira Maria Soto. Be my wife. There can't be any illusions. All you're getting is my name and the man I am when we are together."

Eddy's tears wouldn't stop, and she laughed, knocking over Earl when she tried to jump into his arms. "Yes!" she screamed at the top of her lungs. "I've been waiting six days for you to propose again. I love you, *Señor* Earl Clement, and I'll never need you to be any more than you already are. Do we have to leave tomorrow?"

"Why?" Earl asked, confused.

"I don't want to go home without it being official. I want to go home knowing you are my husband and I am your wife."

"Let's go home, and I promise we'll be back in one month. No matter what is going on, we'll come back and have a wedding with a minister, flowers, music, and family."

Eddy agreed, but neither knew what would unfold at home in the next several weeks.

Chapter 40

THE GOOD TIMES END

A week later Eddy sat at the computer watching the live images of Stuckney and Earl in his vehicle when she heard the shattering sound of fireworks. Eddy refused to believe the sounds were anything else. She heard the loud voices of people screaming. Seconds later the computer monitor went blank.

Jumping up from the office chair, she checked the outlet, and then she flipped the light switch on the desk lamp, inadvertently switching on the home security cameras. It was Earl's idea to install the switches that way.

Her eyes burned from the tears she'd been fighting. Quickly she did the only thing that made sense. This must be Earl's way of telling her to run, she reasoned. Eddy snatched the DVD from the computer drive and shut down the computer. They'd practiced their escape so many times that it came naturally to her.

"The safe," Eddy whispered as she took the stairs two at a time. The envelopes were already addressed and stamped. Quickly she stuffed ten DVDs into cases and began sealing everything. Then she grabbed the already packed duffel bag and any information the police might seize and use against them.

"I remember," she whispered to the picture hanging over the bed. "I didn't forget anything. I love you, Breito." She cried as she ran down the steps and out of the house.

Eddy was safe. All she had to do was keep going. She handed one envelope to the post office clerk and smiled. Racing back to her vehicle, she headed to the parkway that led to I-95. Her distress at leaving Earl behind without knowing whether he was safe almost made her cause two accidents. She'd promised him she would leave, but if she left without trying to save him, she'd be a coward. In all the drama they'd been through, he'd never left her behind.

Eddy stopped at a different post office and mailed off the remaining DVDs.

Knowing she couldn't leave without Earl, she made her way back to the house. After pulling into the driveway, she slid from the car and took out her burner. Slowly she crept into her home through the back door, like a common criminal. She moved to the den and found Stuckney sitting behind the desk, as if he was waiting for her return.

Damn! I can't get taken in on some bullshit, and if Stuckney sees my gun, it'll be all over for me. God, only know what else he'll put on her. She placed the gun on the side table just out of his eyesight and near enough for a surprise attack if she needed it.

"Hello, Ms. Endira Clement. How are things with you lately?"

"Why are you in my home, Stuckney?"

"Oh, you admit that you are the owner of this beautiful house bought with drug money?"

"I admit that you are standing in my den and I didn't invite you here."

"Ms. Clement, oh, excuse me, it's still Ms. Soto, isn't it? Um, I'm here to pick up a package that Earl told me you have in your possession," he lied.

"What's the password?" Eddy asked with a straight face.

She could see his mind working in frustration. Clearly Earl hadn't sent him. He didn't even know that there wasn't a password.

"Fuck you!" he yelled. "That's the password," he said, walking closer to her, hoping to scare her into moving.

Eddy was scared shitless, but she refused to back up one inch.

"Bitch, I'll rape you slowly and kill you slower, if you don't open the damn safe."

A tear slid down Eddy's cheek as she stared at him, but complying wasn't an option. Shit, if he really wanted the money, all he had to do was look in the trunk of her car, where she'd left the duffel bag. "Fuck you, monkey! I ain't got shit for ya!" she yelled.

Stuckney panicked. He never thought she wouldn't do what he asked. Quickly, he gripped her hair in his hand and yanked her around the room, swinging her with force. He could have propelled her through a wall with the strength he put into the spin.

Eddy fell onto the floor, but still she didn't attempt to move toward the safe.

"Bitch, open the fucking safe before I punish you some more!"

Eddy tried to use his reckless anger against him. She understood that if she continued to taunt him, he'd win, and she'd do whatever he asked to get him to stop the torture. She couldn't wait for that. She slowly crawled back toward the end table in the hall where she'd placed her gun. It was her only insurance. She had a fifty-fifty chance of making it there. Either he'd kill her, or she'd kill him.

The neighbors heard the shot and immediately began flooding 9-1-1 with calls. One neighbor even looked out the door, hoping to get a glimpse of someone fleeing the house.

The police arrived and found Detective Stuckney coming into the house through the back door as if he'd arrived on the scene first. His shield displayed in plain sight, no one questioned his reason for being there.

✤✤✤✤✤

Across town, Earl had shot out the camera in his truck, hoping Eddy was watching and would flee, according to their plan.

Bubarcar had grabbed a duffel bag with one hand and pulled his service revolver with the other.

Earl sat stunned for a full moment before he understood the cop's intentions. The tiny space in the vehicle left little room for movement. Earl, however, was able to stun Bubarcar with his own weapon.

The first shots rang out and shattered the interior of the truck. Earl hit the surveillance camera, and then he hit the hydraulics, causing the car to jerk up and down. The gun flew from his hand, and he leaped from the truck, headed toward the cemetery. Stumbling through the park, he found the other members of the crew waiting. A light shined in his eyes as he heard the shot whiz past his ears.

"Surrender, monkey." Bubarcar laughed. "It's all over for you. You have the right to not get shot and face the courts for Gotti's murder."

Meanwhile tapes were appearing all over town.

Eve opened the mailbox and immediately recognized Eddy's handwriting. Ms. Maddy screamed in horror as she stared at the last images of Earl shooting out the camera in his car. The prosecutor's office barely observed the tapes and began marking them as exhibits for the courts. IAB (Internal Affairs Bureau) was all over the offices, trying to locate the rogue detectives on the numerous DVDs.

Buck opened the package, deciding whoever sent the parcel wanted him to view it. Carefully, he locked himself in the den and watched in stunned silence.

Later, a sinister grin plastered on his face, he sat across from Baldy, trying to understand how things had turned out better than any of them could have imagined. The plan hatched in his hospital room was to jam Earl up. Nothing they'd dreamed would have been as smooth as the hole he'd dug for himself.

"Yo, that nigga can't go to jail and escape death. If I got to get caught driving dirty, I'm gonna see that bitch dead," Baldy said.

Buck smiled as he picked up the handset to make a call. "Brian Hopewell, please," he whispered into the phone. "Just be patient, Baldy. Either karma or the devil has placed Earl where we want him. Have you ever known me to let a debt go unsettled? I learned from you that a coincidence to some is careful strategy, when you live the life we living. Stuckney never bothered us, and there were times during our reign when we couldn't help but crank up the heat on niggas. And even then we managed to stay below the radar. It wasn't by sheer luck. Brice Stuckney's parents owned the house next to the building where I lived with my grandmother. By the time they moved I was about ten, but I always remember that family. They were poorer than us, and the father was a mean son of a bitch that beat his wife. My grandmother used to patch up Mrs. Stuckney when her husband went to work. When Brice started working in the seventy-third precinct, I was one of the first people he approached about protection. Imagine that—he had a badge and a gun, but on our streets, even then, reputation protected you. It wasn't until he started moving up on the force that we lost touch." Buck laughed.

Baldy didn't want to ask any questions, but he had to know. "Gotti . . . was that coincidence or strategy?"

Buck didn't hesitate. "I can't take the blame for that, but Stuckney getting turned on to Earl was strategy."

Chapter 41

THE LIGHT

After several days of testifying about his own past misdeeds and crimes, the jurors were finally getting to see the meat of Earl's defense—dirty cops. These cops were not only forcing drug peddlers like Earl to pay bribes to them to conduct business, but as this video showed, the cops had stooped so low as to commit murder.

Hopewell had watched every second of each recording until he was stunned by the only video of Eddy's murder. Quickly, he called Buck for instructions.

Buck didn't change his mind. The plan was the same. "Offer him the best defense your staff can afford, and send me the bill when it's all over."

That morning in court Hopewell prayed his decision to leave Earl out of the loop would give him the emotions needed to outrage the jurors and the judge. It was the only wild card they had as proof Earl was a patsy in the entire coup.

As Earl continued to watch the video that showed one of the NYPD's finest killing his beautiful Eddy, he realized Eddy was still saving him, even after she was gone. He sat on the witness stand in tears, unable to wipe them due to his handcuffs. He hung his head in shame.

His attorney whispered to him to hold his head up high, adding, "They need to see your emotion."

Earl felt like he was cheating. He was winning because Eddy had died. The jurors wouldn't ever know the pure love he felt for her, and he was exploiting that love to win favor in the eyes of the jury. Stuckney had taken the only person in his life that loved him unconditionally.

Earl locked eyes with Stuckney before the detective bolted from the courtroom. They traded looks of hate with one another.

Stuckney knew his time was limited. It was time to cut his losses and run.

Once Earl had his emotions under control again, Hopewell said, "Mr. Clement, those tapes depicted a great deal of damning information. How does it make you feel to see those images for the first time?"

Earl didn't answer. He just raised his head, looked at his attorney, and then looked into the eyes of the jurors. The look on his face was answer enough.

"Mr. Clement, you alluded to the courts that you were just an intermediary for a larger team of dealers. Is it safe to say those dealers are members of the New York City Police Department?"

"Objection!" Colby yelled. "Defense attorney Hopewell is leading the witness and attempting to prejudice the jurors against an entire police department based on the misconduct of a few police officers."

"No, sir, I don't intend to do any such thing. My intentions are to make the direct connection between my client and the relationship between the detectives viewed on those videos."

Judge Dawson had completely lost control of this case. It started out being a simple murder trial, and now all kinds of other problems had developed. He wanted to throw in the towel and give this nightmare to someone else.

"Make your connection, Mr. Hopewell," Judge Dawson said. "My patience has grown short with you."

"What exactly was the nature of the business you did that required Officer Stuckney and his team to receive regular payments?"

"It was my responsibility to pick up drugs from their warehouse and distribute them to all the different locations specified in Officer Stuckney's earlier testimony."

"Are you attempting to tell this court you were a mule?"

"Exactly, except, my employers were the team of police you saw on those tapes. My employer was never Reginald 'Young Gotti' Tanner, as Detective Stuckney stated earlier."

"You've admitted to being a dealer, and you've implicated yourself in all kinds of crimes, so why are we even still in court?" Hopewell asked Earl. "Why didn't you just accept a plea? Either way, you are clearly going to jail for crimes you admitted committing."

"We're here not because I suddenly gained a conscience. I'm here because Detective Stuckney and his team murdered my wife. She was innocent to this game. He murdered her because I wouldn't continue to let him extort me. He murdered Reginald 'Young Gotti' Tanner and his family and tried to frame me. We're here because the prosecutor's office wrote off Eddy's death as another drug-related murder and refused to go after the true culprit."

Colby, his face pink, jumped to his feet and objected to Earl's entire testimony. He literally wanted to leap across the desk and slap Earl Clement out of the box.

As Colby yelled his objections, Earl shouted above him, "We're here because I'm trading my life for Eddy's voice. It can't bring her back, but it can certainly stop Stuckney and his team from doing this to anyone else."

Earl screamed at Colby, "You're a liar. The prosecutor's office is hiding the truth from this court. I'm not the first case brought to your office where Stuckney was extorting a dealer. Your excuses are always the same, starting with the police not being the one on trial, and moving to not having enough evidence. Well, you were provided with the evidence this time, but that still isn't enough."

It was the performance of a lifetime. Earl didn't hold back anything. He gave it all he had as he was snatched from the courtroom.

Hopewell was flabbergasted as his client screamed even after the courtroom doors closed behind him. There was no doubt now that this case would be declared a mistrial.

That night after Earl returned to his cell, he had the same dream he had been having for weeks—He sat in his cell crying over a limp corpse. She was screaming for him to do something, but he couldn't make out her words.

Earl leaped off his bed and looked around for any impending danger, but he was alone. No one was beside him or even near his cell. He sat on the floor and lowered his head into his lap. Earl decided he wouldn't sleep that night. He wouldn't allow himself to feel haunted by the same dreadful image or he might go insane.

"Yo, C.O., I need a shower," he called. "Crack my cell."

Earl gathered his supplies when he heard the familiar sound of the metal release, and the electronic hinges slid open.

"I can't live without you," he whispered to the ghost of Eddy as he showered. "You were the best part of me, and I let you get hurt. Were you crying because I've disappointed you? I am sorry, and I can't fix it. I was a coward. How do I go on without you? I don't want to fight anymore."

Earl had done everything in private that he could do to release the pressure on his mind and deal with the conflict he felt concerning Eddy's death. If only she could touch him or tell him she forgave him for not saving her from Stuckney.

"Why'd you go back?" he whispered after he returned to his cell. "You should have kept going until you were safe."

The dreams came again, except now he was seeing the faces of people he'd hurt over the years. Sasha Richards' battered image took over the beautiful space reserved for Eddy. He could almost feel the fear she was experiencing lying on the floor. As her image faded, it was replaced by the image of Baldy's daughter, stumbling backward as she tried to avoid Earl's gun.

Earl was crumbling under the pressure. He screamed, "Why the hell are you haunting me now? I don't need this stress. Leave me alone!"

Sweat poured off Earl as he leaped from his bed for the second time that night.

"Yo, nigga, shut up all that gotdamn screaming in there!" an inmate yelled. "Don't nobody want to hear all that shit!"

Earl figured he wouldn't be going back to sleep anytime soon that night. Whether he was found guilty or not guilty, he would always have to live with his memories.

Chapter 42

A CHANCE MEETING

"Jahson Holden, you're under arrest in connection with the murder of Sasha Richards. At this time you have the right to remain silent."

Buck was calm despite the number of officers in his foyer and walking through his home. He had been home from the hospital for months and he figured the police had finally come up with more evidence against him, although he couldn't imagine what it was. He was amicable and surprisingly docile.

Attorney Desiree Saunders pulled into the driveway just as the lead officer placed Buck into the squad car. "The processing won't take long," she told him. "Once your prints come back from Albany, you'll be up to see the judge, and there'll be a request for bail. The courts will grant whatever number seems befitting the case. Do you understand?" She winked.

"Yes, Ms. Saunders. Please, you shouldn't worry. I understand, and everything is going to be fine."

"I'm supposed to tell *you* not to worry, Buck," she whispered.

"OK, well, we won't worry together. How long do I have to wait for this process to begin?"

"Not much longer. Just give me a minute or two to show them what a black girl can do when she's mad and outraged."

❖❖❖❖❖

Buck's prints had finally come back after three hours, yet he was still sitting in a holding tank waiting to see the judge.

"Buck, listen, it seems the court is backed up, and I'm afraid you may have to be here until tomorrow morning."

"No problem," he told his attorney. "When you leave here please call Brenda and explain the situation. There's no point in her coming here, only to have to head back home. It won't matter to her that I'm OK. That woman will sit on that bench all night."

"Too late. She's already out front, but don't worry, I'll let her know everything is OK. You should consider yourself lucky that she loves you enough to sit out there, especially when you here for bullshit."

"Stop looking so upset," Buck said. "We knew I was a suspect for months now. At least I was free until they got their act together. We'll both be perfectly fine, as long as you pull it together," Buck said, offering encouragement to his attorney.

❖❖❖❖❖

Things went terribly wrong, so Buck was headed to Rikers Island on a warrant hold. GMDC Block 7 was his new address, until the courts could track down the payments of fines he'd made years earlier after his first release from jail.

Desiree Saunders was in rare form as she tracked down the data that declared her client had made the payments. Her next step was to find her client and get the hold lifted before his transfer to Rikers. Despite calling in favors, she couldn't get him back on the docket before Monday. He would have to spend the next three days there.

Buck soon felt the stress of a time so long ago as the bus rocked across the bridge separating the island from Queens. He felt the humiliation slipping into his crack-proof demeanor. The memories kept pulling at him, but he refused to surrender to them. There was no room for memories and weakness on the inside.

Buck settled into his cell just as visiting hours started. He listened to the names of prisoners being called to the gate.

"Clement . . . Earl Clement on the gate to the dance floor."

Buck's heart felt as if it would leap from his chest. In all the confusion of his arrest, he never thought he'd be placed on the same block as Earl.

Buck needed to get to a phone to inform Quinton about what was going on. As he headed to the phones, he stopped at the first familiar face he saw to get some answers. "Who's running the house, Slim?" he asked, offering him a pound.

"What you need, nigga? I got you. You my family."

"I need the jack for at least fifteen minutes."

"Well, I can help you with the questions you need answered."

Buck didn't bother to state the questions. He stood silently and waited for the answers.

"Yeah, that's the dread that shot you, nigga, and if your next question has anything to do with affiliation, that answer is no. We won't fuck with him in here."

Buck smiled, allowing his body language to speak volumes, along with the hate in his eyes. He didn't need to say what he wanted to do. All he needed was a good plan.

"All right, nigga, thanks for the message, but I still need the jack."

"No problem. It works the same here as in the street. Money talks, bullshit—"

"Will get your ass killed."

Buck got Quinton on the first try and explained everything that was going on inside.

Quinton misunderstood Buck's excitement as stress. "Damn! You don't need this, brother," he said. "It's a matter of three days and we can pull you out of there."

"Nah, then that means I got three days to work. You had better have my money when I get out too, and I don't take IOU's," Buck said, teasing.

Mentally Buck was fighting a war with himself, and the chance to make Earl suffer was the only soothing remedy to the ache. He could see Mia's trusting eyes as she died lying next to him. There was no way he could walk away without letting Earl see his face and feel the pain he had inflicted on others.

Later, Slim slid by Buck's cell. "Yo, Buck," he said, "I got what you need, if you need it."

"Nah, baby, but thanks. I just need a second to get my mind right. Let's keep on the low that I'm here."

"That's gonna be hard since half the niggas in here know Earl is here, and the other half knew you were coming before you did. Anyway, you want to do this . . . then I'm with you. Of course, I could use some of that bounty for my family, and a little for my case."

"I hear you," Buck answered, understanding that just because the scenery had changed didn't mean a damn thing when it came to money. In there money meant even more.

The energy in the house was charged. It was clear something was happening, and corrections didn't have a clue.

C.O. Birmingham had known the Baker Boys since high school. He could call all their names and had even run with the pack a bit when they'd first started hustling. Good sense and his mother's strong prayers led him to his job. But loyalty ran deep when you ran with friends like Buck. He knew Buck wouldn't ask for help directly, but the request would come, and he certainly wouldn't deny his friend.

That night, doubling over in pain, Buck shouted, "C.O., um, I need to see the doctor!"

"Yeah, all right. Give me a minute," Birmingham quickly replied. Instead of a two-man escort, Birmingham escorted his prisoner alone.

"Yo, you know?" Buck asked quietly as Birmingham walked him to the infirmary.

"Yeah, I know," Birmingham whispered. "And when you get back to the house you'll know."

Buck didn't crack a smile or turn to the C.O. The question had been asked, and the answer was given. All they needed to do now was stick to the script.

Sitting in the infirmary waiting area, Buck couldn't help but wish that he was back in his cell. The worst thing for Buck was waiting for someone else to do something he could've very well done himself. He wanted to be there to see the look on Earl's face, to hear his screams. But being off the block was probably the best place for him when things went down. Plus, his stomach pains were very real.

Fuck this, he thought as a stabbing pain settled him into his seat. This was the punishment he'd been forced to live with since being shot. When the stress was too thick, he had to deal with the constant knotting and rumbling in his stomach, but it was a small price to pay, compared to all his success.

Earl was awakened from his sleep by the rancid odor of piss. Someone must have missed the toilet and pissed on the floor. In an effort to kill the stench, he covered his nose, but the odor was too strong to deny. He began sniffing the air in search of its origin. It smelled like it was coming from his cell. Seconds later he saw a lit match fly into his cell as a figure cloaked in the shadows of the darkened hallways walked past, and suddenly a fire erupted on the floor in front of him. The smell had been an accelerant.

"Oh shit!" Earl yelled. Panicking, he backed away from the blaze, snatched the thin blanket off his mattress, and began beating at the fire. He realized his mistake too late, and the blanket quickly went up in flames in the center of the floor.

As the heat radiated in the little box and the flames raged, Earl couldn't move. "Fire!" he yelled, trying to get the attention of the C.O.'s on the floor as his pant leg caught on fire. The cell quickly filled with smoke and had him gagging and coughing.

The blaze continued to rise, and the neighboring cells began yelling as Earl's screams became more frantic and the stench of burning flesh filled the halls.

The fire rescue team rushed in to assist in putting out the blaze.

Earl had minor burns and could barely catch his breath from inhaling so much smoke. None of that stopped him from cursing in pain and frustration. "Blodeclaat muthafuckas trying to kill me. Fuck those bitches. What took you so fucking long to respond? Look at my hands and legs. I swear they better never let me out of here. I'll kill every last one of them muthafuckas."

"I see it didn't hurt your mouth none," a C.O. answered, annoyed at the ranting.

Had Earl not been caught up in the pain, he might have sensed the danger at his back. During Buck's escort back to his cell from the infirmary, he couldn't resist temptation when he saw Earl lying limp on the gurney, waiting for the ride to the hospital.

C.O. Birmingham distracted Earl's escort, allowing Buck to move closer to his nemesis. Buck leaned into Earl's sleeping face and lowered himself to his ear. "Wake up, coward," he said. "Don't you want to look at the man that has set your world on fire?"

Earl's lids danced, but his eyes wouldn't open. Buck knew he'd heard his voice. "When you wake up, you'll be looking for me, and I'll find you when I'm ready for you to see me."

Quickly Birmingham gathered Buck and ushered him back to the house, hoping that no one had noticed the little exchange between the inmates.

Chapter 43

THE HATE

"Yo, that nigga Earl is heading back here," Slim told Buck the next day. "I heard he got minor scarring and they're going to put him back in his cell. What's the plan?"

"That nigga gonna be looking for me, but I ain't ready to show him my face until the very last second. I want him to look over his shoulder, and when he turns back around, I'm going to be there waiting like a deadly serpent."

"Shit, be careful not to run that nigga to the psych ward before you poison him," Slim joked.

"You don't know him like I do. He'll kill himself before he goes telling someone all the shit he's done to hurt people. He really is a coward."

Buck imagined the weapon he'd need to end Earl's life, and he was determined to make it his way. Slowly he worked the thick plastic, manipulating it to the specifics in his mind. He measured it to fit into the palm of his hand, and then went back to the tedious scraping. The shank had to be perfect, and he didn't trust anyone to do this with the same patience. It was a quiet obsession and he nursed it while waiting for his chance to kill.

Buck held the shank in his hand and began moving with it as though it were a part of him. He fashioned a holster out of torn strips of sheets, and kept it hidden beneath his shirtsleeve. With a hard flick of his wrist, the blade slid into his palm.

Quick, short jabs would do the trick if he just wanted to maim. However, Buck was beyond hurting Earl. His intention was to get close and rip an opening from his navel to his heart. He wanted to see the fear in Earl's eyes as he stepped in front of him. He wanted to watch confusion change into pain. He wanted to see Earl take his last breath.

"Yo, *B*, you gonna have to see the dread today," Slim told Buck. "He back, and the only meal that is optional is breakfast."

Buck nodded but didn't say anything. He wanted to stay focused. His eyes were constantly looking for the best opportunity to make his move. Birmingham had offered to isolate the situation, but Buck declined. This was his battle, and he certainly didn't want anyone else in the middle of it. Slim practically begged for the chance to murk Earl, but Buck wouldn't give him the OK.

"Slim, you been nothing but stand-up in your efforts, and I'm going to see that you get your share of the bounty regardless, but this I have to do myself. You understand?"

It was Slim's turn to nod. "Yo, when you done with that, I know where to hide it," Slim said, referring to the weapon he was certain Buck was holding.

"Thanks, but I don't want you catching no come-back from my work. I have to start it and finish it all the way out. No offense, but I can't let anyone catch a charge for trying to protect me."

Slim understood the lengths Buck was willing to go to ensure the right outcome. He respected Buck's ability to think everything through down to the last detail. However, he wasn't sure Buck was ready to stand so close to someone he once called a friend and murder him. He wasn't questioning Buck's strength, but he knew men like Buck didn't normally put in their own work. They paid niggas like him to do it for them.

Once Earl was back on the block, he could feel the danger in the air. He could feel it creeping up behind his back. But every time he found the courage to look over his shoulder, no one was there. He felt the tremors coming back as if it was once again his first day in court. He knew he needed to pray, but he didn't know how.

"C.O., I need to go to services," he yelled from his cell.

"Yeah, all right. Let me see if there's anyone to bring you there," Birmingham answered.

Earl waited about fifteen minutes before he walked to the bubble to see the officer face to face. The inmates who were cool with Birmingham called him Alabama. It was their way of showing respect and being familiar.

"Alabama, you forgot about me," Earl called out. "I'm trying to go to services."

"Nah, dread, chow is up in about twenty minutes, and you know it's chaos right now."

"No problem. Do I need an escort, or can I just make that move on my own?"

"Here, take the pass and see the officer when you get down there." Birmingham pointed to the stairwell.

Buck waited in the hallway, listening to the exchange. It was an opportunity he couldn't let pass. Birmingham walked away from his post, yelling for another officer on staff to cover for him.

Physically Buck was prepared to kill Earl. He was fully recovered and ready to get revenge. Emotionally, though, he was all over the place. He couldn't let the rage swirling inside him get the better of him. He took deep breaths, trying to calm the negative energy.

He counted his steps as he made his way to the chapel area, where he knew he would find Earl. He took notice of the drab walls. He thought about everything except the thing he was about to do.

Earl heard a commotion in the hallway and quickly turned to see what was happening. He heard shouts and screams, and knew things were becoming violent. He panicked when he realized there was no way he could defend himself in a melee. He felt his tremors rising again as he turned, hurrying toward the chapel.

It happened too fast. Buck was walking toward him, practically running to meet him. Earl wanted to turn and run away, but his feet were rooted to the floor. He felt a rush of fear as he stared dumbstruck at the man he thought he'd killed.

"Fuck you," Earl whispered as he stood still, allowing Buck to trap him between the battle at his back and the one coming straight for him. His courage finally kicked in, and he headed for the blur coming toward him.

The weapon appeared from nowhere. Earl hadn't seen it, but he felt it instantly. He felt it digging into the folds of his flesh. He felt it turn and rip his stomach into two. And after taking a quick, deep breath, he felt the pain of trying to breathe.

Buck quickly stepped away, staring at the confusion in Earl's eyes. He waited a moment longer and saw Earl drop to the floor.

Earl's tremors had finally stopped. He was on his way to be with Eddy forever. The nightmares would no longer haunt him.

"Buck, thank you," Earl whispered.

Buck was shook as he leaped the stairs two at a time, heading back to the block. He needed Birmingham to be on his post so that he could head directly to the showers and get to the spot he'd chosen to stash his shank.

Luckily Birmingham was on post, and he quickly escorted Buck to the showers. Buck shoved his weapon in the wall close to a pipe and stood under the running showerhead. He let the water wash away his hostility.

Slim saw Buck heading back to his cell. "Are you good?"

"I will be. I've always been a soldier first, and a leader second."

"Lockdown!" the C.O. yelled.

The deputy warden stormed through the floor, cursing out her staff and the inmates. "You are playing for real!" she yelled. "There is movement on this floor, and I called for a lockdown. You over there, sitting on your ass. That means you aren't working. That can only mean your ass got to go."

The house was quiet, trying to understand the reason for a lockdown. Things had happened too quickly for the drama to filter through the building.

"This ain't child's play!" the warden yelled. "I got a man dead. There are at least two wounded on the same floor. If you can't help, just get the fuck out the way. Anybody come up missing and y'all can't account for him, I promise to sign the form taking your jobs."

Four hours passed and no one left the Island. The C.O.'s and all visitors were stuck, waiting for an accurate count of the inmates. The kitchen, law library, the clinic, and all other facilities closed immediately.

Buck's palms were sweating, and his leg kept shaking. He'd just committed murder, and they were looking for him. They were looking for his weapon, and he didn't know if he could stand the pressure. The cells were tossed, and shit littered the halls. They were confiscating all kinds of contraband. Tempers flared out of control. Inmates were bitter at the violation of their things.

"It's time to go," Buck whispered to himself as his cell was tossed.

The next day Buck stood at the table beside his attorney, waiting for the judge to set the amount for his bail.

As Buck walked out of court after his bail was paid, he stood shoulder to shoulder with Baldy.

"We can rest," Baldy said. "Let it go. You're a free man, and all debts are paid. She can rest, and you can too." Baldy spoke softly, away from the rest of the crew.

Buck looked at his friend and wished he were alone to release his stress.

He wanted to put it all behind him, but he couldn't let go. He still tossed over making things right for Mia. She'd trusted him, and he wasn't able to save her. "I just need to know if she can forgive me," Buck said.

"What you asking me to do, Buck? You want me to lie to you and tell you that I don't feel the same pains you do? Damn it, I do, but because I'm her father, I can tell you she loved you. She's forgiven you, because there was nothing you could do except die or kill the bitch that killed her. You completed the job. Now let that bitch burn in hell where the fuck he belongs."

Quinton saw Baldy and Buck talking and reacted to the exchange before they could start yelling at one another. Neither of them knew how to handle anguish, and getting violent in front of the courthouse wasn't the right place to let go of the drama.

"Danny and Dave were talking shit last night," Quinton said quickly. "They want to catch that ass-whupping on the basketball court."

"Twin, I heard you anxious to catch the beat-down of a lifetime," Baldy yelled.

"Whatever. Come see me when you ain't in your slip and slides," Danny responded. "We won't mind giving you a good workout, old man."

"I hear you talking, but you ain't said shit. You know where the court's at. Let's do it," Buck yelled.

Anissa stood in the middle of all the macho bull and didn't dare encourage a drop of the drama. Instead she did everything to discourage the rough basketball game she knew was coming.

"I don't give a damn how fucked you all get, take your asses to the emergency room. Don't hang around my house whining about a scrap, a bump, a scratch, or blood. I ain't cleaning shit, I ain't stitching shit, and I ain't fixing you greedy muthafuckas nothing to eat, so eat while y'all outside," she said, seething at their idiotic tradition.

"Come on, baby, you got to do your part," Quinton said. "When we get banged up, you get revenge by stitching us up."

"Damn all that! I will not be listening to 'That hurt' and 'That sting' half the night. Do what y'all usually do after the game. Go somewhere and get drunk. Pass out in your cars and wait until the sun comes up to drive home."

"Dang, Anissa, you used to love me. What happened?" Buck whimpered.

"Call Brenda and I'll tell you," she answered, walking away.

"It seems to me you just told him," Danny said and laughed.

"Mind your business, Danny," Anissa told him, "because I ain't but two seconds from calling 'what's her face.' Not that stripper chick either."

The lights of the city shined brightly as the basketball hit the blacktop. Buck stood on the sideline, gasping for air, a bottle of water at his side. Dave and Danny were waiting for the rebound.

Despite the hour, the park was packed, and old heads from the hood were out in full force. Favorite tunes pumped through the speakers of one of the vehicles sitting on the block. Chicks walked back and forth, strutting their stuff and hanging on to anyone who looked available.

"You ready, baby? Quinton yelled. "I'm coming, so you better get out of my way." He pulled up short, letting go of the ball.

"What the fuck was that, nigga? I thought you wanted to play?" Dave yelled when Quinton missed the shot. "You out here acting like you scared. Stop trying to play it safe. Come see me, nigga."

The crowd roared at the banter between the men. They knew it was all in fun. They'd seen many a basketball brawl between these men.

When the crew arrived back at Quinton's spot beat and battered, Anissa cursed so much that Quinton, the twins, Baldy, and Buck couldn't stop laughing.

"Ahh, Anissa, you doing that on purpose," Baldy said when Anissa was especially rough cleaning one of his scrapes.

"I told you to go to the damn ER, but, no, you in my living room with a lump on your head the size of a golf ball, and you whining. Shut the hell up and put this on your big head."

Danny looked at his twin before he jerked his head toward the door. He didn't want to think how mad she would be by the time she got around to bandaging them.

"Don't even think about it. Y'all woke me up, so now suffer the abuse. Muthafuckas can't just get drunk and talk shit. Y'all got to fight each other on the basketball court."

Anissa held out a glass of water and a Valium for Buck.

"What the hell is that?" Buck asked.

"What you care? Just take it and go to sleep before you fall down."

"That must be the good shit!" Quinton yelled, holding an ice pack in his hand.

"Girl, please, those fools are all over my house," Anissa said into the phone. "They got my shit looking like a makeshift hospital. Old muthafuckas were down there crying about the pain."

Brenda didn't say a word. She held the phone to her ear, listening to Anissa gripe.

"What time you coming to see about that man?" Anissa asked slyly.

"I'm not confronting that man in front of his crew. He will embarrass me just to save face."

Anissa was silent. She knew Brenda well, and she knew Brenda wouldn't want anyone telling her what to do.

"You there? I'm here running my mouth, and you're not even trying to help me," Brenda said.

"What am I supposed to say? You've got it all figured out," Anissa countered.

"Don't tell him I'm coming, and don't let him leave. At least, if we have an audience, I won't be worried about him killing me."

"Girl, please, Buck is a gentle giant. A nigga will catch hell, but you are safe with him. I guarantee it."

❖❖❖❖❖

The sound of lips smacking and forks scraping across plates filled the house. Even Mifaith was enjoying farina between the pieces of meat her uncles sneaked to her when Anissa turned her back.

The doorbell slowed down the momentum of their meal.

"Buck, get the damn door. You closer," Anissa yelled.

"I'm tired of fighting with you, woman," Buck yelled back. "I've been fighting with you too long. Quinton, I'm glad you home now. She can order your ass around a little while."

When Buck opened the door and saw Brenda there, he blocked the threshold, waiting for her to speak.

"Hello, Jahson, how are you?" Her voice shook.

Buck didn't answer. He just glared at her until she began fidgeting.

Slowly she backed away until Anissa stepped into the foyer with Mifaith on her hip. Excited to see her Aunt Brenda, Mifaith bounced and squealed.

"Brenda, you better come in before this girl jumps out of my arms." Anissa pushed Buck out of the way and ushered her friend into the house. "Forgive Buddha over there. He ain't finished eating yet."

"Yeah, well, that might be only one of his issues," she said, pointing at her swollen belly.

Anissa nodded. She was glad everyone was still in the house. It might just save her and Brenda from being killed. "Come on, girl, the invalids are in my dining room eating all my damn food," she yelled, pushing Brenda along.

Baldy jumped out of his seat to greet Brenda.

She smiled, knowing he was trying to offer her some support.

"Hey, sister, long time no see. I've missed you," he said.

Antagonizing Buck wasn't his intention, but that's exactly what happened.

The twins shrugged their shoulders, silently asking each other what was going on. Neither had an answer, but they were happy to see Brenda's face.

"Come sit between the two best-looking men in the room," Dave teased Brenda.

Scooting across the floor, they made room for her.

Danny couldn't help himself. He loved the anger he saw in Buck's eyes. "Damn, girl, you looking swollen around the back. I mean, have you been exercising your glutes?" Danny snickered.

Buck didn't dare say a word or he'd explode.

Anissa didn't want the bull to break up her china, so she took control of the room. "Quinton, you remember Brenda, right?" she asked, hoping to get his help in calming the situation.

"Yeah. Hey, Lady B, how's it going?"

"Good," she answered, afraid to meet anyone's eyes except Mifaith's.

Baldy came back to the table with a fully loaded plate and a glass of orange juice for Brenda. "I don't know what you eat," he said, "but I figured I couldn't go wrong if I left off the pork."

"Thanks," she answered nervously.

Mifaith didn't wait to be offered any food. She stretched until she was close enough to Brenda's plate to snatch a piece of toast.

The table erupted with laughter as they watched her hide the food from Anissa, who flew over to take it from her. "Girl, you greedy, just like your daddy."

"Don't blame that on me. Buck is the one that started her stealing food," Quinton joked.

"Don't blame me because my godbaby knows what she wants."

The gibberish coming out of Mifaith changed the direction of the conversation. Everyone except Brenda and Buck relaxed.

"All right, you came here just to look at me, or you wanted to make sure I wasn't dead?" Buck asked.

"Neither. I came to tell you I was pregnant before you found out from Anissa," she answered, ashamed.

"Yeah, well, that's nice. Tell your man, congratulations. I wish you all the best."

Buck left the room and the house before Brenda could recover.

"Just give him a chance to come around," Baldy said. "He's mad, but he'll get over it soon enough."

"You told me he wouldn't accept me if I tried to come back. Well, I guess you were right."

"I didn't want to be right. Don't let him bully you, or you'll be sorry. He'll run all over you. Buck can be a bully, but more than that, he has to respect you."

"I'm not fighting him into talking to me. I came here knowing it could go either way with him, and I'll go home knowing I tried."

"I was listening, and I got to tell you, Brenda, you're full of shit," Anissa said. "You were hoping Buck would just look at you and forgive you for leaving him when he needed you the most."

Quinton was sitting in a chair listening while the twins sat on the floor. Everyone knew Anissa was lethal with her tongue, and they also knew that she was partial when it came to Buck, because of their long friendship.

"All right, Nissa, this isn't your fight. It's between Brenda and Buck," Quinton interjected.

"You're absolutely right, but it's no different than you leaving me and coming back. You had the same entitled look on your face when you returned. But you weren't owed shit, and neither is she. A sincere apology might work instead of the pompous attitude," she told Brenda.

Brenda was angrier than she ever remembered being in her life as she listened to her friend call her out. "Anissa, I explained to you why I had to leave. I thought you understood, and if I had known you were so against me coming back into his life, I wouldn't have bothered coming over."

"I heard every word you said. I sympathized with you, and I was honest with you. I explained to you it was wrong to leave him while he was still fighting for his life. It was unfair to walk away knowing that eventually you'd have to come back and tell him you were pregnant. More importantly, is he really supposed to trust you now, after everything that's happened?"

The twins had been quiet as they watched the exchange between the women in the house. Danny knew Dave was about to speak, and he wished he could shut him up with mind control. As far as Danny was concerned, Anissa was right.

"Anissa, I hear you, but we all know how Buck can be," Dave said. "He's mad now, but he won't be forever, and he'll want the chance to be a father and husband," Dave said, trying to soften the blow of Anissa's words.

"That's exactly what everyone is counting on … that he won't be mad too much longer," Anissa said. "But he deserves more than that. He is owed an honest apology, or at least a good enough excuse. She left, so she should be licking his boots to get back in his good graces, not the other way around."

"All right, Nissa, I'm sorry," Quinton said, thinking the venom of her words was really directed at him. "I left because I didn't know what else to do. I felt like a failure. I wasn't sure I could be the man you wanted me to be. I didn't know if I could be a good enough father to Mifaith. There were a host of other reasons, but mainly it was fear."

"Man, please, this isn't about you. I don't want Buck's feelings hurt anymore. No matter what you might think, he's the only one that kept the promises you all made. While you were away swatting flies, he was here making sure Mifaith and I were all right. He still checks on Chaka's kids regularly. Meanwhile you muthafuckas have retreated to whatever dismal lives you lead. I want to protect my friend because I know I can count on him. Forgive me that I don't care about hurting your feelings, but I want someone for him that he can count on when it matters."

Baldy thought about everything Anissa had said. He wished he could come up with a reason to fight her arguments, but she was right. Buck did deserve someone that would be there for him when it mattered most, but that still didn't mean Brenda wasn't the woman for him. "Anissa, I understand everything you're saying, but we can't choose the person for him. He chose Brenda, so now we have to find a way to get him to hear her out before they both lose out," he said.

"I'm with that, but you better not hurt him. I'll kidnap you and beat you to a pulp," she said seriously.

"I'm not so sure you don't want to hurt me now," Brenda said, "especially after hearing how you really feel."

"I still love you, but I was angry. You still my sister," Anissa said, tears in her eyes.

Danny felt his phone vibrating before he heard the silly chime. Staring at the caller ID, he immediately recognized the number. He headed for the porch to have some privacy.

Dave's phone rang next, and soon Quinton's phone rang too.

Anissa looked at Baldy, hoping for some answers, but he couldn't offer any.

When Baldy's phone rang, he immediately knew the caller without looking at the number. It was Buck's ringtone. "Yeah, I'm headed out. I'll meet you there," Baldy answered cryptically after picking up the call.

"What the hell is going on now?" Anissa demanded.

The men didn't want to tell her, but they knew she wouldn't take silence or no for an answer.

As the cars headed down the highway one after another, Anissa and Brenda led the pack with Mifaith in the car seat enjoying the outing.

"Shit, Anissa, I could have stayed at the house with Mifaith. Me going isn't going to do anything but add more tension," Brenda said.

"This is what I was talking about. He needs to see that you are willing to be there when he needs you. He can't be afraid you'll run," Anissa answered smoothly.

"I'm not so sure this is going to be the right time to be in his path."

"Buck is a brute, but he is also a pussycat. You will understand the depth of his loyalty after this. Just trust me."

Chapter 44

PROMISES

Petra had turned her home into a shrine to the memory of Chaka and her brothers. Pictures, candles, crosses, and Bibles filled the house. Buck wondered when things had gone so terribly wrong for Petra. He noticed the sadness in Petra's eyes, and something else was there too. She was a bit off, talking as if Chaka might walk through the door at any moment.

The children sat quietly, looking at him with pleading eyes, silently begging him to take them out of the house. Buck knew he couldn't leave them. No matter how miserable his life would be without Brenda, he had to take care of his godchildren. They needed him, and he needed them.

Petra had been feeling guiltier than ever, and she needed a break. She was happy to see Buck.

"Petra, let me take the kids for a couple days. It'll give you some time to think about your life and where you want to go from here." Buck knew she needed professional help, but he didn't know how well the idea might be received. He hoped she would be OK until he could come up with a tactful way of suggesting it.

"You know you can always come to get them, Buck. They love you, and Chaka would want them to spend time with his brothers."

"OK, I'll take them for the weekend. We can hang out, eat pizza, watch movies, and play video games."

CJ was relieved to know they were leaving, if only for a couple days. He didn't care if all they did was hang out on the porch. It was better than the misery their mother offered at home.

After the kids were settled in Buck's car, Chanice waited patiently for Buck to drive off, so she could tell him the drama they'd been facing lately.

"Mommy hardly ever comes out of the basement now," she told him. "Grandma said it's her own personal tomb. What does that mean, Uncle Buck?"

"It means she's sad."

"Sometimes she screams at the top of her voice and she doesn't stop for hours," CJ said.

Buck was nervous. He didn't know how to respond. Quickly he tried to change the subject. "Let's play punch buggy. Every time you see a buggy, you punch someone softly and call it."

"Like this? Punch car!" CJ yelled, banging Buck's arm.

"Yeah. Just don't hit me so hard next time," Buck said, pretending to be hurt.

❖❖❖❖❖

Forty minutes later the kids were playing arcade games while Buck was watching the pizzeria's TV, waiting for pizza to arrive. He saw Petra's house on a breaking news story.

"A single mother of two has barricaded herself and her children inside her home," the reporter stated. "She has fired several shots inside the house, and the neighbors believe she might be suicidal."

"Petra used to be a good friend and neighbor," one neighbor stated, "but her family has suffered a great deal of tragedy. We just hope the kids are OK."

"*What tragedy?*" the reporter asked.

"*A while back her husband was murdered, and after that, her brothers were killed. It's been nothing but funerals for those poor people. Sometimes at night you can hear her screaming. It's like she's begging for hell to swallow her too."*

Buck didn't stay long enough to hear the rest of the broadcast. He piled the kids back into his car and called Baldy.

Before he could ask for help, his living room was crowded with the family that was always there for him.

"Has anyone told the police that Petra is home alone?" Anissa asked.

"I didn't know what to do," Buck answered, irritated. "Shit, I've never been in this predicament before."

Danny and Dave took the kids into the game room to keep them busy playing video games.

"All right, Buck, Petra trusts you. Maybe you should go to the house," Quinton suggested.

"OK, then what the fuck am I supposed to do? Stand around with the rest of the muthafuckas trying to see inside?"

"No, asshole. See if you can help. Try to talk her into coming out. No one wants to see her hurt, and if I go to the house that won't help at all."

"Damn that I can't help feeling lucky she let my ass out of there alive with the kids. I knew something was wrong. She was weirder today than usual. Now you're trying to send me back over there to be killed. Fuck you! My promise was to watch out for the kids, and I'll protect them with my life, but that bitch is crazy. I ain't fucking with her."

"You want to explain to those kids why you didn't help their mother when it mattered?" Brenda asked.

"Did you just say something? I know you are not talking to me about being there when it matters. God forgive me, but I didn't think you understood the concept."

Brenda had a smart remark prepared, but decided against it. Instead she sat in the chair glaring at him, hoping he had enough sense not push her any further.

The phone rang, killing the staring contest between Brenda and Buck. Buck answered. It was Petra's mother.

"Petra has finally lost her entire mind," she said. "She's been shooting at the street from the attic window. I've been calling, but no one is answering the phone. I don't know if the children are OK."

"The kids are with me," Buck said. "I picked them up for the weekend. We were in the pizza parlor when I saw the news break. Since then everyone has been keeping them busy."

"Oh my God! Buck. I'm so glad they didn't see it. I don't know how I would explain. I'm going to speak with the police now," she said and quickly hung up.

Petra knew the pain she felt had nothing to do with being psychotic. Guilt was robbing her of a good life. Instead of facing the pain, she played tricks with herself. She imagined Chaka alive and well, all of them living together as a family should—with love. She remembered the moments when they loved so much, they shared one thought. In the beginning her memories helped her move forward and function, but the guilt was now a cloud engulfing her slowly.

The hysteria started slowly in the privacy of her bedroom. The fits of tears and long periods of irritation wouldn't subside. Each time she remembered their lives together, her screams became louder. When the anguish became too much for her to bear and she could no longer continue with her normal life, she fled to the basement.

Her mother called the basement a tomb for the living dead. The words held more truth than Petra could ever share.

Petra knew that her craziness was punishment for her poor choices, and her death was the only way to end the pain. Her children could no longer remedy the pain. If she entered a room, they rushed to leave. If she screamed for them, they hid. If there was an issue to be handled, they talked only to their grandma and Buck.

Back and forth she rocked, smiling and talking to him as if he were sitting next to her. Eventually the one memory that made Petra's pain unbearable surfaced as it always did.

We were in the living room celebrating, laughing, enjoying CJ's cake and telling silly jokes. Chanice was dancing on her father's feet and giggling happily, in love with her daddy. Then the vibrating of Chaka's phone interrupted the fun. He'd promised to stay, but he was preparing to leave.

Without warning Petra, caught up in the memory, leaped from the rocker and fired a shot out the window. The neighbors heard the blast and immediately called 9-1-1. People dove to the ground, unsure of the direction of the shots.

The police arrived, but the shots didn't stop. With every painful memory, Petra fired another shot.

The anger subsided after a while, and she finally sat back down in her chair. She decided there was no way she was ever going to be rid of guilt for the deaths she had caused. Her only option was to leave her children behind. Silently she thanked God for Buck and his foresight to take the children.

Chapter 45

BUCK AND BRENDA

Buck set up the grill in the yard since everyone had come over. Anissa and Brenda were in the kitchen preparing meats and making salads. Petra's kids had both fallen asleep, and the twins were in the den playing video games.

Brenda could feel the nervousness returning. Her stomach churned, and her head hurt from fighting the stress. She just didn't know how things were going to turn out with Buck, and now with Petra and the kids, there wasn't time to talk about it.

"It's a losing battle," Anissa said when she noticed her friend's distress. "Let it go until he takes care of business."

Brenda turned to look at Anissa. Standing in the kitchen, she wanted to curse her and she wanted to question their friendship, but that would only set her off again on another tirade. She had to talk, or she was going to scream.

"Is he ever going to say anything to me at all? I've been here all damn day. He's barely looked in my direction. Fuck this! I'm leaving."

"Brenda, you're real good at running. Try standing still and facing him. You may not like his terms, but at least you confronted the issues. Trust two things. Buck is very much a man, but he loved you once, so he'll hear you out, if for no other reason than what he felt for you. Second, he is a Dozen, and as his woman, you had better learn what that means."

"He loved me *once*? What the fuck is that supposed to mean? I'm standing here with swollen ankles, my stomach churning from all this confusion, and I have to wait for his terms? Sounds to me, Anissa, like you're telling me he'll always choose them first."

"Do you want some very good advice, not as your friend, but just the truth?" Anissa asked, hoping that Brenda would say no.

"Fuck it. I got the feeling I'm gonna need to hear this if I make a decision to stay here any longer."

"They are the Baker Boys, and no fussing or cussing is gonna change that. All those men in there know is the brotherhood they shared from their childhood. Even Baldy can't come between that bond, and Buck loves him like he would a father. Their success depends on their friendship, their brotherhood, and their loyalty. I'm standing here telling you that Chaka almost destroyed their existence when he died, but they found a way to reconnect. I don't know if has anything to do with the secrets they share, but I do know it's the love and respect. There are five men I trust with my life, and all except Baldy is a Baker Boy. I know where I fit, and you will have to learn where you fit in the order of things. He'll love you with his heart, but he is who he is. Don't try to change him, or you'll lose in the long run."

"What the hell is that supposed to mean? If I can't be first, I won't be next in line to a boys' club." Brenda's eyes blazed, and her nostrils flared.

"Then you may as well take your swollen ankles and queasy stomach to the car, and don't come back, because you will lose."

"You're telling me if I ask him to walk away for me and his child, he won't do it?"

"You heard what the fuck I said. I'm done holding your hand. If you ask him to let go, he won't stay with you. He'll see it in another way entirely."

"How can you say he won't leave? He isn't Quinton. He isn't, and he can't be." Brenda was starting to freak out.

"Take your chances, sister, and let me know how that works out for you,"

Anissa answered calmly.

Brenda wasn't expecting the calm. She had expected a challenge, maybe a little prove-me-wrong attitude. Standing in the foyer, she locked eyes with her friend and knew she was telling her the truth.

"I'm not made like you, Anissa. I can't hold down the fort while he discovers himself. I lost my mind just thinking I might have to suffer losing him when he was shot. I don't have that kind of staying power."

"You were right. Buck isn't Quinton, so I'm not exactly sure that he won't walk away. However, I'm certain that he'll be committed to his promises from the first day to his last breath."

Buck had heard half of the women's conversation and had expected Brenda to leave after her admission. Bucks' family was the men he surrounded himself with since he was seven. The drugs were only one entity, and they'd all made enough to walk, but Brenda would never understand he belonged to something bigger than himself.

Anissa knew Buck had heard every word they'd said. She could tell by the sadness in his eyes as he entered their space. "Who did you leave in charge of the grill?" she asked.

"Anyone brave enough to go near the fire is on grill." Buck laughed.

"Oh shit. Buck, you play too much. Get out my way, fat boy, before we are forced to eat only salad." Anissa slid past Buck and turned back to wink at Brenda. Silently she prayed they would find a happy medium. Suddenly she realized she had been hard on someone she called a friend. She hoped that no matter what Buck and Brenda's outcome, they could still be close.

"Tell me it's not true. Jahson, please tell me you won't stay if I ask you to leave," Brenda said once they were alone.

"How do you want me to answer that? I could lie and hang on to you for a little while longer."

"I can't raise a family like this, wondering if you're going to come home or if you're dead somewhere."

Buck looked at Brenda. He stared into her eyes, hoping she could read the words before he said them. He didn't want to hurt her, but she had to know the man she was getting. "Brenda, you can't make me into the man you want me to be. It doesn't work like that, no more than I can turn you into Anissa."

Brenda had reached her boiling point. He was actually telling her he wouldn't leave. "I'm pregnant, and not by some mysterious man! By you. I need an honest answer. Am I going to be able to count on you?"

"I've never been anything but honest with you, so you can't come at me like that. I'll be the best father you've ever met. I'll support you financially, and I'll respect you regardless, but I can't be with you if you expect me to leave the crew." Buck spoke softly, but the meaning of his words came through loud and clear.

His words shocked her into an unbelievable tailspin. "What did you just say to me?"

"I can't trust you, *B*," Buck said. "You left me lying in the hospital. I was dead to everyone in the world, except the people that loved me. That included you, and you walked away knowing I needed you."

"Fuck you! I was afraid. I saw all those tubes and I saw my life without you, and I left you before you could leave me."

Buck wasn't as thick as he pretended to be. He understood her fear. He understood her wanting to be number one, but she didn't understand him. "You made a choice, and I lived through it. You will too." He turned to leave the room.

"Nigga, you stupid if you think that's how this conversation is going to end. You telling me I made a choice. It's not that cut-and-dry. You making a decision to be a street urchin, and I love you anyway. It goes against everything I've ever believed in. And I'm standing here, and you tell me you can't be with me?" She choked.

This wasn't the couple's first argument, and he knew how straightforward she could be with her emotions, but he wasn't giving in this time. Being afraid wasn't enough. He'd heard the stress in her voice, but his feet were planted firmly. "*B*, stop yelling. That's not going to change my mind. It's just going to be very embarrassing for us both later."

"You're absolutely right, and I won't embarrass myself. I've already done enough of that by coming back here. I should have kept going, and then I wouldn't know how you really felt."

Before Buck realized it, he was in Brenda's face. He was seething, and the words of his hurt rolled out of his mouth. "You're very selfish, *B*. You want me to be who you want me to be. You want me on your terms. You want me to do as Brenda says, but you walked away from me. Now I'm cementing the deal. You slammed the door in my face and all that. You didn't even have the nerve to tell me. You let your moms tell me to stop calling. I'm doing you one better. I'm telling you to your face—Fuck you, *B*. Go home. You ain't ready for me."

"What is there to be ready for? A corpse? I don't want a dead baby's daddy. I want a man that knows the meaning of mistakes and forgiveness."

Quinton was the first to enter the house after hearing the shouting. Danny and Dave followed closely behind. They'd heard Brenda screaming, but Buck had responded in kind, and that meant he was beyond his boiling point.

Buck was an absolute gentleman, and women loved his sensitivity because they rarely if ever had to see the hate inside him. He almost never showed it. Brenda had begged him to tell her something, so he had revealed all his emotions to her, uncut.

Quinton felt obligated to stop things before they went any further. "All right, Brenda, you had your say. Let him cool off and think about it before you do or say something you can't take back. Anissa," Quinton called, "come get Brenda."

"Hell no, and y'all get the fuck out of there before they both whip your ass. I'm a nurse, not a fucking referee. Let them box. Maybe he'll learn some respect, and she'll learn some too."

Dave and Danny laughed at her response. It was as appropriate as they could imagine. Buck was a killer, and he was meaner than most when it came to loyalty, but to Brenda they knew he'd cave. That was part of what made him different than the rest of them.

Quinton walked back out to Anissa, looking for some help. Instead he got a look of disinterest. "What's up?" he asked as she began playing with Mifaith.

"Not my business, and I'm staying the fuck out of it. Earlier today you thought I was signifying when I was telling Brenda about Buck. You forgot a few things. We have years together, a child, and a commitment. They're struggling. It's all about respect and control. She'll learn not to bully him."

Quinton laughed at the idea of anyone bullying Buck into anything.

"You can stop laughing, because she wants him to walk away from you, from the Dozen, and from everything he knows, to be with her." As she suspected, the smile disappeared, and an awkward look of confusion replaced it.

"The only thing stronger than us is love, Nissa. He may decide to walk away. Think about it. He may just step. He suffered the greatest loss two different times. Maybe we need to think about letting him go."

"You dumber than she is, if you think Buck is ever gonna walk away from the Dozen. While you were away, he could have, and not one of you would have dared to stop him. He could have taken everything, but instead he stood by his promise. He dug deep and worked three times as hard for the missing links of you and Chaka. He has taken care of every detail. He could leave, but he won't stay away."

"I'll accept that, Nissa, but what does that have to do with the fight they're waging in there?"

"It simply means, every time she can't get her way, she can't run. And he can't make everything about you and them. That's what it means. They have to fight this war until they can come to some suitable agreement."

A silent argument had ensued between Buck and Brenda. Buck sat in his favorite lounger, and Brenda stomped back and forth.

Chanice was the first to notice the quiet when she woke up and walked into the room. She sat next to her uncle. Only seconds later, CJ followed with his head down, looking sad.

"The last time my dad and mommy fought he never came back," Chanice said. "Is that going to happen to you, Uncle Buck?"

Brenda's heart stopped. She felt a sense of panic as CJ crawled into Buck's arms and held on to him.

"Nah, Uncle Buck's gonna live long enough to see you grow up and marry some ugly big-head boy," Buck said.

"That's nasty. She don't want to marry no boys. Then she gonna fight with him, and I'm gonna have to beat him up," CJ said.

Brenda was undone by Chanice's observation. It rocked her to the soles of her feet, and she quickly moved out of the room. Struggling, she thought about the words Chanice had used. Maybe Buck was right. Maybe she was being selfish. But he owed her more than the misery he was offering.

Climbing the stairs, she headed for his bedroom and away from the biggest fight in her life. *Can I walk away from him and never come back?* she wondered. *Does he really want me to go?*

Brenda heard laughter filtering through the house. Despite the argument, Buck had transformed himself to be a great uncle.

Will my child miss out on that because I'm afraid? Brenda sat on the bed reflecting on the things she'd miss if she walked away from Buck. Her last thought before she fell asleep was whether she wanted to be a mother without a father in the picture.

Buck found Brenda asleep on his bed. It was comforting and a curse. She was there for now, but tomorrow was another story. The kids had gone to bed, Quinton and Anissa were gone, and he was alone with this woman.

Brenda sat up in the bed when she heard Buck moving around. She now knew that she couldn't leave. She was still worried about their future, but he had to let her stay.

"You said you don't trust me, and you told me to go home, but do you really want me to leave?" she asked.

Buck looked at Brenda, and his heart softened a bit. He had been thinking about all that he'd lose if she did leave. "I don't know. Maybe you should leave, and then that will be one less look of disappointment I have to face. My plate is full. I have to go tell those kids about their mother. I have to live with the pain they feel because we pretended not to see Petra's illness. And I have a murder trial to attend. It's very possible I might not make it through these battles."

Brenda wanted to disappear, but she didn't move. She sat quietly, hoping he would change his mind.

Buck glanced back at her but didn't say anything.

"I made a mistake," she finally said. "I don't want to go. If I do, I don't know if I'll have the courage to come back. All I know is how I feel, and I can't pretend that I have something great waiting for me when I go. This is my great thing. You are it for me."

"Brenda, I can't be what you want. I've lived my entire life being responsible, and I take the job seriously. I keep my promises, or I'll die trying. Things are all uphill from here. I'm facing a murder charge. You're having a baby, and I just inherited two children by default. No matter what happens, they need me. I can't hold your hand and carry my load too."

"If you hold my hand, I'll share your load. That sounds so corny, but you understand what I'm saying. Anyway, you can't afford to watch me go, and I don't want to. I'm still afraid, but I'd be lost without you."

Buck didn't trust the offer, and more importantly, he didn't want to let her get close to Chanice and CJ. He reasoned that if she left him again, he was a man, and he could snap back. However, the children would be broken if she walked away from them. They had already suffered, losing both parents, and he wasn't willing to suffer another loss after becoming attached.

"Brenda, you don't understand. I can't afford to let you hurt those babies—"

"This isn't about them, Jahson. This is about you not trusting me to stay.

I can't do anything else. I've explained my fears. I've promised to stand with you, but you won't forgive me. I'm so glad Chaka is dead, because I could only imagine what you would have done to him after you found out he used you, if this is the way you are treating me. Fuck this! I'm not begging."

Chanice was waiting by the bedroom door when Brenda turned to leave. Buck was stunned, but he recovered quickly. "Hey, baby, what's up? You OK?" he asked nervously.

"I couldn't sleep, so I started watching TV, and the news said my mommy was locked in the house and shooting out the window. Uncle Buck, we gotta go before they hurt her."

"It's going to be OK. I didn't want to tell you about your mom because I didn't want to scare you and your brother. If you want to go, we can, but I can't let you go into the house until we are sure it's safe," Buck explained.

"My momma didn't mean to hurt anybody. She's just upset that my daddy is gone. He left her behind. She says it all the time. She misses him so much that it makes her very sad. I have to go tell her it's OK. That's the only thing that makes her feel better," Chanice said, beginning to cry.

Brenda wasn't sure of her role with these children, but she knew there was no way she could watch Chanice cry. She let her heart lead her as she wrapped Chanice in a tight hug.

Buck watched, hoping against everything that Brenda wasn't playing with his emotions and using Chanice to do it. Quickly he escorted Chanice to the room to get CJ.

❖❖❖❖❖

"Chanice, we are going to see about your mommy, but I want you to understand, I will not let you get out of this car. Uncle won't forgive himself if something happens to you. Do you understand?"

"Yes, but if I don't go in, how will she know that it's OK? Who is going to tell her for me?"

CJ woke up to his sister's crying. He was confused, until he realized they were in the car. "Where are we going? I don't want to go home. Let's go back to Uncle Buck's," he yelled hysterically.

Buck couldn't take the dual screaming and crying. He pulled over, shook up and unsure of his next move. Clearly he couldn't fix this. He turned to Brenda, hoping she had answers.

Brenda was just as confused, but offered a temporary solution. "CJ, you're not going home to stay. No matter what happens, Uncle Jahson won't leave you. I promise." Brenda spoke as gently as she could.

Chanice's wailing stopped long enough for her to hear the promise. She sniffled and wiped her eyes. "Who is Uncle Jahson?"

Buck laughed because the look on Brenda's face was comical. In an arch of her eyebrows, she looked completely lost at how to answer.

"I am," Buck answered, laughing. "It's my real name. You see how we call CJ by his initials, and that's his nickname? Well, Buck is my nickname."

"Why do they call you Buck?" CJ asked. "You don't look like a buck. You look like an uncle."

The vehicle gently rocked as everyone laughed.

Buck pulled off again, and they continued toward Petra's house.

When Buck, Brenda, Chanice, and CJ arrived at the house, things were calmer. Petra's mother was out front, along with the police, trying to reason with her.

Petra was beyond reasoning, however, wanting to end her misery. She continued to sit still with the gun at her side, remembering the words of her friends and family. *"There were other choices you could have made, Petra,"* Quinton had said, disappointment clear in his tone.

"Now your children don't have a father, and because of some petty squabble. Was it really that important to you to be the only woman in his life?" she heard her mother ask.

"Mommy, I'm not my daddy. You're doing it again, looking at me funny,"

Chanice said.

The last voice, Chaka's, was the one that she hated the most. *"I never thought you would be so angry with me for something so trivial. There was never a competition between you two. You have something she will never have. You are the mother of my children."*

His voice was the one that drove her to the edge. She screamed back at him. "I was good enough to have your children and raise them, but I wasn't good enough to be your wife? I was the woman you hid in the shadows while you paraded her around like some prize!"

"How many times did I explain to you that the decisions I made to work in those streets sometimes led to detrimental situations?" Chaka asked. *"I never wanted you or my children in jeopardy."*

"It didn't matter!" Petra screamed. "It was just another excuse to keep us hidden. You wanted her more. She offered you nothing, and you gave her everything. I wanted you more, and you gave her a ring."

She waited to hear his voice again. Instead she saw his full image standing before her with pleading eyes. His lips moved, but she couldn't make out the words. Finally his words became clear.

I'm sorry.

"No, I don't want you to be sorry for choosing her. I want you to be sorry for this!"

Petra's mother hit the ground when she heard the shot. She knew without checking what her daughter had finally done. She prayed for her soul and hoped that heaven would know her heart and open the gates.

Buck knew instantly what had happened the moment he saw Petra's mother screaming. He didn't bother to hide his tears.

Chanice climbed from the back seat into his lap and rocked with him. "It's OK, uncle. She is OK now. They are going to be together again, my mommy and my daddy."

Brenda waited for CJ to cry, but he sat, holding on to the seatbelt, his eyes as wide as saucers, terrified by all the movement around the car.

Later, hours after the cameras left, the police were gone, and the house was sealed off, CJ still refused to move. He wanted to leave, and decided there was nothing in the house to see, no matter how Brenda tried to coax him.

"You can go inside, but I'm never going in there again," he answered as if some evil lived there.

"Nothing inside that house can hurt you. Your uncle is right here with you. He won't let anything happen to you," Brenda said.

"You promised I wouldn't have to go inside. You said I wouldn't have to stay. Uncle Buck, we don't break promises. I want to leave. Can we go now?"

"Let's go, *B*. We need to go home and figure out what to do next." Buck traded seats with Brenda. He was in no condition to drive, and he wasn't about to force his nephew to get out of the car.

"I want to live with you," CJ said.

"I promise you, CJ, I will make every effort to see that you stay with me. Your grandma may want you to stay with her for a while."

"No, I don't want to go with her. I want to stay with you. Say you promise I can stay with you."

Brenda was heartbroken as she realized the effect that this was having on Buck.

Buck looked back at his nephew. "You won't have to go back in that house. I will make sure that your grandma understands that you want to stay with me. I won't promise that you will stay, but I'll promise that I'll do everything to make sure we are not separated."

Chapter 46

Buck felt the pressure. He felt the pressure from Brenda to be a better man. He felt the strain of not knowing how to be an instant father to Chanice and CJ. And he felt the worry of not knowing if he would be convicted of a murder he didn't commit. The stress hovered over him every morning he woke, and every night before he fell asleep.

He wanted to run for the first time in his life. He couldn't stand it, and he wanted the chance to retreat. CJ followed him around when he was home and cried constantly if he left. Chanice walked around in a catatonic state, barely talking. Brenda was practically pulling out strands of her hair, trying to be supportive. It was too much. She would have run away if she didn't understand the repercussions of such a thing. She had readjusted to his way of life, but she hadn't figured out how to like it.

Finally, after a week had gone by, Brenda ditched the pity. She was tired of being heartbroken by the misery the children were suffering. She found her footing and decided to change their fate. It couldn't be healthy for them not to have any fun.

"CJ and Chanice, let's go. We are getting out of this house right now," she yelled from the foyer.

Chanice walked out of the kitchen, but didn't say a word. She moped to the door and watched as CJ bounced down the steps.

"Where are we going?" CJ asked.

"Out, handsome," Brenda answered. "Now come on before I change my mind."

The sign advertising the skating rink brought smiles to all their faces. CJ and Chanice giggled, thinking Brenda had lost her mind.

"Come on," Brenda said. "But first you have to make some promises. No broken bones, and don't knock out any teeth." She laughed. "I'm not a skater, so you two will have to show me how it's done."

"You've never skated before?" Chanice asked. "How come? Didn't they have skates when you were little?"

"Yeah, but I wasn't any good at it."

CJ took charge. He led the girls to the door and mimicked his uncle, holding open the door. As they headed to the booth to pay, he asked all the necessary questions. "Excuse me, is there a separate fee for children and adults?"

The attendant pointed at the sign above his head before she spoke. "Hi, cutie. There's a special price today for children, but if your mommy wants to skate too, she has to pay regular price."

Brenda smiled at the attendant. "I won't be skating," she said, rubbing her belly. "But hook these two up."

Chanice didn't wait for encouragement. She heard the heavy beats from the music, and the flashing neon lights were calling her to the floor. She hit the floor quickly and was whizzing by to the beat before Brenda could get over to her position on the sideline.

Brenda laughed as Chanice clowned and turned backward. "Look at your sister," she said to CJ. "She's pretty good. I'd love to skate like that. Will you teach me someday?"

CJ watched his sister and then turned back to Brenda with a look of astonishment on his face. "That takes a lot of practice, *B*," he said, mimicking Buck's behavior. "You might wanna sit this one out while we show you how to do it."

It was endearing to hear him talk so freely. She only hoped the happiness of the day would hold out. "Come on, little man," she said, pulling out the camera.

CJ was better than Chanice. Before long, he was twisting and turning forward and backward, doing tricks that had Brenda's jaw on the floor.

They stayed until dinnertime, and then headed home.

Buck was in the kitchen when his family arrived home. He was cooking and wondering where they were when he heard Chanice cracking jokes on his apron.

"Uncle Buck is Mr. Mom. Quick, CJ, look. All he needs is a wig, and he'll be an ugly girl."

"Hey, you not supposed to insult the cook until after you eat. Oh, and for your information, I'm the only person in this house that can cook." Buck splashed the children with water from the sink. He was amazed at the loud laughter and the excitement in their eyes. He knew something was up. "Where have y'all been?" he asked CJ.

"We went to this skating rink. Uncle, it was fun. You should come next time," CJ said, bouncing around the kitchen in his excitement. "Brenda just watched, because she was too scared."

Brenda winked at Buck, happy for the first time she was the source of their excitement.

Buck watched their expressions and he felt pride in the good deed she had done. Maybe it was time to lighten up on her. "You can't skate?" he asked Brenda. "How is that?"

"She can't skate or cook, but she knows how to have fun," Chanice said.

"I bet Uncle Buck can't skate either," Brenda said. "If you so great, let's go back, so you can show me."

"Woman, please, you don't want me to show you up. All right, tomorrow let's go to this rink."

"Can we invite Uncle Q and the others?" Chanice pleaded. "I know Mifaith can't skate yet, but it could be fun for all of us."

Buck pointed to the phone. He wanted the children to feel comfortable speaking to everyone in their family. "It's your idea, so you take the initiative," he told Chanice.

"What's that?" she asked.

"It means you take the first step. You make the phone call."

As Chanice turned to use the phone, Buck looked at Brenda. "Thank you so much for doing that today. It's the first time I've seen them genuinely having a good time. You had me worried for a minute, talking about skating while you all knocked up."

She smiled, and then her expression turned serious. "Buck, this wasn't about getting you to acknowledge my good deed. It was an idea I had because I was tired of feeling useless. I want to be more than a babysitter. I want to be friends with them. I want them to depend on me too."

"I get it, B, and I know we've been a little hard on you. I'm sorry. It was never my intention to make you feel useless. I'm just learning to be a full-time uncle, and sharing the duties is a little tough. I didn't want them to count on you. I'm sorry."

"Maybe I deserved your doubt, but the truth is, I'm here, and all I want to do is be good to them. I've accepted my faults, but that's not what this is about."

Before he could respond, she shared CJ's antics with him.

"He is a mini you. He walked in the rink and took charge. I was very impressed with his manners. We may have to get that boy into some kind of leadership program and find him a good group of kids to play with. He's too serious for his age."

Buck laughed at Brenda's excitement. It was warming, and now he knew that she was going to be a permanent fixture in their lives.

"OK, Auntie B, what do we do about Chanice?" Buck asked.

"That girl got more questions than I can answer. She is nurturing and tough. Let's put her in Girl Scouts, for starters."

"Whatever you say, lady, but when she wants to kill you for being around a bunch of squealing little girls, don't expect me to save you."

"She'll love it. I did. Jahson, you realize we sitting here planning their futures like real parents?" Brenda chuckled.

"Do you realize that we are as real as it gets? Among other things, we need some time alone to talk about our future. Are you ready to answer some questions?"

"That depends on the questions. Furthermore, if it has anything to do with fighting, fussing, or leaving, keep that to yourself," she said.

"Listen to me, B. I'm responsible for those babies, but I need some help. I can't do it by myself. We need to come to some sort of decision about us before we mess up two more lives, plus the one growing in you. I love you without question, but there's still the trust factor."

"Damn that, Jahson. You don't want to trust, because it makes it easy for you not to forgive. I'm not asking for your forgiveness anymore. I'm here. The only problem we really have is simply, if we share custody, and if something happens to you, am I their legal guardian?"

"Well, I guess that's the only problem we have then. It don't matter that we're about to have a baby of our own? It doesn't matter to you that he needs a last name? It doesn't matter that I want to marry you? Yeah, I guess custody is our only problem," he said, a smirk on his face.

"To hell with that! You suck at proposing. Are you the same man that swept me off my feet from the first night we met? Nope, that wasn't a proposal. Try again. And where the hell is the ring?" She laughed when Buck's face turned serious.

Then Buck laughed. He realized Anissa was right. Brenda wouldn't appreciate being proposed to in some casual setting. She wanted the excitement, and he would have tried to give it to her, if they hadn't been so buried by the drama in their lives.

"Who are you? And what did you do with the woman that would have been happy with just a promise of love? Instead I'm shacking up with some broad that wants a big, pretentious engagement."

"Pretentious, my ass. I want to spend some of that hard-earned money on an engagement party that will make some folks jealous. Besides, I'm pregnant, and you have to indulge all my crazy whims."

Buck nodded. It was amusing to him how she could turn him into some docile idiot and make him angry all at the same time. This wasn't one of those moments, though. He wanted to give her a dream party, especially since she'd proven she deserved it.

"I'll propose to you however you see fit, as long as you promise to say yes."

Chapter 47

FREEDOM

Desiree Saunders and Brian Hopewell sat at the defense table listening intently to the prosecutor catalog a list of things he'd present as evidence. All of it was supposed to show that Jahson Holden was a murderer. A life-size portrait of Sasha Richards was on display for everyone in the courtroom to view.

Buck didn't dare hide his face as the jurors looked at him. He didn't hang his head in fear, despite the severity of the charges. He listened as the prosecutor detailed every inch of Sasha's brutal murder. He couldn't hold in his emotions as photographs of her battered body were passed around and displayed. Judging from the reaction of the jurors, he was going to jail.

Hopewell leaned over and whispered, "It's cheap parlor tricks, and we still have an ace."

The room was silent as Hopewell stood. Buck held his breath, waiting and hoping for a miracle. Hopewell declined his right to give an opening statement.

"Judge, I request a meeting in your chambers," Hopewell said. "New evidence recently came to my attention, and it could save the court a lot of time and money."

Judge Philbert agreed to a meeting in her chambers. She had heard about Hopewell's previous antics in the courtroom. After the judge, Hopewell, and the prosecutor were settled, the judge said, "Look, Hopewell, I don't intend to spend my nights at home trying to best you at the games you play, so make it good. Make your point."

"My client has a moving violation in the Commonwealth of Virginia. As a result of failing to pay the ticket, my client is a wanted man. I was unable to get a copy of the warrant, but I do have official paperwork from Virginia explaining everything. It has all the information regarding the violation, including the date on which the violation occurred, which happens to be the date that Sasha Richards was murdered."

"Is there any reason why this information wasn't funneled through the proper channels before now, Hopewell?" the prosecutor hissed.

"I only just received this information. I am not too familiar with Virginia's policies, but my office received a great deal of trouble due to our reluctance to surrender Mr. Holden."

There was nothing more to be said. Mr. Jahson Holden could not have murdered Sasha Richards. The judge dismissed the jury, the prosecutor was pissed, and it was a windfall for Hopewell, and especially for Buck.

After the courtroom had emptied, Hopewell told Buck, "I received the check for representing Earl, even though the case didn't play out."

"See it as a payment for taking the case at my request," Buck said. "I didn't know anyone that could ensure him a fair trial."

"It has never been a problem working with you, Mr. Holden, but your release has made me an enemy with my peers." Brian Hopewell laughed. "I just have one question. How did you get a hold of those videos?"

"My friend, some things are best left a secret." Buck smiled.

Chapter 43

HOLDING HANDS

Brenda was sitting on the lounger when Buck came through the door with ice cream in one bag and a pastrami sandwich in another. Buck stood just out of reach, laughing as Brenda struggled to get off the chair.

The children raced into the room, trying to find the joke. Seeing Brenda rock back and forth hadn't been funny since the first day they noticed her doing it, but Buck still laughed every time.

"Man, I'm ready to eat. It's your fault anyway that I can't get out of the damn chair," Brenda complained. "I'm calling my mother and telling her you mistreating me."

Chanice and CJ shook their heads at their uncle as they both struggled to help Brenda.

"Aunty B, why do you always sit there if you know you can't get out of the seat?" Chanice asked.

Buck was ashamed of himself, but he couldn't stop laughing. He finally pulled Brenda into his arms and kissed her before she could fuss again. "Come on, beautiful, before you starve."

"I can't wait until I go on leave. I promise to punish you by cooking every day. I'll see how you like that." She giggled.

CJ looked at his uncle, and before either of them could laugh, Brenda waddled away. "You not going to let her cook for us, are you?" CJ asked, clearly worried.

"Maybe she can cook, but only on your birthday."

CJ's face couldn't have been more serious if they were talking about school or girls. "That's not funny, Uncle Buck. How come you and Uncle Quinton chose girlfriends that can't cook?"

Buck couldn't stop laughing as he looked at Brenda sitting in the chair with her bowl of ice cream and the hot sandwich dripping with mustard. Instead of answering the question, he smiled at both of the children who had been left in his care. Every day he thanked God for their existence.

Often enough he thought about Petra and Chaka. He thought about the friends and the things he'd done along the way, but he didn't regret taking them and raising them. They were an education all by themselves, and he loved his family.

"My birthday is coming, Uncle Buck," CJ said. "Instead of having a party, I want to go visit my daddy's stones."

Brenda saw the expression on Buck's face. "Is there any reason that we can't do both?"

"I don't know. I just wanted everyone to come with us and say a prayer for him. I want him to be at peace, like the preacher talked about at church."

Chanice chimed in before Buck could answer again. Her eyes pleaded with him. "We can always have a party too. Daddy worried that we wouldn't be OK if something happened to him. Uncle Buck, we OK, right? We just want to show him we're OK."

"It's your day, CJ," Buck finally answered. "Anything you want to do, it's my job to make it happen." Buck smiled.

Two weeks later family and friends placed an array of flowers at Chaka's headstone, and the children read verses from the Bible that they'd chosen.

Quinton, Buck, Dave, and Danny each stood behind the children, representing their promises to Chaka.

Quinton raised his head while everyone prayed. There was a brief moment when he felt himself slipping back to the first time they'd come there.

He turned his head toward the gas station adjacent to the cemetery, and there she was. Eve stood there quietly observing the scene. As the family joined hands, Quinton nodded to her, and she nodded back in acknowledgment.

Eve hadn't gone to the cemetery to pay homage to Chaka's grave, but was surprised by the vigil. Quickly, she calculated her next move. While all heads were bowed, she rushed across the avenue and slid past the observers, not caring about an intrusion. Briefly, she stopped and made the sign of the cross before continuing the trek to her mother's enclosed mausoleum. The closer she came to the tomb, the more her knees shook. Her palms began to sweat, and for the first time since receiving Eddy's letters she had second thoughts. Before she could turn back, she heard the quiet hymn being sung along Chaka's grave and knew she had to give her sister her last wishes. The instructions were specific.

> *If something happens to me, leave me at my mother's side. I'm not asking you to visit. Just leave my ashes with her. It's your responsibility to do this, Eve, because inside the tomb you will find the only thing I have to leave behind. Take it and remember me.*
>
> *Love,*
> *Baby Sister Eddy.*

In the oversized handbag she carried the beautiful decorative urn with the ashes of her sister to the opening of the private house. Suddenly, Eve could feel her heart pounding as she nervously stepped passed the threshold. The darkness almost engulfed her as she waited for her eyes to adjust. Trembling, she took two more steps into the space, and panic took her breath. Tears welled up in her eyes, and she shivered alone with nothing but the memory of her family. Slowly, she stepped further into the darkness and almost stumbled on the floor within arm's reach of her mother's coffins. A muffled scream escaped before she could get her bearings to continue.

After taking another step, she realized an object was blocking her path. Stooping low, she felt around in the darkness, trying to make out the hard casing. Eve stood straight up the moment the attendant was walking by the doorway.

It occurred to him he hadn't opened the door all way, and the built-in lights weren't on. "Ah, Ms. Soto, I see you are here already. I'm sorry I wasn't here to meet you, but we had some unexpected mourners today," he said.

"No problem," she answered. "I arrived a little ahead of schedule, and since the door was cracked, I came in to say a prayer," she lied.

The attendant regarded the situation and quietly began backed out of the area, but as an afterthought, he told her about the place. "As long as this door stays open, those overhead lights and the floodlights along the floor will be on. If you need anything let me know."

Eve's eyes immediately rested on her mother's coffin, and slowly they fell on the chest at her feet. It was no ordinary footlocker-style chest, but a miniature replica of the casket like her mother's. With shaking hands Eve toyed with the lever before flipping the case open. With a quick look over her shoulder, she realized she was once again alone, and she rushed to see the contents. The stacks of money were neatly wrapped and bound, causing Eve's eyes to bulge. The smirk appeared before she had even a second to pray over the souls of her deceased mother and sister. Her only thoughts were how to get it from there to her car.

MELODRAMA PUBLISHING ORDER FORM

WWW.MELODRAMAPUBLISHING.COM

Title	ISBN	QTY	PRICE	TOTAL
Myra	1-934157-20-1		$15.00	$
Menace	1-934157-16-3		$15.00	$
Cartier Cartel	1-934157-18-X		$15.00	$
10 Crack Commandments	1-934157-21-X		$15.00	$
Jealousy: The Complete Saga	1-934157-13-9		$15.00	$
Wifey	0-971702-18-7		$15.00	$
I'm Still Wifey	0-971702-15-2		$15.00	$
Life After Wifey	1-934157-04-X		$15.00	$
Still Wifey Material	1-934157-10-4		$15.00	$
Eva: First Lady of Sin	1-934157-01-5		$15.00	$
Eva 2: First Lady of Sin	1-934157-11-2		$15.00	$
Den of Sin	1-934157-08-2		$15.00	$
Shot Glass Diva	1-934157-14-7		$15.00	$
Dirty Little Angel	1-934157-19-8		$15.00	$
Histress	1-934157-03-1		$15.00	$
In My Hood	0-971702-19-5		$15.00	$
In My Hood 2	1-934157-06-6		$15.00	$
A Deal With Death	1-934157-12-0		$15.00	$
Tale of a Train Wreck Lifestyle	1-934157-15-5		$15.00	$
A Sticky Situation	1-934157-09-0		$15.00	$
Jealousy	1-934157-07-4		$15.00	$
Life, Love & Loneliness	0-971702-10-1		$15.00	$
The Criss Cross	0-971702-12-8		$15.00	$

(GO TO THE NEXT PAGE)

MELODRAMA PUBLISHING ORDER FORM
(CONTINUED)

Title/Author	ISBN	QTY	PRICE	TOTAL
Stripped	1-934157-00-7		$15.00	$
The Candy Shop	1-934157-02-3		$15.00	$
Sex, Sin & Brooklyn	0-971702-16-0		$15.00	$
Up, Close & Personal	0-971702-11-X		$9.95	$
				$
			Subtotal	
			Shipping**	
			Tax*	
	Total			

Instructions:

*NY residents please add $1.79 Tax per book.

**Shipping costs: $3.00 first book, any additional books please add $1.00 per book.

Incarcerated readers receive a 25% discount. Please pay $11.25 per book and apply the same shipping terms as stated above.

Mail to:

MELODRAMA PUBLISHING

P.O. BOX 522

BELLPORT, NY 11713